Stud Princess

MAY 18

CH

Stud Princess

N'TYSE

URBAN BOOKS

www.urbanbooks.net

Urban Books, LLC
300 Farmingdale Road, NY-Route 109
Farmingdale, NY 11735

ISBN 13: 978-1-62286-645-8
ISBN 10: 1-62286-645-2

First Trade Paperback Printing April 2018
Printed in the United States of America

10 9 8 7 6 5 4 3 2 1

This is a work of fiction. Any references or similarities to actual events, real people, living or dead, or to real locales are intended to give the novel a sense of reality. Any similarity in other names, characters, places, and incidents is entirely coincidental.

Distributed by Kensington Publishing Corp.
Submit orders to:
Customer Service
400 Hahn Road
Westminster, MD 21157-4627
Phone: 1-800-733-3000
Fax: 1-800-659-2436

Stud Princess

by

N'TYSE

"Bitches don't choose, they get chosen. So quit babysitting time and go make me some money!"

—Chyna, America's Stud Princess

A Note from the Author

*So here we are diving back into the gritty world of
Sand, Rene, and Chyna. Hopefully, you will enjoy* Stud
Princess, Notorious Vendettas *as much as you did* My
Secrets, Your Lies. *I'm often asked, "Where did Sand
and Rene come from?" Well, the short answer to that
is the DNA of my first two characters was inspired by
those who I felt were being left out of literary fiction. I
had read my fair share of urban and street-lit books
back when the genres were making their introduction,
but I had discovered that there were not as many that
featured characters who identified as being part of
the LGBTQ community. I made it my goal to create a
fictional world that included characters from all walks
of life. MSYL was my first book baby, and I am proud to
be one of the first wave of authors who featured stories
told or inspired from these perspectives. As always, I
appreciate your unwavering support, and I look forward to your thoughts, so do reach out and let your girl
know how you feel. And before I forget, be sure to check
out the documentary "Beneath My Skin" on YouTube.
Peace and blessings!*

N'TYSE
www.ntyseenterprises.com
www.facebook.com/author.ntyse
www.twitter.com/ntyse
E-mail: ntyse.amillionthoughts@yahoo.com

Also by N'TYSE

My Secrets, Your Lies

Twisted Seduction

Twisted Vows of Seduction

Twisted Entrapment

As Editor

Gutta Mamis

Cougar Cocktales

As Producer

Beneath My Skin (Documentary)

Behind the Mask: My Naked Truth (Documentary)

Before the intermission . . .

It was exactly 11:34 p.m. when Chyna pulled up in a pearl-white Lexus on the corner of Second and Berleck Street. She knew from the way Rene was standing that the girl was scared shitless about meeting so late and at such an unusual spot.

The wind was bone chilling, and while Rene was trying to keep warm in her thin jacket, Chyna was hotter than sizzling skillet grease. One glimpse of Rene and her mind thought all kinds of nasty thoughts. And if seeing her from a distance did as much as it did for her now, she couldn't wait to see the reaction she would get once she was face-to-face with the fresh meat.

Rene spotted the Lexus as it made its approach. She knew then that it had to be the woman she had spoken to over the phone. After seeing her get out of the car, she didn't look as threatening as her voice made her seem. But she still couldn't help thinking that Chyna had to be psychologically messed up in the head to suggest such a crazy place to meet. Rene's guard came down a little. *Hell, what am I scared of?* she thought. Realizing how her hands had been shaking, she stuffed them into her pockets. She was no longer terrified, but just in case this bitch was crazy, she gripped a full container of pepper spray, ready to aim and shoot if the situation got out of control.

Chyna stepped out of the car nice and slow, throwing her mink on over her dress. "Hello. I'm glad you were able to meet with me tonight," Chyna started out, undressing

Rene with her eyes. *Damn,* she thought, *why would such a pretty feminine female want a butch like Sand?*

"Look, half that money is spent, if that's what this is about."

Chyna was still contemplating having Rene her way, but she had to catch herself and remember that she was there to conduct business. "No, dear. That's not what this meeting is about. I don't want your money, honey. I just want to ask you a few questions and see if you can help me recover what's mine, that's all."

Rene eyed Chyna, trying to remember where she had seen her face before.

"You see, your old boss, Albery, owes me for a job he didn't complete."

Rene was lost and wondered how any of this could involve her. She saw herself to be no help and was curious if Sand really had anything to do with this woman coming there after all. "I don't think I follow . . . uh, what was your name again?"

Chyna raised her brow a bit, then confidently rattled off her government name. "I'm Chyndra Wilson, but people around here call me Chyna." The smirk on her face was intentional.

"Okay, Chyna. As I was saying, I don't think I can help you."

There was no need for Chyna to continue to waste time—her time. "I think you can. As a matter of fact, Sand assured me that you can," she reminded Rene, hoping she would reflect back to the words in the letter that Chyna herself had forged and had hand delivered right to Rene's best friend's doorstep.

Rene looked around, checking her surroundings and listening for any trains.

Why the fuck did we have to meet up on a railroad track? she wondered.

"Look, all I need for you to do is conduct a simple transaction. One time is all it would take."

Rene's eyes roamed back to Chyna.

Chyna saw the uncertainty planted in her face. "I'll tell you like this, ma. You do this thing here for me, and you and Sand will be given the best life has to offer. I'll even throw in an incentive." She lifted her brow and batted her eyelash. "This is a sweet deal, honey," she added while imagining the money she could make off Rene if she was one of the girls on her team. But that was another conversation that she would have to remember to have with her. For now, Chyna was determined to psych Rene up.

The longer Rene took to answer, the more irritated Chyna grew. She was hardly giving this young, naïve fresh meat an option.

Rene considered it for a second. "And what would that incentive be?"

Chyna grinned. When someone responded with a question that showed interest, they usually wanted a piece of the action. And that was all she needed to hook Rene.

"That's for me to know and you to find out."

Rene's hair blew with the wind. She was still curious. "How much are we talking that he owes you?" she asked.

"Let's just say the numbers are up, and it's tax season."

"So, if I do this for you, you'll pay me off, and Sand will come back home to me?"

"That's what it is," Chyna said.

Rene stopped for a moment to gather her thoughts. A fresh start—a break like this—was exactly what she and Sand needed because she knew the money she had pinched from Albery's company would only take them so far. Chyna's proposal sounded more secure.

"All right. What have I got to lose? The son of a bitch tried to fire me on some bullshit anyway." Rene couldn't wait to avenge Albery for threatening to terminate her because she wouldn't agree to be his little office whore. She'd love to empty his bank account to a negative zero. She laughed inside at the thought. "I'll do it," she said finally.

Chyna smiled. "That's my girl. In the meantime, here's a cell phone. It can only receive incoming calls, and only I have the number. I'll contact you when everything is set up. Now, to the right of you, over there under that rock," she looked over in that direction, "there's an envelope with your name on it. You can thank me later. Until then, you better get off that track. A train's coming."

At first, Rene didn't hear a train. Then suddenly, the loud horn of a locomotive was banging in her ears. The light from the huge, oncoming train was blinding! She hopped off the tracks so fast that she leaped over a wide ditch.

Chyna smiled wickedly as she walked back to her car, knowing she had proven her point.

Rene headed for the envelope. She tore at it eagerly to see what was inside. She thumbed through several bills. *This is about five thousand dollars!* She stuffed the money into her purse and couldn't get in her car fast enough. As she cranked up her engine and drove away, she neglected to notice the red Honda that had been trailing her all week.

and so the saga continues . . .

1

"Illusion! Ty know your ass in here taking a gotdamn nap while she out there working the room?"

Illusion pretended to be deaf. Before Fletch stormed in like a maniac, she was lying peacefully on her backside, peering up at the opulent decor. She'd been in hundreds of hotel rooms, motels, and Holiday Inns, but none of them compared to the luxuries of this one.

"Say, girl, I know you hear me talking to you," Fletch hollered again.

"Nigga, mind ya own. Shit, I needed a fucking break. Them horny-ass old men ain't going nowhere with they drunk asses," Illusion snapped, whipping her head around to face him. "She can manage. Hell, she's been wanting to prove herself this long. Now, here's her chance."

"Yeah, well, fuck all dat. While your ass in here meditating and shit, you know what I'm saying, you sitting on Chyna's money. And I don't think she's gonna go for that," Fletch said, posting up in an OG stance.

Illusion rolled her eyes at him. "You know what? Fuck Chyna and her money! I'm tired of you running 'round here like her gotdamn puppy scout. Patrolling and worrying 'bout what the fuck I'm doing," she shot. "Needs to get you some bidness and stay the hell up outta all mine!" She gathered every strand of her fourteen-inch weave, and then let it all fall across her right shoulder.

She cut her eyes coldly at Fletch. Just his being there was annoying the fuck out of her.

Fletch waved his arms and waited a full whole minute before he said anything else to piss her off. "You need to calm all that down. It's ya boy," he reminded Illusion, in case she'd forgotten who in the hell she was talking to. He extended his arms as if he was measuring something as wide as himself. "I'm just looking out and making sure you straight. That's all." Fletch could tell by the look on her face that he was talking for nothing. He tossed his head up at her. "Come on, ma," he said as he poked out what he called "a real man's chest." "Don't get all hostile on a brotha and shit."

Illusion stared him up and down. White-on-white Jordans, Sta-Flo starched baggy big boy jeans, crisp white 4XL shirt with Sean John's signature scribbled across it, jailhouse tattoos that covered every piece of skin belonging to his neck and arms, and eye-candy flash from wrist to ear.

"Kodak nigga," Illusion mumbled, then frowned at the mere idea of him having bragging rights to say he fucked her. The dreadful memory alone left a sour taste dancing around her mouth. Telling herself that she'd slept with worse, Illusion let it go, equating Fletch with all the other johns that had to drop a big face on her. She closed her eyes, trying her hardest to shake off those plaguing memories. When she finally reopened them, Fletch was still standing there, smiling, desperate, and as pathetic as they came. Illusion didn't have to say a word because the sickened look transfixed on her face spoke loud enough—so loud that his ass pretended like he couldn't interpret what the fuck she was saying.

"Fletch, go have a drink, roll a joint, fuck some pussy, do something. Just get off my tip," Illusion shot, turning her lips up once again until they were kissing her nose.

He wasn't even standing that close to her, and his bad breath was hitting her smack in the face. She shook her head and eyed the shine in his mouthpiece, wondering if a trip to the dentist to take care of that halitosis would be asking him for too much.

"Yeah, a'ight. I see how you gon' be. Ha ha ha. You got jokes." Fletch was able to steal himself an eye-quickie up Illusion's backside as she crossed one leg over the other, exposing a double dose of the smoothest, thickest brown thighs he'd ever seen. He stood there imagining his tongue showering them, then spreading them farther and farther apart, making room for his face to go down-town. She was showing all skin tonight. The sexy red-hot number had peek-a-boo slits cut throughout the entire dress, and it stopped an accessible inch below the dip of her ass, revealing the ultrathin black lace of her G-string.

Fletch's teeth grazed his lips. He could still taste the assortment of juices flowing from her chocolate sugar-cane fresh on his tongue as if it were only yesterday that he was deep-sea fishing between her folds. He recalled her sun-kissed sienna legs and ass sprawled over him, taking the length of his wood to her maximum, slowly, then at full speed. She rode him long, hard, and deep in every position his overweight body allowed him to fuck in.

That night was programmed in Fletch's memory to autoreplay, and every time he fantasized about it, his jimmy jumped upright. He could vouch that Illusion fucked better than she danced and gave brain so mean, she made Supahead look like a spokeswoman for Oscar Mayer wiener.

A few men often told Illusion she resembled the model Naomi Campbell. In fact, she favored her so much that women who shared work in her line of business often complained about losing money whenever she came on the scene. And although Illusion hated having her looks compared to another woman's, other than the woman who birthed her, she rolled with it.

With her back to Fletch and no indication that she wanted him in the room with her, Illusion remained in a world of her own.

"With your mean fine ass," Fletch quipped. He was practically fucking her with his eyes. He glided his hands across his genitals, feeling the rise in his pants as he toyed with the possibilities.

Even when Illusion was mad, she was sexy. Five feet ten without her heels, handpicked apple bottom, and round, firm, perky titties . . . Just the way he preferred them. He was damn near drooling and didn't even know it. Illusion was a showstopper. She held it down and living up to her name, every guy that came in her direction wanted something that they couldn't get anywhere else, something to keep coming back for—a sexual illusion.

Fletch knew that it was time to get the hell up out of there. Illusion was playing with his head—both of them. "I'll be in the front, but you better not keep these folks waiting long. They paid for two-girl action, not one," he stressed. There was bass in his voice that had not been there before.

Illusion just lay there. Fletch was fucking up her groove and invading the bit of privacy and quiet time she tried to enjoy before she went to work.

"If this shit gets back to Chyna, you already know," he warned. While his job was to direct the traffic and play watchdog, he wasn't about to be cramped up in a room with a bunch of no-pussy-getting old men who all looked like they just escaped from the nursing home. They couldn't harm a flea. And Chyna said they had long money, but shit, you couldn't tell from the looks of what they were throwing out to Ty tonight.

Fletch's manhood was throbbing. His attention was still chasing those wonderful memories of his dick parked between Illusion's Grade-A servicing factory. He couldn't take it. He needed some pussy right now.

"Shit. Fuck it. I'll be downstairs in the car for a minute. I gotta check something out," he said, now more anxious than ever to pop in that new, uncirculated DVD his boy Slick bootlegged for him. Cherokee's big booty ass could not be kept waiting a second longer.

Illusion fanned him off. "Bye, nigga. Poof. Be gone." She didn't want to hear shit about what nobody paid to see tonight. While that was only half the truth of why he busted up in there like a full-force police squad, Illusion knew the real deal. Fletch wanted a free show, but fuck that. He'd pay for the goodies just like she made him do the last time they got together. Today was no different. If H2O wasn't free, there was no way in hell her pussy was going to be. She felt like her pudding was the grandest thing on the face of the earth, and for that reason, her rates weren't negotiable. Just like the stock market, her prices could rise in the blink of an eye. Her pussy had value—black market value. There wasn't anything mediocre or second best about it, so niggas had to pay up to lay up.

As Fletch's footsteps faded, Illusion's heart began to race. The adrenaline rush from the pill she'd swallowed minutes earlier was gradually taking her on a journey to her next euphoric high. If she had to go out there once again and grind on old tart-breath men who smelled like they'd been bathing in mothballs and Old Spice, then she'd make damn sure she was high enough to do it. And if the room was anything like she left it, there were at least six seniors in there, all gray-haired or balding, in suits and bow ties ready to get things jumping. The only thing that wasn't quite a turnoff for Illusion was the fact they all were high-end clients of Chyna, meaning the scenery was greenery. But knowing Chyna, they'd already paid an upfront fee that included the gratuity because Chyna didn't like certain customers placing that kind of money in her hoes' hands. It'd give them a reason to leave her, maybe consider working for themselves. And Chyna couldn't have her bitches thinking. At all. Because she did it for them. She simplified that part of the game. All that was needed from her hoes was to obey the orders they were given before going out on a sex date. And still after only ho'ing and showing for Chyna for two months, Illusion knew she wouldn't be able to keep this up. She'd been better off working the streets alone, without a pimp "looking out for her" and "watching her back," as she recalled all the crap Chyna sold her on.

Illusion waited a few minutes more while admiring the mosaic sculptures and art framings that embellished the room. Her focal point, a beautiful piece of hanging artwork and its array of rich, bold colors, softly blended with splashes of vibrant reds, emerald sea-greens, and indigo-blues. She found herself daydreaming about sweet nothings that included empty promises and dreams that never became realities. Then her thoughts drifted to someone else—her daughter. She wondered if her baby girl would remember her if she saw her now. No telling with all the hateful things she was sure her grandmother fed her. Last time she saw her baby, it was for her third birthday. Baby girl looked like a pretty little princess in all that pink and white, but that was over five years ago. Now her princess was eight, probably in the second or third grade.

Illusion hated everything her life had become and regretted all the bad decisions she'd ever made leading up to this very moment, starting with her daughter, a product of the streets that her mother still served. When Illusion gave birth to her daughter right in the breezeway of a vacant apartment building, instead of throwing her baby in the garbage can or leaving her in the backseat of a city bus for someone else to find, she gave her a better home, right on her mother's doorstep.

Illusion wiped away the solo tear that snuck down her cheek. She had come to terms with herself a long time ago, so there was no need to sit and feel sorry all over again. That chapter in her life was closed—forever. But there wasn't a day that went by that she didn't dwell on her past and wish that things had turned out differently. Unfortunately for her, that was life. It was shitty like that, to some. There was no Magic Marker or Incredible Crayon that could erase all the shit she'd done and been through. Everyone couldn't be a doctor, lawyer, or teacher. Somebody had to be the pimp, ho, drug dealer, and homeless man on the corner with a "will work for food" sign. If not, the rich and famous, accomplished and privileged wouldn't be so successful after all. Everyone would be common folk, average, and no better than the next.

That's exactly how Illusion had come to view life. But she knew she could do better than turning tricks for money—much better. Illusion wanted and needed that change, but until change came, she had to do what a moneymaker had to do. Spin those tricks and get that money.

Illusion blinked back the tears threatening to fall from her eyes. The room was spinning. She recognized this. The X Fairy had come to visit, and the bitch was working her magic spell. As it came down on her, Illusion surprisingly found herself crawling under the 600-thread count Italian sheets, when normally, she'd be horny as hell and ready to fuck the first thing with a hard dick. She could faintly hear her theme music in the background and knew Ty was pulling in a double. As T-Pain remixed that he was in love with a stripper, Illusion visualized the men spanking Ty's ass and yelling for her to take more clothes off, to give them their money's worth.

Her eyelids gradually folded over the glossed whites of her eyes, then rose again. All she wanted was to dream—dream about the life she always wanted, the life she never had. She forced her eyes shut, and everything turned black. A sense of calmness comforted her. Sleep was the closest thing to death, and if death meant peace, then she'd pray to God that she would never wake up.

2

"I know this bitch ain't finally show her face after I done did all the damn work!" Ty huffed loudly, straining the vessels in her skinny neck. "Uh-uh. Hell, naw. Fuck that! Take me to the house, Fletch, and leave this bitch here!" she ordered. "I ain't playin'. This ho ain't ridin' with us."

"Ty, calm all that shit down, girl!" Fletch yelled. "I got this." He turned to face Illusion. "What happened, ma?"

Illusion rolled her eyes upward. "Shit, I fell asleep. Blacked out. Hell, I don't know. And why didn't your ass come back up and get me? Thought you were looking out," she went off, mimicking his earlier remark. She felt a headache coming on. If it wasn't for one of those drunk-ass men trying to slip in the bed with her, she would probably still be asleep, dead to the world. When the old man told Illusion the party was over and that her friends were leaving, she jumped up, knocking him to the floor, and hauled ass to the elevator, catching up to Fletch and Ty as they were getting into the Hummer.

"Remember, *you* the one told me to leave your ass alone," Fletch hollered back, refreshing her memory. "I tried to tell you these people paid for a two-ho show tonight. Not one, but two," he repeated, waving the peace sign directly in her face. "Besides, I was outside watching the door. Making sure y'all's asses were safe," he seethed.

Illusion wasn't buying that. "Yeah, sure you were. Your ass was probably down here jackin' off," she huffed. "Everybody know what you do in there with them windows rolled up," she blasted, putting him on front street.

Her gold chandelier earrings dangled across her shoulders every time her head swayed from side to side. "You ain't fooling no-damn-body. And so what? Y'all was just gonna leave me here?"

"Come on now. You know good and well I was—"

"You ain't gotta explain shit to this bitch!" Ty shot, cutting Fletch off mid-sentence. "She knew what time it was when we got here. And now the bitch acting brand new all of a sudden," she raved. Ty didn't give a flying fuck that Illusion was standing right there in close enough range to hear every word she said. "Now she thinks she's too good to work a call like this, leaving me in there all by my damned self." Ty balled her hands and pumped her fists, then slammed the door. "Trifling bitch," she spat under her breath while finding it hard as hell to believe that she got played.

Illusion was reading Ty's lips. "*Bitch?* I ain't gon' be too many more of your bitches, I'll tell you that much! Ya li'l young high-yella ass need to learn how to respect your fucking elders," Illusion chastised, knowing she was probably only a few years older than Ty. "Better get your little Chocolate tie-a-shoe or tie-a-whateva you want somebody to tie-lookin' ass on somewhere." Illusion combed through her hair with her fingertips, then neatly tucked her mane into a tight knot, just in case something popped off. After a minute or two, she pulled the back door handle, attempting to get in, finding it locked.

Fletch instantly looked over at Ty. "Ty, quit playing. We ain't got all fucking night for this shit. Unlock the damn door!"

"Hell, no! That bitch about to walk her ass to Midlothian. Hope them feet ready, bitch!" Ty sang. "Now, sleep on that," she laughed.

"Ty, give me the keys," Fletch said, holding his hand out to her.

Ty rocked her head from side to side. With her lips poked out like a bird's, her eyes open wide, and her short, spiked hairdo, which was highlighted a royal blue and honey blond, she looked just like the peacock the girls in the house jokingly called her. But she thought the style was tight, and Chyna never said otherwise. She smacked her lips and popped her tongue. "Make that bitch walk some of the fat off her ass. Horse-built skank. Hell, she ain't running a damn thing over here," she said as she gripped Fletch's keys tighter and relaxed back in the seat, unfazed. She rolled up all the windows in Illusion's face, bringing her yapping down to a minimum.

Illusion tried the door again, but it was still locked. Her high in less effect, she began hitting on the windows for them to let her in. She couldn't see through the illegal tint, but she knew, without a doubt, that Ty was getting a kick out of everything. Her patience had already run thin, plus, it was too damn cold to be standing there playing childish-ass games. Illusion was wishing like hell that she hadn't showed up to work the party tonight. Chyna knew better than pairing them up because Illusion didn't want or need a sidekick. She was good on her own. So all the extra Chyna sent along with her was a bunch of BS.

The smell of rain brushed across Illusion's nose. Recalling the weatherman's forecast about cool temperatures and scattered showers, Illusion became infuriated at the idea of getting her fresh hairdo wet. She shot Ty a murderous look through the glass. "Bitch, I'ma whoop your ass! Believe that. I betcha won't jump your ass outta the car!" Illusion challenged, pointing her long French-tipped nail at Ty. Illusion held her hands in the air, calling Ty out. "Come on. Get ya ass outta the car, ho!"

Illusion's angry expression and her cat-eyed look frightened Fletch. He thought he was watching a scene from the *Exorcist* as curse words flew like flaming darts from each of the women's mouths.

"Get out? Bitch, I don't have to! *I'm* not the one who gon' be walking. So get a head start, trick ho!"

Ty was pissed off and felt like she had every valid reason to be because Illusion had left her alone to strip, dance, and do whatever else she was asked to do for six stank-breath, wheezing old men. All six of them had begged for her to go down on them for a little something extra, and like a true moneymaking ho, she adhered to their every request. She sucked their wrinkled sac dicks without hesitation until each of them came one by one, believing she'd prove to Chyna that she was a ride-or-die chick for the paper.

"Ha ha ha. Come on, y'all, stop. It's too late for all this shit," Fletch finally admitted, lowering his driver's-side window some more so Illusion could see all of his face. Although he was tempted to video his own Ghetto Brawl catfight and sell the DVDs for ten dollars a pop, he was tired and ready to get home to some pussy. Enough was enough. "My girl at home waiting on a nigga, so y'all needs to chill the fuck out and kill that noise, mayne!" He looked down to check his cellular. Aggravated, he sighed loud and hard, then pressed his head back against the headrest. "It's almost one in the fuckin' morning, and y'all muhfuckas out here arguing over some dumb shit." He turned his whole body back to his right. "Give me my damn keys, girl, before I make your skinny ass walk right along with her. That way, both of y'all asses can shut the fuck up and raise up outta my ear with all dat!"

Ty flinched and turned up her nose. His breath was kicking, and he was starting to sound just like both of them. "Fletch, if you let this bitch in this car, I *promise* you, I will push her ass out into moving traffic. Do . . . not . . . test . . . me," she forewarned. She was getting madder by the minute.

"All right, all right. Damn," Fletch laughed, finally giving in to Ty. He slid his hands over his smooth baby soft face—the only other admiring feature that women saw in him in addition to his made-to-suck-pussy-eating tongue and lips.

"Yeah, nigga, remember who sucks your dick without the payment plan," Ty scoffed, referring to him not having to pay Chyna for the services he got on the side. Of course, he knew if Chyna ever caught wind of that shit, it'd be all over for him. That was like stealing food out of her kitchen.

"Aww, shut the hell up! That's favor for favor," he shot back. Fletch already didn't like being manhandled and threatened by a woman, let alone being blackmailed and punked by another. If the money wasn't right, he would have told Chyna to kiss his ass long ago. But it was, so there were never any complaints out of him. He was paid to stick around and play LoJack. Not only that, he used to move weight for her uncle back in the day, so he was like part of the family, the way he saw it.

Just as Fletch was turning around to tell Illusion he would come back for her, she was already making her way around to the passenger side of the car where Ty had reclined the seat and gotten comfortable once again. Illusion unballed her right fist, letting the huge rock in her hand fly. Fletch saw the rock coming and ducked in record time. Illusion then took off her left shoe.

Raising up quickly as shattered glass covered her lap, Ty's face was immediately met with Illusion's size nine-and-a-half, six-inch heel, and a fist that showed no jealousy when it came to redecorating her face. Illusion used the heel on her shoe as the weapon it was never imagined to be and sliced and diced Ty's face like she was discovering a new pumpkin-carving technique.

"Ho, I told you I was gon' get that ass. Ugh! Now what? Talk all that hot shit now, you bald-headed tramp." Illusion swung wildly, every intended blow landing on Ty's once-flawless face. Not even the MAC makeup she wore would be able to disguise the damage from the ass beating she was receiving.

Ty tried to fight back, but the seat belt secured around her offered no advantage.

Fletch hurriedly jumped out of the car and ran to Ty's rescue. His unzipped fly confirmed Illusion's earlier accusations. "Illusion!" he screamed.

"Let me go, Fletch!" Illusion grabbed as much of Ty's hair as she could fist, then pounded her face nonstop, using her shoe as a backup punch that intensified every unsparing hit.

"Stop it! You trippin', girl." Fletch managed to pull Illusion away from the car and snatch the shoe out of her hand. He threw it to the ground. "Man, stay yo' ass right here! I'll come back and get you!" he hollered, almost out of breath. "Y'all actin' like some gotdamn five-year-olds!" He turned to face his ride, raising his hands over his head at the sight of it. "Shit! Why y'all always gotta bust out a nigga's windows? Does my ride say 'fuck a nigga shit up'?" he yelled.

Without a mark or scratch, Illusion stepped back, allowing Ty space and opportunity to hop out of the vehicle and take her on for round two. This time, face-to-face. Fist-to-fist. She made sure her bun was still tucked tightly in place. She knew females always went for the hair, and she'd be damned if she let Ty get the best of her in any way. While her eyes remained on the passenger door, she tuned out Fletch's ranting and bitching about breaking his window. Wasn't like it was the first time a woman had bust out his car windows, and it probably wouldn't be the last. She looked him up and down as if she was sizing him up, then looked back down at the fragments of black glass that covered the curb and sidewalk.

Ty was still strapped in her seat, screaming, "My face! Awww! Look what this bitch did to my face!" The unending blood that dripped onto her shirt scared her even more.

"What I tell you? I told your ass not to fuck with me. Don't let the good looks fool you, bitch," Illusion boasted, feeling like Laila Ali.

"Illusion! Keep yo' ass right here," Fletch pointed at the ground. "I ain't playin' with you either, girl. I'll be back soon as I drop Ty off," he said. He hopped back into the Hummer and sped off.

Halfway down the road Illusion could still hear Ty's screaming crybaby ass. She stepped back into her $200-designer shoe, wiggling it a little. Her heel was still intact. She could hardly believe it because she knew she had just whipped the shit out of Ty with it.

She struggled with whether she should wait on Fletch, get a head start and walk, or just turn around and go the other way altogether. She was already sick of living in that house. All those women. All that drama. Making way less money than she walked in with, and dealing with way more madness than she signed up for. There wasn't much to think about. Illusion made a few bad choices in life, but she was no dummy. She didn't need Chyna to survive. Hell, survival came with a how-to kit and that kit was tucked tightly in between her legs.

Illusion started for the opposite direction. The city slickers and street kittens were all out at play. Midnight had turned into one in the morning and for the scavengers, goons, and hustlers on the block, the day was just beginning.

3

Chyna had been trying to reach Sand for over an hour now, only for the calls to be redirected to the motel's switchboard. She was getting more irritated by the minute. Before she could dial the number again, her phone lit up. It was Fantasy calling her from the house.

"Chyna!"

"Speak to me."

"Where are you? It's Illusion!"

Chyna listened closely to the background noise on the other end of her line. "What about her?"

"She done beat this girl up! She bleeding every-got-damn-where. Her eye, her nose, and her lip is busted. She's gonna need stitches," Fantasy rambled uncontrollably.

"Slow your roll, Fantasy! Beat who up?" Chyna snapped as she proceeded slowly through the blinking traffic light. She turned on the windshield wipers and attempted to wipe away the falling rain that made everything before her a constant blur.

"Ty!" Fantasy was cringing just from looking at the poor girl. "You gotta see this damn girl's face."

"Where's Fletch?"

"He left to go back for Illusion because his dumb ass left her at the hotel."

"I'ma kill that bitch! I swear that ho don't know who the fuck she messin' with. Just watch me. That bitch got it coming!"

Chyna could hear Ty screaming and cursing in the background. "Tell Ty to shut all that noise up. I'm on my way."

"All right, I'll let her know," Fantasy said. "I love you," she added quickly before Chyna could hang up.

Chyna knew it was coming. "Keep it that way," she replied, then abruptly ended the call.

The house was noisy, but what else was new? Everybody bragging about all the money they'd made for their pimp that night, betting each other on who outdid the next and sold the most pussy or tricked out the most johns.

Fantasy remembered boasting and engaging in the same immature arguments, but now, she liked to think of herself as "privileged." There was a lot of shit she got away with simply because she was who she was and that was all there was to it. But she still wore the same shoes that every last one of those girls in that house wore, except hers were padded and laced with special treatment. Hell, she slept with men for thousands, even women paid for blissful nights of pleasure with her, but what separated Fantasy from the rest wasn't her pussy-selling techniques; it was the relationship she established with Chyna long before any of the other girls ever entered the picture. A time when it was just the two of them and only a few others that Chyna later ended up contracting to amateur pimps that were fresh in the market and ho hunting. Fantasy was the number one, and number one in the game meant being the bottom bitch.

Chyna wanted all dimes on her team and those hoes she had before Fantasy were far from it. They smoked whatever they could get their hands on and injected anything, anywhere in their bodies for the sake of getting high. Chyna didn't want women like that repre-

senting her name or jeopardizing what she was trying to build, which was her very own empire. Chyna
was a businesswoman before anything else, and the
clients she had her eyes set on weren't going to take
her seriously if she had women that looked like Star
Jones rejects. She wanted women that men would lie,
cheat, and steal for. The kind that silenced the room
when they stepped in the door and, with a lick of the
lips, could suck the come out of every dick present. She
wanted women that would make the president himself
take a risk at getting some ass. And if they weren't that
way when she got them, then they damn sure had to
have the potential. But most importantly, they had to
be loyal.

Chyna scoped out hoes from sunup to sundown, desperate to replace her uncle's hand-me-downs. It was a
match made in heaven when she came across Fantasy,
at the time, Fat Cat. Fantasy was very well known on the
streets, and even though she was already on contract,
Chyna had to have her. She was sexy, driven, and knew
that her place was behind her pimp. It wasn't too much
longer before Fantasy was being promoted, soon to
become the wife of her pimptress. Chyna needed someone in her corner she could trust as she recruited eligible
women, one at a time. There was no one better to fit the
bill than Fantasy. She was Chyna's main bitch practically
from day one. She already knew the game, and for what
it was worth, she didn't mind giving all her money to
Chyna, so it was just that much easier for her to convince
the other hoes to do the same.

Chyna rescued Fantasy when nobody else would. She
snatched her out of a rugged lifestyle and introduced her
to a better one. One that paid real money. Chyna pulled
up in a Jaguar late one Wednesday evening and asked
Fantasy if she wanted to turn that chump change she was

making into $5,000 paydays. Being the loyal ho she was, up until then, she only gave enough info to qualify herself as a player in Chyna's league, fearing that if it got back to her pimp, she'd be rotting by morning.

The very next day, her pimp was dismissing her cold. Chyna told Fantasy she had paid Big Benz off to clear her debt with him. So that meant she was free to walk and serve under Chyna's reign.

Fantasy found out that very same night that Benz was found dead in his green Cadillac with half his brains blown out. Some said it was a dispute between him and a few roughnecks in the hood, while others believed one of his hoes did him in. Fantasy didn't care because all that mattered was that the motherfucka was history, and he would no longer be abusing her. She never asked Chyna if she had any association to his murder. She really didn't care. But while she was free from Benz, Fantasy quickly realized that he didn't have a damn thing on Chyna. It would only take her a few short weeks to figure out that Chyna wasn't just another young, ruthless hood legend, but also the niece of a drug lord with a notorious vendetta.

After proving her loyalty to Chyna, it wasn't long before Fantasy was being crowned wifey. That title alone gave her status and made her superior to the rest. Every woman in the house knew automatically who had permanent keeps. And Fantasy played her position so well that the girls flocked to her when they were too afraid to go to Chyna if they didn't make their nightly minimums, which was nothing short of a grand. Fantasy's relationship with the girls was tight. She took care of them, coached them, and made them believe she was on their side in order to keep everything in Chyna's eyesight. She earned their respect only because she gave them the street game that they couldn't get anywhere else for free. And she kept them fly, so they were always dipped in the latest designer fashions from head to heel. And every now and then, so they'd really feel special, they'd throw extravagant parties on special occasions or even holidays. They were one big happy family; however, Fantasy had her favorites. What mother hen didn't? Still, she tried her best to keep them all under her nose because when it came down to Chyna's money, there wasn't a bitch in the world worth dying for.

Fantasy headed for the downstairs bedroom where she and Chyna slept, but not before warning the girls of the destruction yet to come. As she moved graciously across the second floor of the mansion, her voluptuous ass and breasts bouncing with every step, she squeezed the money bag which held all the cash the strollers pulled in from their Friday night regulars.

"Chyna's on her way, so for you hoes who ain't got dates tonight, you better go walk the stroll, 'cause if you know like I know," she paused, "it's about to be some shit up in here!" she announced. She passed the four rooms on her left, peeking inside every last one of them. "I'll see y'all in the morning," she hollered to the remaining few that chose to sit around in their rooms, polishing their toenails and gossiping about the crazy run-ins that night.

"All right, Momma!" the youngest of the bunch replied.

She then made her way back to the room that Ty, Peaches, and Illusion all occupied. Ty was still ranting about how she was going to stick it to Illusion something serious.

"Oh, and Ty," Fantasy interrupted matter-of-factly, "if you were about that life you wouldn't have caught the beat down that you did, so kill all that noise 'cause you fucking up my high." Truth be told, she couldn't stand Ty or the ground her flat-footed ass walked on. Because Ty was one of the youngest in the entire house, barely eighteen, she felt like she had to prove something to everybody. Fantasy made it a point to let Ty learn the hard way. All the women in the house paid their dues and earned their stay under Chyna's roof. If Ty wanted to walk around like she couldn't be touched, parading and carrying on like her pussy was golden because she was still young and tight, then Fantasy would let her believe that shit. By the time Chyna was done with her, she'd be begging for somebody to pull out a needle and thread to sew her stuff back together.

Ty was left to nurse her cuts and bruises alone. She yelled obscenities at the mirror while she wiped away the crusted and dripping blood that trickled down her face and neck. It was a painful sight. Her swollen top lip was split wide open, putting her out of blowjob commission. She pulled the handheld mirror closer. Her right eye was nearly closed shut. She tried to open it, but the pain was so excruciating that she gave up. "Bitch!" she screamed and cried nonstop. *This ain't over, Illusion. Hell to the fucking no.*

4

Calling the room again, Chyna wondered who Sand could have been on the other line with this late. There was still no answer after several tries, and it was beginning to piss her off. She tossed the cell in the passenger seat, spinning a full U-turn back to where she and Sand had been lying low for the past couple of months. While Chyna had eyes on the streets, in the clubs, and back at the house, no one was watching Sand. That was a separate issue she chose to handle personally.

The day Chyna walked in on her mother's dead body was the day she also died. Someone had taken away the only person that ever meant anything to her. It was that day that she sold her soul to the devil. She didn't care about anyone but herself, and she terminated anyone that stood in her way. Just like her mother, money was her motivator. But unlike her mother, she'd be damned if she sold her own pussy to get it, not when there were always so many others ready and willing to do it.

Her mother worked the tricks like she worked her hair when she needed it just right. That bounce or that curl had to be perfect, not a strand out of place. She would freshen up, slip into something provocatively sexy, throw on a Marvin Gaye album, light some sweet-scented incense, and then wait for the knock at the door. She and Chyna had lived in the two-bedroom duplex unit for

years. It was in one of the worst crime-ridden neighbor-
hoods in South Dallas, but it was a roof over their head.
They had even learned that a murder-suicide had taken
place there. The landlord was never really able to rent
or sell the property for that reason alone. So when her
mother came along and offered him a deal he couldn't
refuse, he handed her the keys, accepting her deposit and
first month's rent in the form of sexual favors until she
could establish herself a source of income.

Chyna's mother made sure her precious five-year-old
daughter was fast asleep before letting her sugar daddies
inside. There was no way in hell her baby girl would ever
know, if she could help it, how her mother earned a living.
How she paid their bills was grown folks' business. But
sooner than later, and now a teenager, Chyna became
inquisitive about her mother's male friends, as well as
the nickname she'd heard them call her in the middle
of the night. And sometimes it didn't matter where they
were—grocery store, church, or school function—they'd
stop her mother and whisper just enough to get her to
squealing and carrying on, then they'd wind up at their
house later that night, in her mother's bed. Chyna could
hear everything through those cheap walls, more than
her mother ever knew.

Chyna's friends teased her constantly at school, cracking jokes about how her mama was the sidewalk of everybody's neighborhood. At first, the jokes made no sense;
then they became clear once she sat down and pulled it
together for herself. Her mother was a prostitute, and the
whole world knew it.

Her mother's promiscuous activities came to a tragic
end the day Chyna got home from school and found her
mother's bedroom door wide open, and her mother's
naked body lay sprawled across the bed with a black
garbage bag covering her face. It was the first time she'd

seen her mother helpless without an ounce of fight in her. It was the first time she witnessed death up close and personal.

After her mother's death, Chyna fled, refusing to be taken into the legal system. As the streets called, she greeted them with a handshake. They took care of her, introducing her to a newer reality. The one her mother tried to keep hidden from her.

Shortly after spending a few weeks on the run, Chyna began asking folks in the hood if they knew anyone by the name of D'Troy. As luck would have it, D'Troy was an established household name on the streets. Everybody who fucked around knew who he was or knew someone who did. D'Troy was her mother's only sibling and the elder of the two. Chyna heard her mother mention him a few times but never enough to indicate that they were close at any point. Regardless of the relationship he had with her mother, Chyna knew D'Troy was the only person she could turn to because he was the only real family that she had left.

Her mother hardly ever went around her own brother, and after moving in with him, Chyna believed she knew why. People in his hood referred to him as Killer-D, the ice-cream man. The women who walked the street corners knew him as their pimp. Her mother and D'Troy were from two different worlds but still apples under the same hopeless tree.

Spice 1 pumped out gutter rap lyrics through the worn-out, makeshift speakers hanging on the living-room walls by a nail. Baby bottles topped off with a concoction of cold syrup and codeine, crushed beer cans, empty baby food jars, baking soda, razor blades, scales, foil, and freezer bags cluttered the tabletops of D'Troy's operation, right next to bowls of weed and empty cereal boxes that stored most of the working supplies. Base heads would beat at the door all times of night, hoping to score some dope or establish themselves a layaway plan. The few workers D'Troy did have grinding for him would also come by numerous times to re-up on product or make a drop. They'd come in empty-handed and leave with a loaded box of Lucky Charms, Cheerios, or Frosted Flakes, holding enough work to last them a week. And the women D'Troy permitted to enter his domain rolled through it like a Soul Train line—dropping payment, scoring, and sometimes doing both. It was a trap—a trap to make money and a trap to lose it if the wrong person stepped foot inside.

It wasn't long before D'Troy was getting word from one of his insiders that his name was dropped in a routine drug bust as being the supplier. He knew then his entire empire was at stake. His confidante became the only woman he ever allowed to eat, sleep, and shit on his dime. He knew his days were limited, and it was that time to pass the torch to Chyna. She had watched him run his enterprise for three years, learning every aspect of it from the supply and demand of the dirty snow to the prostitution ring he clandestinely led. D'Troy knew that if Chyna was her mother's daughter, he wouldn't have to worry about a thing. He trusted her to manage and oversee all of his dealings just as if they were her own. He had taken his niece under his wing when she needed him, and now it was time for her to take him under hers.

Just days after Chyna turned eighteen, D'Troy immediately transferred all of his bank accounts and real estate into her name. Before the feds could come kicking in his door, he called up Albery Johnson, the lawyer he'd been paying in advance for well over six years to prepare him for the day he got knocked. Little did D'Troy know, Albery was not only a dirty lawyer that specialized in shady business, but he was also a sellout. When Albery found out all the charges that D'Troy was facing, he knew he could have gotten him off on a lighter sentence, a sentence other than life. But instead of paying them off, he sold the case, putting D'Troy in the mouths of the wolves that wanted him off the streets forever.

While Albery believed he was walking away scot-free, he had no idea that D'Troy had inherited a business partner along the way. What he also didn't know was that the day he sold the Donald Troy Wilson's case, aka D'Troy, his life, just like his defendant's, had been traded. Albery had a rope hanging around his neck so thick, and Chyna, on the other end, was itching to tighten it.

Turning into the Super 8 parking lot, Chyna decided to try the room again. This time it rang without being redirected back to the operator. On the third ring, Sand picked up.

"Yeah," she answered dryly, already knowing who the call was coming from without having to read the caller ID display.

"So, you're up?"

"Tsk. Well, it ain't like I'm getting much sleep lately," she answered sarcastically.

Sand's sour attitude didn't surprise Chyna at all. She held the phone as close to her ear as it could go. She listened for any other voices in the background. All she could hear faintly was the television. Her voice dropped to a whisper. "Well, why don't you come on down. We're staying at the house tonight," she informed Sand.

"I thought we were chillin' here for a minute."

"That situation has been handled. I got the all-clear on that earlier today," Chyna interrupted, referring to the detective that had been following them around. That was all Sand needed to know. "In the meantime, I have an

issue back at the house I need to deal with. I'm waiting
out in the car, so make it quick." Not allowing time for
Sand to reply, she pressed the *End* button. This was
another big test, and Chyna could feel herself losing control. She didn't like that shit. It seemed everyone needed
a reminder of who she was, and she wanted Sand to be
there to witness it, just in case the thought of pulling a
fast one ever crossed her mind.

Chyna adjusted her rearview mirror. She caught a
glimpse of herself. She was strikingly beautiful, just like
her mother had been. Her smooth ginger complexion,
naturally blushed high cheekbones, and long, thick
black lashes that enveloped her beautifully slanted eyes,
earned her compliments from both men and women. She
never needed makeup to enhance her beauty because she
looked perfect without it. Her mother would always joke,
"You're mama's li'l porcelain doll."

Chyna rubbed her temples. Her shiny lips were notice-
ably plump. From top to bottom she had *sexy* written all
over her. She was not the average five-foot-eleven-and-a-
half woman. She rocked a Coke-bottle figure with enough
breasts and ass to lend generations to come. She even
wondered herself sometimes how she managed to be so
blessed with a body that most women would kill for and
every man desired.

She studied herself in the mirror. It was time to put her
game face back on. She relaxed her thoughts, reassuring
herself that she was in control. This was her courtyard.
She called the shots. And it was about time motherfuckas
recognized that.

Ta-ta-ta. Sand tapped on the window. Chyna had the
engine still running, and her wipers were singing a tune
of their own. She unlocked the passenger door.

"Shit, it's cold out here," Sand complained as she
flopped down in the seat of Chyna's vanilla-pearl Lexus,
tossing her bag of clothes behind her.

Chyna ignored her comment. There was other shit running through her mind. She stared straight-ahead, the car still in park. "Who were you on the phone with?" She squinted her eyes, observing the different vehicles that pulled in and out of the motel's parking lot.

Sand blew into her hands and rubbed them together in an attempt to get warm. "I don't know what you talkin' about," she said.

Chyna tilted her head sideways. She stared deeply at Sand, studied her for the right answer, a better answer other than the one she was getting. Her danger-filled eyes warned Sand that she wasn't in the mood for the dumb shit. "I called. The line to the room was busy." She stopped and raised her brow some. "So you might wanna tell me who you were on the phone with." There was a hesitating moment of nothing. "My customers' profiles are strictly confidential, and I believe we've already had this conversation," Chyna reiterated to Sand. But Chyna knew she was a long way off from the direction she was headed. She already knew that Sand hadn't compromised her clients' profiles, but she threw the fish out there anyway. She wanted to know if Sand had spoken to one individual in particular, and that's all she cared about at the moment.

Sand finally said something. "I was just checking in on some things. You know, making sure Sabrina and Angel made it to the spot okay."

Chyna suppressed her laugh. She could smell bullshit, taste bullshit, and hear bullshit, so Sand was pushing her luck. Fantasy was in charge of all the check-ins, and the last time she checked, Sabrina and Peaches were the ones that were working the call because Angel had a special request ticket with another private client in Las Vegas. By now, she was laid up in the Bellagio, escorting a highly favored city councilman to his own pre-Christmas party.

Chyna's teeth slid over her bottom lip. "Humph. Really? So I guess everything was fine?"

Sand's eyes were locked on Chyna's. "Yeah, everything straight. They made it." The menacing stare Chyna gave Sand was intimidating, but underneath her clothing, Sand knew she was still a pussy, and because of that, she wasn't threatened, at least not now. She sucked her teeth. "You asked me to handle this business for you, and that's what I'm tryna do. I'm handling it so I can be done with this mess you done pulled me into."

Chyna admired Sand's wit and valor for trying to play her the way she felt that she might have been doing. She found the entire performance amusing—but worthless. Chyna turned her attention back to the road, then roughly shoved the car into *Drive*.

"By the way, when's the last time you spoke to your girlfriend, Rene?" she asked snidely, getting down to the real question at hand.

Chyna glanced at her passenger. Sand was handsome, and the color she wore complemented her best. A solid red Polo sweater, starched black jeans, black high-top Air Force Ones and a red baseball cap with a bold, solid black S mid-center. Her biracial genes gave her a smooth sandy-red complexion that won over plenty of hot chicks. Women practically threw themselves at Sand. Gay, straight, bisexual, young and old. It didn't matter. They would serve their pussy on a platter and feed it to her with chopsticks if they could. Sand was suave, that much Chyna would admit. Even more now with her hair cut low and faded, bringing out the tomboy in her stud-appeal. The long braids she once had were all gone. But in conjunction with her fine looks and boyish swagger, it was obvious Sand needed a recap of whose ship she was on.

Right then, Sand felt like her lungs had collapsed and her breath stolen at the mention of her ex. She inhaled, looking at Chyna like she was the Grinch who stole Christmas.

"It's been like three months or something like that since I last talked to her." She twisted her lips and screwed up her face. "Why you asking?" she inquired, giving Chyna a once-over. She was wearing the same white strapless corset dress she'd seen her leave in earlier tonight.

Chyna wanted to play this game along with her. She shrugged her shoulders. "Just concerned. I mean, we *are* family, Sand," she smiled impishly. "Anyone that works for me, I consider family. We look out. Make sure each other okay. I'm sure you can understand how important that is, right?"

Sand pretended to be listening, but the mention of Rene's name distracted her from anything else Chyna had to say. A million things ran through her mind. She wanted to scream, *"Fuck that bitch! That ho played me like a Pac-Man game. She fucked off and got pregnant on me. That bitch violated me. I don't wanna hear her name no-fuckin'-more. She can eat shit and die for all I care. Rene don't give a fuck about me, so why should I give a fuck about her? Man, she played me. All that time she was just playin' me. Playin' me like a damn fool."* But that was her own business.

Chyna believed she'd found Sand's weak spot judging by the look in her eyes. As they rode in silence all the way back to the house, the only sounds to be heard were the raindrops splashing against the windows and the slow train of tears that crept down Sand's face.

5

With $5,000 stuffed in her pocket, Rene felt like she had just committed highway robbery. She sped down a dimly lit two-way street, determined to get the hell out of the hood. As she flew over railroad tracks and drove through a secluded warehouse district, she couldn't help wondering if the money Chyna had just given her was even real, or, better yet, stolen. But stolen or not, she could use the cash, especially after everything that had transpired over the past few months.

Rene counted her blessings and was thankful every morning she woke up alive and kicking because three months ago, she could have been lying up in a hospital bed—or even worse, six feet under. Death had knocked on her door, found a key, and let itself in. She'd seen her life flash right before her eyes the night her fiancé, Vincent, pulled a gun on her, ready to determine her fate. That was right after she was raped by his accomplice. She kept telling herself that her intentions were never meant to hurt anyone. She tried for as long as she could to deal with it alone, but still, somehow, Vincent haunted her thoughts. She recalled the feel of his breath blowing against her skin while his hands rubbed her protruding belly. It was impossible to block out those memories of her unborn baby's father.

For too long she hid behind shadows, pretending she was happy when deep down, she was hurting—hurting because she was confused. Confusion never granted a painless transition, so why should she expect any mercy? Over the months, Rene wondered why it was so hard to live and love without limitations. She needed someone to make her understand how being in love could be wrong and why people were so threatened by *her* sexual decisions. And if love was supposed to be free, she wondered why in the hell she almost had to pay for it with her life.

Thinking about her ex-fiancé, and then her lover, reminded Rene why she was in the position she was in. She failed to make a choice between the woman she loved and the man who she had foolishly believed would make for a perfect future. But tonight, for once in her life, she was ready to face those truths. Sand was who she loved and wanted to spend the rest of her life with. She was also the reason she was about to put her life on the line.

6

The red Honda Civic was only a car's length distance behind. Deja had been following Rene for close to a week now just like clockwork. She had learned her routine, and everything about the woman was consistent. When she first spotted her that day leaving the barbershop that her best friend Nessa worked in, she knew right away it was Sand's girl. She looked exactly how she imagined she would look, if not better. Rene's jet-black hair was long and wavy, her skin the color of simmering honey, and her Bambi eyes a shade or two lighter. Together, they glowed like the moonlight. She was more gorgeous than any other woman Deja had ever laid eyes on, and she could see why it may have been hard for Sand to detach herself. But deep down, despite Rene's abundant beauty, Deja could sense that Sand wasn't happy. She didn't need a crystal ball to see through their relationship when the vibe Sand fed off spoke to her loud and clear. Sand wanted more, needed more, and Rene was nowhere around to provide, at least not from what Deja could see.

She didn't recall her being there for Sand on several occasions when she needed her to be. But the person that was there and came running was Deja, even when it wasn't her job to do so. Although it all was done out of the kindness of her heart, Deja believed *that* kindness had grown into something else. *Love.* But the last thing Deja wanted to do was wreck a happy home. That was beneath her character, but she felt she owed it to herself to find out for sure if those feelings that intruded her thoughts late at night were anything but wrong.

Rene turned left. Deja sped up, catching up to the light before it could turn red again. The rain began falling harder, making it difficult to keep up without being noticed. Rene's beam lights guided them down a narrow, dark road without a streetlight in sight. Deja held her composure. She was determined to find out what was going on with Rene and attempt to put together this crazy mystery that would hopefully lead her to Sand.

Deja's last recollection of Sand was her being hauled off to jail like some escaped felon. Then her mind raced back to the fonder memories and that one night she cherished the most, opening night of Sand's nightclub, Sandrene's. As Deja remembered it, Sand passed out at the club. She had been drinking the entire night, drinking her problems away, Deja reasoned. She didn't know who to call or where to take her, so she drove her to her place.

They staggered through the house, into the guest room, and onto the bed. As Deja turned to leave, Sand grabbed her by the arm. "Come here for a second," she said.

The touch, the feel, Deja knew where this was going. "You're drunk, Sand," Deja professed, trying to pull her arm away from the embrace that sent electrifying shock waves all through her body. "Don't do this to yourself," she kept saying in her weakest of voices. "You're drunk, so this isn't happening," she said truthfully.

"It is happening, and I know you feel it too," Sand slurred. Her drunken drawl sounded like Ebonics slang. Her hands soon slid from Deja's arm to her wrist.

"You have a woman, remember?" Deja painfully reminded, poking Sand in the left arm where Rene's face stared back at her—giving her an uneasy feeling in a compromising situation. Rene wasn't even in the room, and Deja felt her presence standing between herself and Sand, watching their every move.

Sand's hand moved up Deja's arm. "Yeah, but she ain't real with me," she exclaimed, staring into Deja's eyes. "You keeps it real with me. That's what I need, ya feel what I'm saying? Somebody that's gon' keep it real all the time." Sand's hazel eyes were barely open, but she refused to let Deja go.

The liquor on Sand's breath was so strong, but Deja wanted nothing more than to lie in her arms and allow those intoxicating vapors to seduce her all night long. She shook her head slowly. While her mouth was saying all the wrong things, her pussy was voluntarily translating the opposite. "Please don't do this. Don't tease me this way," she pleaded, disappointing herself as she spoke those betraying words. She wished like hell Sand knew what she was saying because if she did, she'd realize that every word that fell from her lips made her pussy wetter and wetter. She was going to dismiss the fact that Sand had a woman and that their timely affair could never be more than just a last-minute call for affection.

Sand pressed her forehead into Deja's. "I just need somebody to hold me," she said.

"You're drruu . . . unkkk." Deja dragged, her head falling back once those uneasy words full of unwanted excuses made way through her lips.

Sand's leading hand maneuvered its way underneath Deja's dress. "I want you," she whispered. She began pulling on Deja's clothing with her teeth, her hands freely exploring all the speed bumps on Deja's body where her curves molested every inch of her frame. Deja had to speak up. She was losing herself. "We can't do this. Ummm . . . This ain't right. Oh shit. Umm, it ain't right," she purred like a kitten standing in-between Sand's legs. Her head almost fell off her shoulders.

"Just hold me," Sand repeated. "That's all I want you to do right now."

Deja reached her arms around Sand's neck and pretended that they were slow dancing to the melody that played in her head. She didn't refrain when she felt her dress hiking up above her waist, lifting over her shoulders, and sliding down her arms. Sand unclasped Deja's bra with only the two fingers she used to trace the small of her back. She slipped it off slowly with her teeth, greeting Deja's breasts anxiously with premoist lips. The tip of her tongue caressed her swollen nipples like silk. She bit down softly, taking them one at a time between her teeth, then sucking them both as if they were tiny raisins waiting to spill their sweet juices.

"What if—" Deja stopped, feeling her thong being ripped to shreds right off her ass.

"Ssshhh," Sand silenced her with her tongue. She dropped her head and began kissing her way up and down Deja's bare neck and chest.

Deja was frozen. She held Sand tighter as the long stiffness of two of Sand's fingers suddenly began parting the lips of her begging pussy. It felt so good, so right. She spread her legs some more, assuming responsibility for what was already taking place. Those two fingers moving between her were soon bathing themselves in her sticky wetness.

Sand's voice was just above a whisper when she asked, "You see that?" She mingled the juices that coated her fingers as she slid them in and out of Deja's pussy with ease. She proceeded to suck off the marinade she'd helped to create, swallowing and savoring every last drop.

Deja was in another world. "See what?" She could barely catch her breath as she panted, her breasts rising and falling against Sand's come-coated lips. She opened her eyes for just a moment, then quickly closed them because the ceiling looked as if it were caving in on them.

"See how it talks to me?" Sand asked as her fingers took another cruise along Deja's warm opening.

Deja's juices made all kinds of sounds that she never heard it make before. Squishing sounds just like when her clothes washed or when a tide settled in against the shore. Her pussy was communicating with Sand in a language that only its interpreter could understand. It was letting Sand know that she could have it all. It was hers if she wanted it.

"You wanna feel me inside of you?" Sand asked her lover.

Deja couldn't speak. She felt numb all over. She wanted to pinch herself to be sure it was really happening. But real or not, she was right where she wanted to be—at her climactic peak. Without answering Sand, she just held on tighter, feeling herself being lifted onto the bed, and leveled onto her back. The golden heels of her four-inch pumps sank into the comforter and poked at her pillow-top.

"You want me between you?" Sand asked again. "Tell me yes. I wanna hear you say that shit."

Deja moaned even louder. How much more could she take? "Oh, yesss!"

"Keep holding me," Sand managed between kisses. She dragged her tongue from Deja's earlobes all the way south to meet her belly ring that was identical to the rainbow-colored ball in Deja's tongue.

"I'll keep holding you," Deja squealed in delight, her eyes completely shut.

Sand lifted Deja's legs and placed them over her shoulders. Her head fell between and her tongue not too far behind. She placed her mouth on Deja's swollen pussy lips. That sweet and tasty desire revived her lonely soul.

"Ummmm. Damn, Sand," Deja cried out in pleasure. She felt like she was being rocked into a trance as each breath she took sounded weaker than the last. Sand's snakelike tongue was moving feverishly in and out of her pussy, activating all the sensors that controlled how wet she could actually get. She almost died when suddenly Sand's mouth began sweeping across her clit in soft, then heavy broom strokes. She felt like she was being swallowed whole as Sand's fanatical flesh backstroked, dived, and floated in her creamy sea. And Sand's sensual slurps were confirmation that she was collecting every drop that oozed through her folds.

"I'm coming, Sand," Deja moaned, biting down on her bottom lip so hard it started to bleed. With her arms in their same position, Deja was ready to give birth to each nut that Sand had impregnated deep inside her. "Oh yes!" she cried out mercifully, wishing she could be at the other end of that bed, posed in a sixty-nine. She wanted Sand to feel it too.

"Hold me," Sand said as she buried her tongue deeper inside, ready to catch those children of hers with a tongue for a mitt.

Sounding like a wounded animal, Deja called out in satisfaction, "Oooh." Her legs wrapped themselves around Sand's body as tightly as they could until their bodies molded into one. "Oh God!" She couldn't take it anymore. Sand's lips were brushing against her pussy fast and slow, playing it like a harmonica. The more she squirmed around, the harder Sand's nose rubbed and knocked against her poking clit.

In between slurps, Sand encouraged her lover. "Take it. Don't run," she coaxed, French-kissing the lips of Deja's love some more. "Don't fight it. *Slurp*. Take it."

"Ew shit, baby. I'm com . . ." Deja didn't even have asthma, and she felt the need for an inhaler. Her squeeze then faded into seizurelike convulsions as her body began to shake and tremble irrepressibly. As Sand rose from between her legs, all Deja could do was lay spent.

The energy she once had was gone, and that ceiling that was caving in was now spinning around, taking her in circles. She remained quiet, but the inside of her pussy was still humming from the aftermath. She looked over her shoulder at Sand. Deja knew how guilty sex looked and as she fought back the desire to challenge her for another round, she sensed that Sand was already battling her regrets. Maybe even practicing how she would feed those apologetic lies to her girlfriend later—much later—long after the liquor wore off and the stench of their sex corroborated its own version of the truth.

Deja checked herself, then slid off the bed wrapped in complete nakedness. What had *she* done? What had *they* done? She took one last look back at Sand, wishing like hell she'd offer her a spot beside her. Between her. But she didn't. She lay selfishly alone, drifting in and out of an uncomfortable sleep. Deja patted her hair back down on her head because she could feel it all over the place. She gathered her thong, bra, and dress, suddenly feeling like a puppet with loose strings. Partly embarrassed, she left the room, quietly closed the bedroom door, and then made her way to the master bedroom. She could only wish and hope that their little episode wouldn't be the last time.

The next morning they ate breakfast like two strangers in a foreign place. The night before never being mentioned between either of them, although the passion marks on Deja's inner thighs told a different story that she couldn't get enough of.

Rene's car began slowing down. She was riding her brake lights. Deja had to let up. Make it not seem so obvious that she was on her tail, but she needed to find Sand. She *had* to find Sand. And she knew Rene was the only person who could take her there.

***

Rene walked past Deja so fast that she didn't even bother looking up to apologize when their shoulders collided. Her worried face was full of questionable sadness that Deja felt somewhat responsible for. She watched Rene jump in her car and speed off. Deja hurried into the barbershop, looking for her friend, Nessa.

"Nessa, was that—"

"Sand's girl? Yep."

"What was she doing in here?" Deja tried hard to not seem jealous, but it was written all over her face.

"What you think she was doing up in here?" Nessa flung her hands on her hips and looked at Deja like she was crazy. "Hell, she wanna know where her girl at. She say she got my card out of some jeans or something. I told her last time I seen Sand was at Sandrene's, and that the last thing I heard was that she was in jail because she killed somebody."

"And what she say?" Deja was more than just curious. She had to know.

"She said that Sand would never do anything like that," Nessa said doubtfully. "She thinks Sand being framed by somebody. She didn't go into too much detail, and I didn't ask no questions. And believe this," Nessa said, way too excited, "she had the nerve to start questioning me and shit like I know something. I told her like this. I'm her braider, that's it. I don't know nothing, and I ain't seen nothing. I ain't tryna be caught up in no conspiracy-type shit. Y'all can keep that drama all to yourselves. I have my own issues."

"What?" Deja's eyebrows folded in as she watched Nessa sweep up her last client's hair.

"Girl, you heard me. I got kids. Leave me outta that mess y'all got going on," Nessa rambled, giving Deja a dismissive wave. "I'm too old to be sitting up in somebody's courtroom or jail cell. Shit, I ain't trying to be funny, but I get up in there, and they might try to turn a bitch out. Have me all fucked up and shit, knowing I can never leave my Mandingo-dick nigga alone. He puts it on me too good."

"You talkin' crazy," Deja laughed. "Ain't nobody gonna turn you out. And they'd be crazy as hell if they even tried." She rolled her eyes at the thought.

"Naw, but I'm serious, though. Sand my girl and all, but if she done killed that girl in them townhomes like rumors have it, hell, ain't no telling who she coming for next," Nessa carried on, her face as serious as it could get.

Deja had heard enough. "Girl, quit with your paranoid butt!"

"I ain't paranoid. You said it yourself that the police pulled y'all over and took her down. Now, what would they do that for if they didn't have proof that she went off and murdered somebody?" Nessa shook her head and resumed her sweeping. "Just talking about it got me spooked. Look, girl, I'm breaking out in a chill." Nessa showed Deja the tiny bumps rising on her skin.

"Nessa, please. Sand ain't kill nobody! I'm sure that it was just a mix-up and will all be handled once it goes to court. If it even goes to court because I can guarantee that it's one of those mistaken identity cases."

"Girl, you just met her. Hell, and you talking like you've known her all your life. I'm the one introduced y'all. So unless y'all jumped in a time machine and took a trip back into time, you don't know shit about her either." Nessa began waving her finger. "See, I done told you a thousand times that you never know a person when you think you do," she continued. She was lit like a fire-cracker ready to blast off. "People do some of the craziest shit. You watch the news. You better get hipped and open your eyes. And what I gotta convince you for? Hell, you know how people can just snap, firsthand," Nessa said, reminding Deja of the beat downs she used to get from her ex-girlfriend, Toni.

"Okay, okay, Nes. Jeez. You've made your point already. Please spare me the I-told-you-sos and four-hour pep talks." Deja pulled her hair behind her ears. She knew Nessa would take it there, and suddenly, she was ready to leave without even getting her hair done. Nessa was always bringing up Toni as if Deja needed to be reminded of what almost drove her to suicide. She'd rather not think about Toni's ass at all. "My God, just bump my hair already," Deja shot, exasperated. She flopped down in the leather swivel chair.

Nessa emptied the dustpan into the trash bin underneath her station. She whipped out the cape, swung it over Deja, and snapped the clasps together. "And why haven't I seen you in the past couple of months? What your ass been up to, heifer?" she asked, switching the subject. She could read Deja's face as well as feel the steam shooting out of her ears.

"Keeping busy," Deja answered dryly.

"Uh-uh, school out for the holiday break, so come again." Nessa playfully popped Deja on the shoulder with the tail end of the wide-tooth comb.

Deja took a deep breath. "I'm running the club."

Nessa glided the comb through Deja's hair, then stopped. "What club?"

Deja tightened her body. She took a sip of her diet Coke before laying it all on her. "Sandrene's."

Nessa swung the chair around so that Deja could face her. "Say what?"

Deja didn't feel like she owed Nessa an explanation, but she gave her one anyway. Twisting her bottle cap back on and sighing deeply, she said, "I'm looking out for Sand's club until she gets out," she admitted. "Somebody has to do it. You know she worked too hard to build that club for it to just go down the drain over some—"

"Stop it right there. I don't remember how and when that became your problem. Deja, do you *know* what you're doing?" Nessa widened her raccoon eyes as she spoke. "You don't even know what kinda shit that girl involved in and you—"

Deja interrupted her the same way she had done. "Nessa, I'm a grown-ass woman. I appreciate you looking out for me, but I can handle myself." Deja was ready to jump out of the chair because she refused to listen to a second more of Nessa's nonsense.

"Gurl, sweet Jesus." Nessa grabbed at her heart.

"Aghh!" Deja held up her hand with a stop signal gesture, the same way kids did when they played Simon Says. That conversation was over before it could even begin. She didn't expect Nessa to understand, and she wasn't asking her to.

The very next day, Deja woke up to her normal Sunday start. She drove across town to the 24 Hour Fitness she joined years ago in an effort to ditch the stress weight she'd packed on over the years. Pulling into the parking lot, she spotted the car immediately. It was Rene's car. A silver Chrysler Sebring with chromed wheels. The same car she'd seen her in at the shop. She knew it had to be too good to be true to coincidentally bump into this woman two days in a row. She pulled in right beside it, hoping it would be her lucky day.

When she entered the gym, there stood Rene with her hair pulled back into a ponytail and feet slapping away at the black conveyor belt. Rene wasn't as aware of her surroundings as Deja expected her to be because had she been, she would have recognized her from the day before. She stepped on the treadmill next to Rene. She placed the earphones over her ears and began pacing her walk.

She listened to over twenty of the songs compiled in her playlist before she was able to finally get a break.

Rene grabbed the towel hanging over her shoulders and wiped the shirt-drenching sweat from her face and neck. She decreased her speed, bringing her workout to a halt. Deja's eyes moved with Rene all the way to the service station where she tossed her towel into the basket and headed for the door. Deja followed Rene, unnoticed, all the way to her car. As she pulled out of the parking lot, Deja pulled out right behind her. Every day from that day on, Deja followed Rene's faithful workout schedule, believing all along that it was a sign that she and Sand were meant to reunite.

Rene looked in her rearview mirror a second time. She saw the red car when she made the left at the light. It had turned with her. She realized she was being followed. She knew it. Chyna had set her up. She slammed on her brakes as hard as she could, skidding from lane to lane. The car behind her zipped around her to avoid hitting her from behind, doing a full doughnut spin in the middle of the street. She shifted into *Reverse*, then back into *Drive*, taking off down a narrow truck- and van-favored residential street. She looked behind her. No car. She kept straight until she ended up back on the main road. She drove at a raging speed in a hurry to get back to Shun's place. Nearing her destination, she grabbed her prepaid cellular and hurriedly dialed the number Chyna had hand delivered to her months ago while she was recuperating at her best friend's house. Rene couldn't punch all the numbers in fast enough. She was ready to give Chyna a piece of her mind. This wasn't the deal they'd made. She didn't agree to being followed.

Chyna's cell phone rang many times until suddenly, all Rene could hear was someone in the background scream- ing for dear life. And then she recognized the voice.

"Chyna, come on. Stop it. That's enough. Let me pay you off whatever she owe you. Don't do her like that, man!"

It was Sand, loud and clear. Rene wasn't sure how she had gotten them into this predicament, but she was determined to get them out. She hated that she ever had anything to do with her old boss Albery because that's what she believed this was all about anyway—his debt to Chyna. And if she could help it, she'd make sure that Chyna got every dime she wanted out of his raggedy ass. But in the meantime, all Rene wanted was for Sand to be okay.

She began screaming into the phone hysterically. "Please, let me talk to her! I'll help you get your money back," she wept until the tears falling from her eyes became blinding.

7

Her first customer pulled alongside the curb in a silver BMW blaring upbeat reggae music. Illusion stopped walking. She was soaking wet. Her hair and her clothes were sticking to her skin, making her feel icky all over. She gave dude a second look and hoped this was her money trick because she needed to get the hell out of the rain and off the streets. "Whatcha lookin' for, honey?" she called out to the driver, cautiously walking up to the passenger side of the car.

The driver lowered his window more so he could read her invisible *"pussy for sale"* sign. He looked like he had just come from a nightclub judging by the way he was dressed. He wore a black and gold long-sleeved polyester shirt, the first three buttons undone, and a suede hat with black and brown feathers sprouting out of the left side. The gold rope necklace was short enough to be worn as a choker, and not to mention so thin that it played disappearing tricks on her eyes.

With his hand rested on the steering wheel and his top three buttons undone, it was evident that he wanted Illusion to get a full view of the nappy hairs on his hairy chest as he leaned forward, marveling at her stature. "I'm looking for whatever you offering, pretty lady," he replied finally, giving second and third notice to Illusion's backside where a greater portion of her assets sat.

Illusion picked up on his Nigerian accent. Foreign men turned her on in a weird kind of way, but it was too damn cold for her to just be wasting time on some window-shopper that wanted the goods but couldn't afford the price tag. She leaned over into his vehicle, cutting straight to the chase. "You the police, motherfucka?" she asked boldly, hoping he wasn't vice. But she was still in Chyna's district if he was. All she had to do was breathe Chyna's name, and that would be her keep-out-of-jail free card.

"Come on now. You look much smarter than dat," the trick told her, not realizing his insult.

His eyes were bloodshot red. Illusion didn't have to assume anything other than this nigga was high as a kite. The lingering smell of marijuana bum-rushed her nose. Whatever he'd been hitting was so potent that she swore she was making contact. She casually disregarded his last remark. She looked over in the backseat. He was riding alone. She searched for a wedding band. There wasn't one, unless it was MIA, but since when had that ever been a concern of hers?

"So what you doing out this time of morning?" Illusion had to feel him out. "You looking for a good time, playboy?" she answered for him, lifting her head up every now and then. She was keeping a watchful eye out for a black Hummer sitting on plus-sized rims. She was paranoid as hell, to say the least, and with her back turned the way that it was, she felt like Chyna could have snuck up on her at any given moment and took her out where she stood, especially after leaving the post. She just knew Fletch was riding up and down the street looking for her ass.

"What da ya say you get me outta this rain and take me somewhere where we can talk in private?" Illusion suggested, her eyes darting from this fella of interest to the empty passenger seat. She allowed him a full view of her wet, voluptuous breasts that suffocated themselves against the fabric of her dress, causing them to resemble two perfectly round oil stains. Her engorged nipples only taunted her potential customer as all he could imagine was how they looked up close and personal. Her nipples were dark as ripe berries and shaped like mini gumdrops, and they tasted just as sweet.

"You want to go somewhere private?" he asked, ready to adhere to her last request. "Hop in. I'll take you there."

Illusion smiled. That broke the ice for her. She let herself in. All she wanted was out of the cold and rain, and if she could, make some paper on the side. She didn't have a dime on her. The only thing that was in her purse besides her roughed up ID was a makeup case, condoms, liquid KY, spearmint chewing gum, and a half pack of cigarettes.

"Okay, here's the deal," she said, throwing everything on the table. "You spot me a nice, clean room, and throw me, say, three hundred dollars"—Illusion looked like a financial representative going over the final numbers with her client—"and I'll be all that you need tonight," she smiled seductively. The heater was blowing strong. She reached over, turning all the air vents in her direction. "It's just so cold and," she let the words hang from her lips, "I'm all wet."

The man couldn't take his eyes off her. She was a fox. "All mines, huh?"

"All yours, daddy," she reassured him. Illusion knew she could wing this. She felt extremely confident. This was what she did before she got caught up with Chyna. She called all the shots, set her own prices, and kept 100 percent of the profit. She didn't need somebody else auctioning off her pussy.

"Sounds like a sweet deal to me," her date said without having to reconsider an offer so grand. "Me likes the show already." His English was fairly good, but his accent weighed heavy on every word. He stole one last look at her and couldn't wait to get her to that "private place" she spoke about. "You going to let me babysit you all night, huh? I think that might mean trouble for you, little girl," he warned, shaking his head and grinning at the idea of sexual punishment.

Illusion nodded while driving her tongue across both her lips. "Did I mention, I love pain?"

He bounced his head when he asked, "What hotel?" He was tired of talking. He'd let the anaconda he was packing speak for itself.

"Anywhere but Zaza." Illusion quickly strapped herself in, leaned back, and anticipated the events to come.

"By the way, what's your name, beautiful?"

Illusion was taken aback. She had never heard a man call her beautiful before. She was used to all the other labels they gave her, like Sexy, Badd-Bitch, Top-Ho, Silver Dolla, and the list just went on. Not one made her feel as special as, *Beautiful.*"

"It's Illusion," she told him, admiring his sincerity but thriving off the fact that she'd stumbled upon a square.

"El-u-john?" he pronounced, stretching his neck out like a rooster as he sounded out every syllable in her name.

She nodded. "Um-hmm." Oh, was she gonna have fun with this one.

"That's a pretty name for a pretty girl," he smiled again, his lips distending past his jawline.

When he volunteered his grill, Illusion wanted to scream. His gap was so wide she could have parallel parked a semitruck between it. "And what's your name?" she asked, almost afraid he'd flash that signature smile of his again, but she was determined to butter him up and stake out his value before the night was up.

"Muhedio," he smiled broadly from ear to ear. Either he loved saying his own name or Illusion had him so far gone that all he could do was smile and be happy.

Illusion returned a weak smile. "Can I call you Mu for short?" she asked.

"Sure. I don't see why not." Muhedio's head was in the clouds.

Illusion raised her dress a little, exposing two naked thighs. "Mu, have you ever seen a woman as fine as me?"

His wide red eyes grew even wider. "No. Never," he cheesed.

"So have you ever," she spoke slowly, "paid for pussy cat?" She slid her index finger in her mouth and around her tongue. Then she swung her right leg over the dashboard and let her thighs part ways.

Muhedio appeared to be in shock as he watched Illusion reveal her crotchless G-string. Beads of sweat invaded his forehead at the sight of her Brazilian waxed snatch. He'd give anything just to kiss it.

Illusion amped up her game. "Ever pay for a good fuck, Mu?"

His answer was shaky. "Nnnnooo," he swallowed hard, licking the ash from his naturally two-toned lips.

"Do you want to know why men pay for my pussy, Mu?" she asked him.

Muhedio nodded his head more than once, trying to drive in between the white broken lines ahead of him while being distracted by Illusion's pussy lips that hung off his passenger seat. She was disrupting the small amount of concentration he had left.

Illusion slipped her saliva-drenched finger inside of her opening. Her legs were now spread wider than before. She stirred up her juices, then eased her finger back out, never taking her eyes off Muhedio. She brought her finger up to his nose and made a sizzling skillet sound with her tongue and teeth. "Smell that." She slid the entire length of her finger across his upper lip, slowly enough for him to receive a whiff of it. His nose flared up as he strongly inhaled the musky scent wrapped around her finger like a breath of fresh air.

"You like the smell of that, Mu?"

He couldn't deny it. "Oh yeah," he nodded. He liked it so much that he was ready to eat her pussy right off her finger.

"You wanna know what this pussy tastes like, Mu?"

Muhedio's dick was bulging through his pants, struggling to break out. She had him so hot he was perspiring. "Yeah, I wanna taste the pussy cat on my tongue," he said, excited.

Illusion saw the huge lump in his pants. She reached for it. He was large. Larger than most. "Mama gon' take real good care of that as soon as we check in. Don't you worry." She lifted her other leg, spreading them both into a V shape. She was wondering if the Ecstasy pill that she had taken earlier was beginning to take effect all over again or if she was just too damn excited about this money she was about to make, because at the moment, she was so damned horny that she couldn't stop touching herself. Her pussy was aching to be fucked, her nipples were harder than stones, and she was salivating at the mouth just thinking about sucking the skin off his succulent love stick.

"I want to fuck you all night long too," Muhedio agreed, joining along in her dirty talk.

Illusion began cross-selling her goods in advance. "You do? You want this ass too, don't cha, Mu?" she moaned, grabbing her own ass and wiggling it like jelly in the seat.

"Hell yeah. I wanna put my dick in your ass too." Muhedio drove faster, totally ignoring the 35 mph speed limit. He had to hurry before he ended up exploding on himself. He squeezed his balls, trying to calm the urge.

About seventeen minutes later, he was pulling into the Adams Mark Hotel. The two of them stepped out of the car, and Muhedio ran around to Illusion's side, throwing his leather coat around her shoulders. He paid the parking attendant and led her inside the building.

When they got to their room, the first thing they did was head for the shower. Illusion blow-dried her weave and waited for Muhedio to finish. He came out of the bathroom with a white bath towel wrapped around his waist. Muhedio was at least five feet seven, medium built with extra storage, and mahogany skin smoother and darker than the richest chocolate. He was slightly bow-legged when he stood at a certain angle, and hung so far down to his knees that Illusion couldn't help wondering if he suffered lower back problems. His hair was cut low, and the only facial hairs he owned were the tiny beads under his chin that shriveled up like ground meat.

Illusion spread her pussy open, advertising it. She made it talk some, then used her muscles and made it yawn and blow bubbles. Muhedio was captivated watching it like a circus act the way Illusion's kitty box thumped as though it had two heartbeats. His mouth shot open as he watched her stretch herself like elastic, getting bigger and bigger, then shrink back to normal size—all right before his eyes.

As Mu stared in amazement, Illusion got excited even more. But right when Muhedio's dick began to nod at her, she hurriedly closed her legs back together like scissors.

"Hey, I wanted to see that," Muhedio pleaded with her, not wanting her to stop what she had been doing.

Illusion grinned, her titties saluting him. "I take cash only. I saw an ATM downstairs in the lobby." It was time to conduct business on her level now.

"I have the money already in my wallet," he whined. "Open it back. Do that thing again. Make it clap for Muhedio," he begged, stroking his shaft for a stiffer erection.

Illusion's face couldn't look any more serious. "Let's see it," she told him, raising her foot to his hairy stomach and denying him the privilege of getting any closer. She didn't trust tricks for a very good reason. The first and last john she ever let get over on her ended up talking her into doing all kinds of crazy shit like sucking him off while he fingered her ass. He even made her piss on his stomach while he worked himself up. He never wanted to stick it in because he was married and didn't want to cheat on his wife with a kid. He had told Illusion that he had a Social Security check he hadn't cashed yet in his pocket for $800. But after everything was all said and done, he didn't have shit on him but some change. So just like that, sixty dollars walked off, and she was left with his come smeared all over her chest and chin. So money first became her golden rule. She wasn't that strung out teenager like she was back in the day, selling her ass for weed, clothes, and new kicks. It was a new day. If it wasn't speaking dollars, then it wasn't speaking at all.

Muhedio walked over to his pants that were strewn on the floor. He reached in his pocket and pulled out his wallet. As soon as he opened it, Illusion spotted at least five credit cards. She batted her lashes when he held up six crisp $100 bills.

"See, I keeps money, baby." He waved the money in her face. "Muhedio wouldn't cheat the pretty lady." He handed Illusion all six of them, putting her mind at ease. "Keep the change. I know you'll be more than worth it," he spoke confidently, sucking in his bottom lip while he imagined all the positions he would be flipping her in. Now that the business was done, they could get down to it. "What are we about to do?" he asked Illusion, joining her in the bed.

Illusion pushed in the light switch on the lamp, turning the room pitch black. Inside, she was turning cartwheels because she knew she had lucked up and hit the jackpot.

Now, all she had to do was cash his ass in. With the money balled tightly in her hands, she told him, "You are about to lie back and enjoy this ride." She crawled over him, bowing between his legs. She parted her lips, slid out her tongue, and wrapped it tightly around every fraction of his stiffening ten inches. She deep-throated him like the professional she was. No amateur shit. One lick and swallow and Illusion knew he'd be ready to change his religion. His dick was exceptionally long, harder than tree lumber, and the biggest thing swinging in Texas. But Illusion couldn't allow herself to lose focus. This was business. Pleasure hitched a ride off her train a long time ago.

Three nuts, sore jaws, and an ass fucking like never before had Muhedio out like a light. He was sound asleep, and it couldn't have happened soon enough. Lying next to him and pondering her next move was all Illusion could do. She wondered if Fletch was still driving up and down the strip looking for her, or if he decided to run home to the new chick of the week that occupied his late nights. She even wondered if Ty's eye was still bulging out of the socket, looking as though somebody played ice hockey on her face. She tried her hardest to hold in her laugh at the image she saw clearly in her mind.

Ppppffff!

Illusion turned her nose up. *"I know this motherfucker didn't just fart,"* she cursed under her breath in disbelief.

Ppppffff!

Illusion couldn't take it. He had done it again. She clamped her nose together with her fingers and held her breath. She inched her feet to the floor and slid off the bed slowly. Then she pulled the sheets back over Muhedio's shoulders and got ready to make her break. It was cool while it lasted, but she was running a tight schedule, and whether or not he knew it, he had already maxed out his playtime. She wasn't trying to turn *Hooker to Housewife,* and this damn sure wasn't a *Pretty Woman* scene. He could save that shit for the next ho waiting in line behind her because she had moves to make, tricks to fuck, and money to get.

She threw her clothes on so fast that she hardly realized her dress was turned inside out, and she could have cared less. She had to get the fuck up out of there, pronto.

Muhedio's pants lay there in front of her with his wallet partially hanging out and in clear view. She bent down slowly and held her breath for as long as she could to keep from inhaling the long lost rat that crawled up his ass and died. As her sore knees popped, she quietly slipped his wallet under her arm. Then she fished for his car keys and quickly grabbed her purse. She kept her eyes on him as she backed her way to the door. Silently, she turned the knob slowly to the left. When she could hear the slight screech in the hinges, she slipped through the crack and bounced faster than a double-dribble half-court play with six seconds left on the clock.

8

Chyna's hotline buzzed like crazy in the cup holder. It startled Sand who had dozed off. Chyna hooked her earpiece over her ear and then hit the side button to answer it.

"Yeah?"

"Chyna, man, I don't know where the fuck Illusion at. Her and Ty got into it tonight. Fighting and shit, busting out my windows. Man, just going crazy!" Fletch rattled off, completely unaware that Chyna was already abreast of the situation.

"And where is Illusion now?"

"Man, I'm rolling 'round out here, and I don't see her ass. I don't know where the fuck she at right about now." Fletch was looking around as he drove up and down the street. Weren't too many black folks loitering in the area this early in the morning, so all he had to do was look for a tall, black female with a big ass and too-big-to-be-real titties, in a short, tight red dress.

"Well, keep looking until you find her," Chyna told him in her sternest of voices. "I want Illusion back at the house tonight. Whatever it takes."

If Chyna could have seen Fletch, she would have caught him mouthing the word "*bitch*" at her. He didn't have time for this shit tonight. He wasn't running a damn day care.

"And who in the hell told you to leave her there?" Chyna wasn't letting him off the hook.

Sand listened intently as she engaged in a heated discussion.

Fletch had some explaining to do, and he didn't know where the fuck to begin. "Her and Ty kept going at it like nonstop and—" The rest of what he had to say got lost along the way.

Chyna cut him off before he could piss her off any more than he already had. She rephrased her question so maybe he could interpret it better. "Who in the fuck told you to leave her there?" Her pitch dropped a few octaves.

"Man, Ty was bitching and shit and wouldn't let her in the damn car. That's when—" he stopped, realizing that his poor attempts of reiterating what went down were pointless.

Chyna had to take a breather before she completely lost it. She spoke calmly, resurrecting every angry spirit that consumed her. "Fletch, if Illusion ain't back at the house in an hour, it's your ass. Ya feel what I'm saying? Now get off my phone," her lips moved in slow motion, "and go find my bitch!" She disconnected the call.

Sand sat up, fully awake now after overhearing every bit of Chyna's fiasco. She couldn't figure out how a chick that looked like Chyna and donned all the feminine qualities a woman could possess could put die-hard fear in people's hearts the way she managed to do. But once she thought about it, it wasn't about the looks in this particular industry. It was about your rank. If you had street credibility, your name alone was a threat, without anybody ever having to see your face.

Chyna pulled into the Silverman Estates, where not one house in the division was valued at anything less than a million dollars. She punched in her code, then drove past the iron security gates as they began opening for her. Her MTV cribs look-alike was a two-story ranch-style, mini stucco mansion with well over 15,000 square feet of living space. There were parts of the house that not even she saw on a daily basis. It was the home where she housed all of her hoes who meant anything to her. Hoes that were costly to replace. Hoes that she kept under her radar.

As they entered the four-car garage, Sand eyed the impeccable fleet of foreign selections. All a different year, color, and price. She followed Chyna through a side door that led them through a mazed walkway and into an open view and rounded kitchen. They made their way through the dark and quiet house. Everyone had to be asleep. Sand found her way to the brown leather sofa, hoping to get comfortable enough to rest her head until daylight came. She lay her head back and flipped up the footrest. Then she took off her cap and placed it over her face.

Chyna was walking around flipping on every light switch she walked past. She made her way over to the spiral staircase where she began peeling off her clothes, stripping down to just her white sheer bra and matching thong. The heels of her shoes echoed off the twenty-foot vaulted ceilings as she climbed each step with dangerous anticipation. She made her way down the elongated hallway, her stream of hair bouncing against her back with every stride. She peeked into three rooms before entering the one where Ty had been sound asleep.

Only a scented night-light plug-in offered her a full view of all the injuries Illusion had inflicted upon her property. A minute later, Ty's entire body was yanked and dragged from beneath the sheets.

In an instant reaction, Ty grabbed and pulled at the tightness being roped around her neck. She couldn't scream, only wince in agonizing pain while trying to figure out what the hell was going on. She grabbed and plucked at what she thought might have been a rope but instead, had been the extension cord from the nearby wall socket.

"You think you running shit, huh? You in charge now, Ty?" Chyna screamed like a drill sergeant.

Ty shook her head, and her eyes pleaded with Chyna who was seething over her. Tears rushed down Ty's face, hunting for mercy, but they only made Chyna draw the cord tighter. Ty's veins strained themselves against her neck and forehead as her face flushed in multiple shades of reds.

"You in charge, Ty?" Chyna screamed again, this time waking all the girls in the house. "Ho, you running my fucking show now?"

The girls all ran out of their rooms to see what was going on, praying and hoping that they weren't next. They watched Ty laid out in the room on the floor with the black ten-foot cord wrapped around her throat and wondered what she could have possibly done to deserve the late-night ass beating.

Ty kicked her feet, knocking over everything they touched. Her cut and bruised face burned like fire, and her blackened eye was swollen shut. The girls gathered just outside their doors, facing the stairway and bearing witness to Ty's punishment, some seeing Ty's wounds for the very first time, having no clue that they were the markings from an earlier altercation. For all they knew, Chyna had caused them all, which terrified them even more.

Chyna nodded her head vigorously, "Oh yeah, Ty running shit now," she repeated madly, dragging Ty across the carpet by the electrical cord and down the hallway.

The women gathered around each other in panties and bras, some in neither. A few had silk scarves and bandannas tied around their heads, protecting their latest investments. Like a horse, Chyna raised Ty to her feet, then dragged her down the flight of stairs, backward, in a choke hold grip.

Sand jumped up when she heard all the crying and commotion leave from upstairs and make its way down. She was soon witnessing Chyna wrestle Ty to the floor. "Chyna, what you doing?" Sand asked, seeing how Ty's face was all beat up.

"Sand, stay out of this! This between me and my bitch," Chyna warned, overpowering Ty's strength. Chyna could hear her earpiece ringing in her ear. She didn't have her phone to see who it was but with her earpiece programmed to autoanswer, it came on after the fourth ring. Chyna hoped it was Fletch calling back to tell her he'd found Illusion. But it was not Fletch that she heard screaming in her ear. It was a woman.

"Chyna, come on. Stop it. That's enough," Sand kept telling her. "Let me pay you off whatever she owe you." Sand couldn't bear to watch. "She can't even breathe like that."

Chyna had Ty laid out in the middle of the floor for everyone to see. She wanted them all to receive the message loud and clear. Even the woman in her ear was constantly yelling for her to stop without any idea of what was happening. She finally began unraveling the cord. Not because she gave a fuck that everyone was yelling for her to stop, but because she didn't want to scratch up her merchandise any more than it already was. That shit had to be resold. She had calls lined up for Ty for the rest of the week, and she'd be damned if she was about to lose any money over her and Illusion's stupid asses. She was already calculating how much she would be out if Illusion didn't show up for the gig she had hired her out for the following night. Chyna was riding on ten grand that she'd already collected from her client as down payment. Half of the product he needed was packaged away in a leather guitar case, and the other half was walking around Dallas.

Ty struggled to turn to her side. She clutched her throat and immediately started choking on phlegm and blood. Her sobs turned into violent screams after finally catching her breath. Chyna squatted over her. She pinned Ty down until she was flat on her backside, and then roughly began yanking off her bra and panties.

Sand stood back feeling helpless. She couldn't watch what she felt Chyna was about to do to Ty, as if beating her to the ground and almost strangling her to death wasn't enough. Sand turned her head. She felt sorry for the poor girl.

Ty lay unclothed and groaning in pain with her fists balled tightly at her sides. She was boiling over with anger. Although she was only able to see out of one eye, she knew everybody was there, watching from upstairs and ignoring her cries for help. They wouldn't dare run to her rescue for fear of what Chyna might do to them.

Chyna paired two fingers, then roughly shoved them into Ty's dry opening without warning.

Ty's body jerked, and the muscles in her stomach tightened. "Aghh!" she hollered.

Breathing down Ty's neck, Chyna yelled, "You feel that? This is mines. I own every piece of pussy that walks around this motherfucka!" Chyna pumped her fingers into Ty faster and harder than before until her cold fingers folded into a fist, turning Ty's vagina into her own personal punching bag.

"Awww! Awww!" Ty hollered out in pain every time Chyna fist-fucked and slapped at her belly.

"I *own* this shit!" Chyna yelled louder. She gripped Ty by the throat, digging her nails into her skin until she drew blood. The markings from the cord were still visible, but Chyna knew it was nothing a few rubs of cocoa butter couldn't fade. "Look at me, dammitt! I *own* it," she said, jerking Ty's neck so hard it popped.

"And believe me, I will kill you if you ever forget that shit. Do you understand me?"

Ty nodded repeatedly as tears continued to pour from her eyes. The pressure from Chyna's knee in her belly had her folding over, clutching her stomach. She didn't know which hurt worse. Her eye, her stomach, or the constant pounding in her pussy.

Everyone was quiet as Chyna stood to her feet, half-naked in heels. She picked her keys up from the end table and tossed them to Sand. "Take this bitch to Parkland. They ask what happened, you found her that way." She gave Sand a serious look that dared her to disobey. "Have 'em patch her up and send her back to me. Ain't no sick time on my clock!" she hollered, looking in the direction of upstairs where the girls were all packed together.

Chyna didn't give her girls any reason to not maintain their full potential dollar limits. Each of them was on some sort of birth control shot that prevented them from getting pregnant and eliminated their monthly "visitor." She didn't want anything throwing them off rotation and interfering with her cash flow. So not even Mother Nature could come between her and her money. Not if she could help it. Chyna had this escort business down to a tee. When it was time to get out there and make that money, that's exactly what she needed to happen. No excuses.

She walked into her downstairs bedroom, closing and locking the door behind her. It was the only place she felt safe in her own house, but even there, she had countless nightmares of ending up like her mother, stretched out naked with a black bag tied around her head, waiting for someone to discover her body. She tried to shake those paranoid thoughts, but there wasn't a night that went by when those fears didn't haunt her in her sleep.

Sand stood in the same spot with an incredulous look across her face. Chyna had just beat the living shit out of this girl, and now she wanted her to go to the hospital and get stitched up. Sand was missing something entirely. She hurried over to Ty. "It's all right," she tried consoling her as she helped her up from the floor.

Ty wrapped her arms around Sand's lean body. "Please get me out of here. I'll die if I stay in this house!" she cried out like a baby while bloody saliva dangled from her bottom lip and skated down her chin.

"Let me just get you some help first, 'cause you bleeding pretty damn bad," Sand told her as she unknowingly made faces at the sight of Ty's wounds. She guessed that Ty would need at least ten to fifteen stitches. The gash above her left eye had reopened, and squirts of blood oozed down her face. Sand tried her best to remain calm, but the sight of all that blood made her nervous, especially when Ty had two bruised eyes, scratches, and cuts that looked like knife wounds to go along with it.

Sand knew she didn't want to risk being questioned about Ty's condition. She knew the picture it would paint of her. So to avoid all that, she had already made up her mind that she would be dropping Ty off and leaving the rest of that shit for Chyna to handle. She wasn't about to get involved in her whorehouse drama.

"Go get some clothes on," Sand told her. "I'll wait down here."

"Ooookkkaaayyy," Ty sniffled. She barely made her way over toward the stairs without her sore bones cracking. All eyes were glued to her. A few of them with evil smiles spread across their faces, clearly making it known that they thought the shit was funny and that she deserved every brutalizing blow. Ty moved at the pace of a crippled person as she climbed the stairs one at a time, using the iron railing for support so that she wouldn't drop to her knees or fall to her messed-up face. Her ribs hurt so badly, and the excruciating pain that shot around her pussy felt like rape to another degree. With every step she took, rampaging anger soared through her body, but she couldn't react. At least not now.

Where Ty was physically incapable, her psyche was not. She was on some flip mode killer-type shit. If she had a gun, she'd blow Chyna's brains out and feed the pieces to the first hungry stray dog that came her way. Never had she felt so humiliated. Never had she felt like murdering a bitch. The blood flowing through her veins was so hot it was boiling. She cut her eyes at each and every last one of Chyna's girls as she passed them by. All of them had watched her get her ass whooped and did nothing.

"What the fuck are you laughing at?" she charged at one of them. But no one was stupid enough to say anything. "Fuck every last one of y'all. You, you, you, and you, bitch!" Ty spat angrily. She made her way into the bathroom, slamming the door behind her. She was gonna get at every last one of them hoes in due time.

9

Sand pulled up alongside the fire lane in front of Parkland's emergency room. She kept her hand on the steering wheel and made no attempt to move.

"Aren't you getting out?" Ty asked before opening the passenger door.

"Naw, I think it's best I come back and get you. I don't want no part of this shit."

"I'm not going in there by myself. Look at me!" Ty pointed to her face as she wiggled her neck around. Frustration settled in every crease of her skin, starting with the lines in her forehead.

"I see you," Sand said, "and you need stitches, or else you gonna be walking around here with a hole in your face."

Ty shook her head again. "I don't wanna go in there by myself. Please, Sand. Come with me," she whined.

"Look, I'm not about to get involved with all that. Now we here. Go do what you gotta do."

"I'm not going in then," Ty stated, copping an attitude.

Sand looked around, then back at Ty. "Excuse me?" She started digging in her ears, determined to clear out the wax that was obviously causing her hearing dysfunction. "What was that? I didn't hear you," she said, leaning farther into Ty.

"I said, I'm not going in there. Fuck it. Might as well walk around here looking like a fucking mutt rat. Better yet, just take me to my kinfolk's house. I'll get her to take me." Ty waved Sand off. She had made her mind up, and that was that.

Sand was shaking her head. "Naw, naw. See, that wasn't the plan. You gon' either go in there, or I'm taking you back where I got you. Anything else ain't going down on my watch."

Ty threw her hands up, clearly frustrated. "I'm not going in there by myself. What part are you not understanding?" she snapped.

Sand had to catch herself. Before the counseling, before the countdown sessions, before the long walks of bringing herself to calm down, her temper was off the charts. She had scared Rene so bad one time that she wouldn't come out of the bathroom for three straight hours, and when she finally did, she threatened to leave Sand if she ever did anything like it again. Although Sand never laid her hands on Rene, she couldn't fight back the anger that consumed her when they would have their moments. That would be when walls got punched in, dishes got broken, pictures got ripped, and whatever was nearby got smashed. Her temper was always the reason for having to replace a broken picture frame or a new lamp. So now, with Ty, she was on the brink of losing it, and she barely even knew her ass.

"Look, ma," Sand paused, "I ain't got time for no extra bullshit tonight, a'ight? I already got enough shit on my mind." She slapped her hands together and interlocked her fingers. "Better yet, fuck it! I'm taking you back to Chyna. She can deal with it 'cause I ain't the one."

"Uh-uh." Ty reached for the door handle, and as soon as she did, Sand locked it. "Let me outta this motherfuckin' car! I ain't going back there," Ty yelled in a fit. "Take me home!"

Sand threw the car in *Drive* and slammed on the accelerator, burning up the asphalt in the emergency room's parking lot. She didn't slow down, and she didn't stop for the pedestrians that walked right out in front of her, only to be sent back running for the sidewalk. She gunned the engine heading back to Chyna's. As she changed lanes, she heard it—the sound of a loud siren.

"Shit!" Sand cursed once the flashing red and blue lights pulled behind them.

Ty looked in the rear. "Oh my God! They gon' haul us to jail. You got a license, right? I mean, you do know it's illegal to drive without a license?"

"Chill with that shit for a minute. Let me think."

"Oh my God. I can't go to jail," Ty panicked.

"Listen, just let me talk. I got this." Sand could feel her forehead perspiring as well as the tingling of her armpits. She was nervous as ever. She lowered the window once the officer approached her side of the car. She squinted her eyes as he pointed the flashlight directly in her face. "How you doing there, Officer?" she waved. "Everything a'ight?" she asked in a casual, *I'm-innocent-until-proven-guilty* tone.

Ty continued to stare straight-ahead as if she had been ordered to do so, trying her best to not make any sudden moves.

"Pop the trunk," the officer instructed.

As nervous as Sand was, her fingers fumbled underneath and around the steering wheel, trying to locate the trunk release.

"It's right here," Ty said through clenched teeth. She was praying he'd let them go with a warning.

Sand pushed the button, and the trunk instantly popped open. She tried to appear unnerved. The officer walked back to the rear of the car when another set of headlights pulled in behind him. Sand's breathing became labored as she watched from the rearview something being lowered into the back of Chyna's trunk.

She was trying to keep calm, but Ty wasn't making the situation any better as she rocked back and forth while sucking on her thumb like a lost child.

"Oh God. What they doing?" Ty asked after they both felt the car rock and a loud thud hit the floor of the trunk. "I can't take it no more. That's it. I need to call my mama. Do you have a phone I can borrow?"

"Ty, give it a fuckin' rest. Shit!"

Ty faced Sand. She couldn't stop her lips from trembling. "You don't understand. I can't go to jail. That's not a place for me," she wailed hysterically.

"Ssshhh. Ain't nobody going to jail. Just keep cool, okay?" Sand promised, rubbing Ty's shoulders. She was good at hiding her feelings because she was really just as scared as Ty was. She couldn't go to jail either, not tonight.

The officer slammed the trunk closed and knocked on the hood two times. When Sand looked in the rearview mirror, all the men she'd seen hovering around behind them before were getting back into their cars and pulling away. She waited a few minutes. The patrol car drove around, half-saluting her as he pulled off and proceeded through the traffic light.

After a moment of silence, Ty decided she'd speak up. "So, you ain't wondering what they done dumped in the trunk?"

Sand released the car out of *Park*. Her right hand navigated the steering wheel while the left stroked her chin. It was a habit she had when she was bothered or just contemplating things. "I don't wanna know what's back there. It ain't none of my business." She kept straight, looking around for anything suspicious. She obeyed the 35 mph speed limit sign until she finally came up on the freeway.

"You the one driving this motherfucka. It could be a bomb for all we know, and you ain't worried?" Ty asked her. "Well, *I* am," she said before Sand could respond. "Stop the car!"

"We ain't stopping, Ty. If you wanna know what's in the fucking trunk," Sand raised her voice above her norm, "then get Chyna to show you what's in her damn trunk, okay? 'Cause I ain't doing it."

Ty suddenly got quiet. The wheels in her head were spinning. "You owe her for something?" she asked out of nowhere. "You came short on some weight? What is it?" she asked, ruffling more than Sand's feathers. "Oh wait, I bet I know," she smiled, lifting her finger as if she was in somebody's classroom. "You fuckin' one of her bitches," she said, already convinced. "That's it, ain't it? You feel obligated to stick around 'cause ya bitch caught up. I ain't mad," she laughed, rolling her neck. "Chyna will take it however she can get it. I'm surprised she ain't got your ass out here selling pussy and shit. 'Cause you look like you'd bring in a killin'. I bet bitches would drop big dollars to fuck you," she quipped, getting underneath Sand's skin. "Yeah, just wait, though. It won't be long before she sniffs your ass out."

Sand cut and rolled her eyes over her shoulders. "You sure gotta lot of fuckin' lip for somebody that just got they ass beat. *Twice* in one night!"

"I'm just saying. She's got you running her errands and kissing her ass like you owe her for something. Like *you* her bitch," she said, getting back to her original point. Her head bobbled, showing straight attitude, but apparently, she was prepared to go down in honors because her mouth was on the verge of getting her face reconstructed. Permanently.

Sand slammed on the brakes and sent Ty's body jerking forward. "See, that's why your face all busted up now. It's your disrespectful-ass mouth!"

Ty was taken aback. She couldn't believe Sand had the audacity to come at her like that, all because she was speaking the real.

Sand reversed her breaths. "Look, you don't know me. Don't twist me up. I don't owe nobody for shit. I'm doing Chyna a favor, and I'm looking out for an old friend in the process. So, with that being said, you need to stay the hell out of my business and worry about how you gon' repair your face."

Ty bore witness to Sand's other side.

"I've dealt with scarier people in my past," Sand enlightened Ty, looking her over.

Ty rolled her eyes. "Regardless of all that you're talking, we *still* have the right to know what's back there." Her perfectly arched eyebrows folded in. "It could be a dead body."

As Sand thought about it harder, Ty was making perfect sense. She didn't want to be framed or set up for something she didn't do. And knowing Chyna, she was capable of anything, including letting others go down for her dirt. That's how people got caught up sometimes—being in the wrong place at the wrong time. She was already facing similar drama with Jasmine's murder. A murder she was being blackmailed for by Chyna. All Jasmine had been was an old fling. Now she was a concrete example of what Chyna and her ruthless crew was capable of. Sand didn't want the same thing that happened to Jasmine to happen to Rene. She would never be able to forgive herself.

Sand finally came to an agreement. "If you so concerned about what's in the trunk, you go look for yourself." She pulled the car off to the side of the freeway and placed it in *Park*.

Ty looked like a curious, yet scared little girl. She looked in the side-view mirror as well as behind them. The coast was clear. She gave Sand an unsure look before sliding her hands across the door handle.

Sand popped the trunk once again, infuriated but just as curious to know what was back there as Ty was. She adjusted the mirrors and pushed in the button to activate the hazard lights.

Ty eased out of the car, leaving her door slightly open in case she needed to go running back. Her whole body ached as she made her way toward the back of the Lexus. She tried her best to avoid the caked-up mud and instead, stepped right into a huge puddle of muddy water, splashing her legs.

"Dammitt," she hissed. Cars constantly flew past them as if the roads weren't wet at all, nearly sending her flying like a kite. She felt like a fool for wearing thigh-high cut-off shorts and a shirt with no sleeves as cool as it was out. Both scared and anxious, she lifted the trunk cautiously with the tip of her fingers until what was inside grew visible. She reached in and began unzipping the gym bag slowly. Her eyes widened, and she covered her mouth with both hands, backing away from the car in disbelief. "Oh my God. Sand!" she called out. She sucked in small amounts of air, then found herself stuttering to complete her sentence. "Come, come see this shit!" Her mind was on one thing—and one thing only.

As Sand rushed to the back of the car, Ty's face said it all. Sand took one glimpse at what had Ty's eyeballs about to pop out. Neither one of them could believe what they were seeing. Sand quickly slammed the trunk closed, looking around and over their shoulders, "Come on. We gotta get the fuck outta here."

Ty nodded. She understood. And for once, they were on one accord.

10

Rene leaned over into the sink, cupping her hands under the running faucet. She splashed warm water on her face. She had been in the kids' bathroom for over an hour without realizing it, trying her damndest to figure out where in life she went wrong. Just when she thought she understood her purpose, she came to the realization that she didn't. She wondered if all this was a hoax, just to see how far she would go or how long she would fight for real love. She even rationalized all the bad shit that kept happening to her as being some sort of sick curse. Maybe it was something she had done as a child that was just catching up to her now. Or maybe it was her mother who cursed her. Rene didn't know why life dealt her the hand she was given, but what she did know was that the shit wasn't fair.

Tossing around every justified reason for her bad luck, Rene cried all night and into the morning until she emptied her tear ducts dry. Every ounce of troubling regret reminded her that it was all worth it. She had to see it through. Chyna told her that if she did what she asked of her, Sand would come back home. Rene knew it wouldn't be long now. All she had to do was be patient and play her position. She missed Sand. She missed her so damned much that she made herself sick every time the possibility of not seeing her again entered her mind. She longed for her touch, her kiss, her compassion, and everything else they shared as lovers.

Whenever Rene stopped and closed her eyes, she could almost feel Sand's fingers climbing up and down her body. She missed their lovemaking. Those sex-filled nights of passion with them holding hands as they grinded to the rhythm of their headboard slapping against the wall. It was music to their ears. It was art. It was romance.

After lathering her hands, she reached for one of the Spider-Man hand towels that were neatly stacked on the linen shelf behind her and blotted her face with it.

"Rene, honey, you all right up in there?" Shun asked, tapping at the bathroom door.

Rene hadn't realized that Shun was awake. She didn't expect her to even be up so early since the boys were out of school on holiday break. "Yeah, um," she cleared her throat, then fixed her face and swung the door open. "I'm good," she lied, fiddling with her clothes. She wore denim skinny jeans and a fuchsia tank with a gold rat posing across the front. Underneath it were the words, "*Got Cheese?*" Her hair was disheveled, and that wasn't the only thing she was careless about this morning. She had on one white ankle sock and a faded red one.

The left side of Shun's face was pressed against the door just before Rene yanked it open. Shun wasn't the least bit surprised to find Rene up at the crack of dawn, crying her eyes out again. For the past few weeks, Rene had been waking up in the wee hours of the morning, some days as early as five, moping around as if something was bothering her. Always being known as the nosy one, Shun decided this time she'd let Rene come to her on her own without forcing the issue any further, the way she'd done so many times in the past. Their friendship was just starting to get back on track since all the mayhem that went down with Rene and Vincent, and she wasn't going to give her friend any reason whatsoever to not trust and confide in her again. She'd made that mistake, and she felt horrible every time she heard Rene crying late at night, feeling deeply that she was partly to blame.

"I'm gon' whip up some pancakes before the boys wake up. You want me to throw you on some?" Shun asked her friend.

Rene forced a smile. "No, I'm not really that hungry," she said, leaning the back of her head against the door. She rubbed at the shooting pain that had suddenly found residence in her left shoulder, debating whether she felt up to going to her yoga class this morning. Rene looked at Shun who was wearing a long, red housecoat with holes and permanent grease spots too big to go unnoticed. Shun's plastic Jheri curl cap was puffed out at the top, and she had paper towels tucked around the edges to prevent curl activator from dripping down into her face. Shun was Rene's best friend, but all in all, Rene saw her more as the family she never had. When Rene found herself struggling with her differences between loving men and women, she confided in Shun, but only to have her agree with all the others that criticized her open sexuality. She and Sand would have heated arguments over how Shun was just trying to tear them apart, and Sand couldn't stand Shun as far as she could see her and didn't have a problem making sure Rene knew that.

"She ain't no real friend," Sand would holler. "She just using you to watch them damn kids while she go gamble them welfare checks off. Shun ain't nothing but a hypocrite, and you know that shit. She won't even accept the fact that you gay. You see how she act when she come around me. Like I make her uncomfortable and shit? Talking about I'm fucking yo' head up. Where she get off coming at me like that? I can handle myself, Rene, but that's your girl! You supposed to check her ass. I don't even see why you fucks with her!"

With all the convincing Sand tried to do, Rene refused to believe that Shun meant any harm to their relationship. And it wasn't long before Shun's speeches soon began to make sense and have an effect on Rene. She began seeing the light Shun spread upon her for herself, and decided that life with a woman was not what she envisioned for herself. She wanted a man, any form, any fashion. Just as long as his birth certificate read boy or male child. She felt she needed to be a part of something she didn't have to explain—something that she didn't have to be ashamed of admitting about herself. Rene wanted someone she could show off to the world without being questioned about her beliefs when folks saw the two of them together, holding hands. But most of all, she wanted the family she never had. She dreamed of one day becoming a mother.

Rene knew that Sand couldn't promise her things that she wanted, but she so badly wished she could. All Sand could ever assure her was that she would be there, but for Rene, that wasn't enough. So when Vincent came along and swept her off her feet, wined and dined her, took her places she'd never been, and taught her things she never knew, Rene believed he was the one she was destined to be with, the man that would make her life complete.

When she became pregnant by Vincent, Rene thought she'd lose her mind because that part of her happily-ever-after plan wasn't supposed to happen as quickly as it did. Because not only had she deceived her fiancé, but she had also betrayed the true love of her life. She tried pulling away from that life that held her prisoner for so long and soon found her feelings for her girlfriend slowly unraveling. She no longer cared about her whereabouts or if she came home late, or at all. Her interest was in someone new. She made herself believe that in time she would eventually get over Sand, and with the course of life, fall in love with Vincent. She had a plan for escape, a plan for life, but she was scared. She was so scared that she said nothing and did nothing. She played the selfish role and kept her feelings a secret for as long as she could from both Sand and Vincent, which eventually led to an abundance of lies that triggered more lies on top of those she had already told.

But up until a few months ago when tragedy struck home did Rene ever believe that God would send her a wake-up call. She had almost been killed behind all her lies. But she was done with playing games with other people's hearts. She was done listening to what naysayers had to say about who she slept with. Hell, she wanted and deserved to be happy. She needed to be loved, and she wanted to love the relationship just as much as the person she was in it with, which was more than she could say for some.

Shun had that look on her face like she knew Rene was hiding something from her, but she couldn't blame her. "What's been wrong with you lately? You ain't been actin' like yourself," Shun confessed, making it sound as though some sort of psychic instinct had tapped in. "I can tell when something bothering you because you start lookin' feverish, and your forehead kinda wrinkles, then your nose starts frowning," she said jokingly.

Rene walked past her, trying hard to erase her worrisome face. "I've just had a lot of stuff on my mind lately, that's all. Just crazy stuff. Things you don't wanna know," she assured, shaking her head.

"Baby girl, I've just been sitting back and keeping my mouth shut because I do realize that I played a part in some of this, and I know I was the cause of some of them arguments you and Sand used to have," she acknowledged. "That much I can admit to your face. I could tell before I even walked in the house good that y'all had been arguing. I mean, I may look crazy, but I ain't. I notice things too." Shun swung her hand on her hip and walked around Rene, heading back into the kitchen where she'd been mixing up the batter for the pancakes. "I know Cassandra can't stand me." Shun paused. "I mean Sand. And I can accept that. Hell, I don't even think I blame her." She turned back to Rene. "But, sweetie, I was only speaking from how I was brought up. Back in my house, whooo—" she exhaled a mouthful of morning breath. "If you brought home a fag, better yet a dyke," she watched the way Rene's eyes lowered and how she rolled her neck to pop out a crick, as if that terminology made her ache, "you were asking for a Southern-style beat down." Shun's eyes widened. "You might've found your head at one end of the house," she used the spoon and pointed in different directions of her house for emphasis, "and your body down at the other. That was just shit you kept to yourself. Ya know what I'm saying? That was business you didn't discuss out loud. Humph. And my daddy was a preacher, so you know he didn't go for that foolishness under his roof." She scooped a tablespoon full of store-brand butter and then dumped it into the skillet. "So you have to excuse my ignorance. I don't mean to say the things I say to hurt nobody." She shrugged her shoulders. "I just talk that way 'cause all I know is how I was raised. Forgive me for judging you."

Rene raised her head and squinted her eyes as she listened, trying to grasp everything Shun was telling her. "Shun, where is all this coming from? I mean, you've already apologized like a hundred times already. None of this is your fault. I'm a grown woman. You didn't do anything," she said. "I did it to myself, and I'm the one who has to live with it for the rest of my life. I'm the one that cheated on Sand and got pregnant by someone that tried to kill me, someone I thought I wanted to spend the rest of my life with. You didn't take any part in that," Rene revealed to her. "Even if you hadn't slipped up and told her about Vincent and the baby, she would have still found out. It was just a matter of time. Secrets like that don't stay hidden forever," she said.

Shun exhaled. "Okay. Now I don't feel so bad," she laughed, making light of the conversation. Rene joined her laughter. Shun had missed Rene's bright smile for the last couple of months that she had been staying with her and the boys.

Rene walked over to her. "I love you, girl, with your crazy ass," she mused, throwing her hands around her to steal a hug. "I don't know what I would do without you."

"I love you too, honey." Shun let out a sigh. "Now that we're understood on this," she looked around making sure her four rug rats weren't up yet. She was already about to renege on the promise she made to herself. "Tell me what you were crying about in that back room late last night when you came in here. Are you hurting? Is something bothering you? Talk to me." She brushed the back of her hand across Rene's forehead.

Rene closed her eyes, then opened them. She inhaled a nose full of blueberries that filtered through the small, stuffy kitchen.

"Is it Sand?" Shun pressed.

Rene nodded her head once.

"Is she in some trouble?" Shun asked, concerned.

Rene's eyes began to water while her face twisted into a frown. As if on cue, tears automatically came rushing down her face. She swiped at them, feeling the swollen bags underneath her eyes that Shun must've seen as well.

"She . . . She's in real bad trouble," she sniffed. "And I don't know where she could be."Shun pulled Rene closer to her and allowed Rene's head to drop to her shoulder. She rocked her gently as if she were her own child. "It's gon' be okay," she consoled her. "Is there something I can do?" She felt Rene shake her head. Shun never thought she'd say this, but she opened her mouth and let her heart do the talking. "Y'all will get through this, honey. I promise y'all will. The two of you were meant for each other. This is just a test. You remember what the pastor said last Sunday, don't you?"

Rene's cries grew louder.

"If you want something bad enough, you'll fight for it. Even when it seems that the battle is lost," Shun quoted from memory. She offered her more advice. "Fight for what you believe in. If it feels right to you and right for you, then, hey, so be it. Do what makes you happy," she added.

"And you know what's so messed up?" Rene lifted her head, as never-ending tears made a pool out of her face. "I can't even tell you the last time that I told her I loved her."

Shun lightly dabbed at the corners of Rene's eyes with her thumb. "She knows you do, hun."

"The holidays and everything," Rene carried on. "Oh my God. We have never spent the holidays apart," Rene sobbed like a young child in great pain.

"Y'all are gon' be all right. I promise you that. It won't be long before y'all both running around here all cuddled up, hugging and kissing like the lovebirds y'all are." Shun circled Rene's back with her right hand and tried changing the subject to keep Rene from crying herself sick. "Speaking of holidays, you see that Charlie Brown tree in there?"

Rene forced a chuckle out of her cry. That tree was the first thing she spotted when she walked in the door late last night. She recalled thinking to herself, *What Dumpster did Shun pull that one out of?* Rene raised her head and wiped her wet face.

"I'ma need you to help me get the lights up on it," Shun said, snatching up a pork link from the strainer. She bit off half of it and chewed as she talked.

Rene looked over at the naked tree. The only thing on it were the handmade ornaments the kids made for it at school that read, "*My mommy knows Santa Claus,*" and the other, "*We want a PlayStation 3 this year.*" She uttered a laugh. "Well, I guess we both know what the kids want this year," she sniffed, almost forgetting about what brought on her tears in the first place.

Shun grabbed the bowl of batter and began pouring the last spoonfuls of it into the skillet. "Yeah, but I don't think I can afford a video game that costs almost six hundred dollars. Hell, I don't even think," she looked around the house, "that anything in here costs me that damn much."

They both scanned the room. Shun was probably right. Everything she had was either given to her or bought at a clearance sale, garage sale, white sale, tax sale, or close-out sale. Shun was the thriftiest shopper one could ever know because she didn't believe in spending a lot of money on unnecessary things that would eventually wear down or give out on her. She'd rather put that money to use somewhere else, like a trip to a Louisiana casino to increase her odds. She awaited that big payday like everybody else she knew on welfare and prayed for the day she could walk proudly into that Human Resource office to tell her attitude-having caseworker who intentionally screwed up her paperwork every six months (delaying her food stamps, welfare check, and children's Medicaid), to kiss her crusty, dusty black ass. That'd be the day.

Rene reached in her back pocket and pulled out the folded brown envelope that she received as a sign-on bonus from Chyna the night before. Shun, on the other hand, continued to flip the pancakes as if she worked as a cook for IHOP or something. She would even shake the pan a couple of good times to even out the butter, imitating her favorite cook show host, Chef G. Garvin.

"Shun," Rene paused. "I want to give this to you." She extended her hand with the envelope flat in her palm. "It's for everything you've done for me these last couple of months," she smiled softly.

Shun turned her body around and accepted the envelope, smearing pork grease on it before it was fully in her grasp. She wiped it on the side of her robe, giving Rene a strange look out of the corner of her eye. She wondered what it could be. She finally lifted the flap, noticing how the security seal had already been broken. Her eyes shot wide open, and her mouth dropped with shock as she flipped through every single Benjamin big face. The white and brown bold printed currency strap tucked down inside read $5,000.

"Where'd you get this kind of money?" Shun blurted, trying to collect herself. She had never seen so many $100 bills at one time, all crisp and clean as if they'd just come from under the iron. "I can't. I mean. You just . . ." Shun was speechless. All she could think was that Rene had seriously lost her mind. "You carry this type of cash on you, girl?" she finally got out.

"It's hard to explain, to be honest, and I'd rather not try," Rene told her.

Shun held the big faces up to the light fixture in her kitchen, checking for the money's background features.

Rene laughed. "It's real, Shun. I've already done all that."

"Oh my God! All mines?" Shun asked. Rene nodded her head. "Well, hell, you can come on and move in since this how you show your gratitude," Shun fell out laughing, slapping her hands together. "You want my bedroom? You know all you gotta do is say the word."

Rene laughed at her friend's silliness. "I'm just fine where I am. Thank you, though," she giggled.

Shun just stared at Rene, still surprised Rene was seriously giving her all that cash. "Thank you!" She started screaming as if she just hit the lottery. "Thank you, thank you, thank you." Shun was spinning and jumping around in her kitchen as though she'd been touched by the Holy Ghost. She looked at the ceiling, then back at Rene. "God knows I've been praying for a miracle like this. My boys need clothes, shoes, haircuts . . ." Shun had been cutting their hair for so long now that she couldn't recall the last time that she was able to afford a professional cut for them. And the kids in the neighborhood had teased them so much about having plugs in their heads that Shun just stopped cutting it altogether. She turned to her friend and held her tightly. "Now I can give my babies *their* idea of Christmas. God knows how much I needed this." She stopped to just really look at her best friend. "You have no idea how grateful I am," she sniffed, and her voice began to crack with every word.

"You deserve it, Shun. Now, come on and quit all that silly stuff, woman. You making me cry again." Rene vainly wiped at her own tears that started to trail down her face again. "Let's put some clothes on that tree," she coughed and laughed simultaneously.

"Forget that tree," Shun shouted, turning off the burners and piling hotcakes, links, and sweet buttered rice onto the four plates. "I saw another one way better than that. They got 'em on sale at Walmart. Wake the boys 'cause we 'bout to go shopping." Shun rushed around her kitchen pulling spoons and forks from the dishwasher. She shuffled things around in the pantry, trying to locate the syrup.

Rene took a step closer to her friend. "But before we go anywhere, we gon' do somethin' about this hair of yours because this," Rene lifted the plastic cap from Shun's head, "will not win you a diva award, ma'am," she teased.

Looking over her shoulders, ready to explain why, "Girl, I been knowing that," Shun stated. "That just goes to show you how long it's been since I've done something for me." She picked up one of her curls. "This hair right here is a sacrifice and a reminder of what being single and raising four kids can look like."

"Well, it's a brand-new day, and all that's about to change. It's time, Shun, to start doing something for Shun. Don't you agree?" Rene tilted her head sideways.

"You're absolutely right. I don't even know how it feels anymore to look worth something," Shun admitted embarrassed. "Maybe that's why I can't find no damn man," she laughed, apparently figuring out the answer to her problem.

Rene joined her. "Maybe," she laughed. "But you'll see what wonders a little makeup and a fine-tooth comb can do." She popped her tongue and winked her eye. "Just leave the beautifying up to me. I'll show you how to work it."

"And I know you will." Shun turned off all the burners. "Now, let's eat."

Rene grabbed a pork link right off the pan.

"Now that ain't that rabbit food you be eating on," Shun warned. "So don't come hollering about you've been poisoned when your gut pokin' out like mines."

"Yeah, I know. Sand buys these all the time." She wiped the grease from her lips with the back of her hands. She missed Sand so badly.

Shun began placing all the plates on the dining-room table. "Why don't you call her?" Shun asked matter-of-factly, figuring it was as simple as that.

"She doesn't answer," Rene pouted.

Shun yelled at the top of her lungs, "Boys!" She could hear the doors in the back room starting to open.

"I think right now Sand is just taking a break from all of this. I can't expect her to be any more understanding than I would if I were her," Rene sighed truthfully.

Shun stood up from the table. "Yeah, but nobody's perfect. We've all made our mistakes."

"Humph. I hope she sees it that way. I wouldn't forgive me if I were her."

"Rene, you're human. Let it go." As the boys filed in one line, Shun issued their forks. "And don't touch nothing until you've said grace," she told them.

"God is great. God is good. Let us thank him for our food. Amen."

Shun looked at them crazy as they rushed through the prayer. She shook her head, watching them all dive in.

Rene picked at her pancake with a fork. *Let it go. And how exactly am I supposed to do that?* she thought. Once again, she had lost her appetite.

11

Deja woke half-naked in a bra and boy shorts with the Saturday morning sun slicing through the vertical blinds of her bay window. It reminded her that she had more to do than just lie up and daydream. She tossed the quilted covers back, knocking two of the square tasseled pillows to the floor. It was one of the coldest December mornings she recalled in weeks, and yet, the sun was shining brightly. But that was Texas weather for you. One day you're sporting flip-flops and spaghetti tanks, the next, a fur coat and snow boots.

Deja swept the floors with her bare feet, rushing toward the thermostat. It was sixty-one degrees freezing in her house, according to the digital display. She kicked the heater on, then stood there for a second until she could hear the air vents coming alive. She walked around the house, room to room, searching for her red faux fur slippers. Making her way into the media room, she could hear Whiskers, a belated birthday present from her aunt, purring and scratching at the closet door. She slid the door back and loaded him into her arms.

"Hey, boy," Deja said, rubbing the top of her cat's brown and white fluffy head. "How'd you get yourself in there, huh?" Just as she was turning to shut the door, she spotted her feet warmers.

Ding, ding, ding!

Deja put Whiskers back on the floor. "Just a second," she called out, almost running back to her bedroom to find some decent clothes to slip into. She wasn't expecting anyone, so she wondered who could be ringing her doorbell, especially this time of the morning. She snatched off her satin scarf and allowed her freshly permed hair to fall in place with only a few shakes.

Deja punched in the security code on the keypad, deactivating the alarm. She lived alone, and with all the criminals lurking freely, she had to practice extreme safety precautions. She zoomed in the peephole to get a close-up of the five-foot-ten individual staring back at her. When she flung the door open, her expression gave an unwelcomed greeting.

"What up, boo? I see you still looking fine as hell!"

Deja's face held its sour stare. "Toni, what are you doing here?" Deja peeped farther outside her door, making sure none of her neighbors were out like usual, just in case Toni decided to cause a scene like she was known to do.

Toni sucked in both her lips and then grazed her teeth across the bottom one, taking in Deja's new body. She was sexier than she last remembered, but still pigeon-toed, five feet eight, and at least a buck forty with a curvaceous backside. She was a five-star chick on the real. Toni used to do things with Deja she never attempted with anyone else. And the very thing she definitely couldn't forget—Deja was an undercover freak!

"Ain't you glad to see me?" Toni beamed. "I mean, damn. I should be getting a hug, kiss, or something like that." Toni's mouth quivered with every flashback. She could bite the shit out of Deja's ass right now. That's how sweet she looked in those tight-ass aerobic tights and top. And the way her nipples stood at attention, Toni was positively, without a doubt, sure that Deja wasn't wearing a bra. "Damn, girl, what you been doing? Pilates or something?"

Deja stood there unamused and suddenly sick to her stomach. Agitated, she said, "Toni, what do you want with me? Why are you here?" Deja's hand rested on the doorknob.

"Come on, now. This the type of welcome I get? Don't be like that, baby. We too good for that." Toni took baby steps forward, moving closer to the woman she used to call hers.

Deja eased back into her house, the door barely open. "Look, Toni, you know you ain't supposed to be around me, so why in the hell are you over here?" Deja reminded, ready to whip out the restraining order she had placed on Toni last year after one too many physical altercations.

Toni threw up her hands. "Damn! I ain't tryna start no trouble for you, ma. I'm just checking on you. You all right? Life treating you good? Shit, I ain't seen your ass in what, a year?" Toni exhaled. "You actin' like you scared of me or something." She continuously looked Deja up and down, undressing her like the good old days. Only this time her eyes had to do all the work. "I've been thinking about us lately. You remember how we used to kick it?" She was damn near begging Deja to reminisce back to those wonderful times that seemed like only she could recollect. She subjected herself to a calmer approach. "I made a few bad choices," she confessed, "but goddamn, a nigga done changed."

Deja rolled her eyes upward, her brow waving the people's eyebrow. This whole routine was all too familiar, and the same way she was sick of it then is the same way she was sick of it now. She wasn't buying into any of Toni's bullshit tactics to try to win her back. She'd heard it all before. And suddenly Toni wanted to admit to being wrong. Please. Now was not the time for a confession session, so she could save that mess for church. As far as Deja was concerned, Toni could pocket that bullshit for somebody who gave a damn. She gasped as she had replaying flashbacks of the broken noses, the busted eyes, even all the hair she lost from just putting up with Toni's abusive and jealous, bipolar ass. Deja wanted to grab the mop from behind her door and give it her best shot—right up her ex-girlfriend's ass.

"Toni, I gotta go. Thanks for being even slightly concerned, but I'm not going there with you again."

"What? You got somebody up in there?" Toni asked, stepping back and doing a double take. She spotted the chameleon-painted Chevy Caprice parked in the driveway beside Deja's red Honda Civic. "Oh, I get it," she pointed to Deja. "You tied up," she gathered, unleashing a phony sense of concern. "I'm cutting into your mix and shit, huh? That's what that is, D? You occupied up in there?"

Deja stood there hesitating to speak another word, although she'd already said more than enough. Her face was as blank as a drawing board, but inside, she was applauding Toni for finally getting the picture. She was now even gladder that she had Sand's car towed to her house instead of to the address on the insurance card because now, it was proving to be the perfect prop. Although no one else was in the house with her, she knew it was probably safer for her to lead Toni into believing there was.

"So, you giving up my pussy?" Toni whispered, feeling disgusted by her own accusation. "You letting another motherfucka have my goods? Hit my shit?" she lashed out.

Deja remained quiet. Even the birds that crowded around her front yard tree could figure this one out. It wasn't a secret that Deja contemplated seeing other people before, during, and after their breakup. And it wasn't even up for discussion because what she did was her own business. She didn't have to answer to Toni, nor did she owe her an explanation of any kind. They were finished the day she laid her hands on her for the very last time.

"I can't believe this shit," Toni sneered loudly.

"Toni!" Deja said again. "I really have to go."

Toni stepped back onto the welcome mat. She inhaled the aromatic lavender and chamomile scent that seeped from Deja's pores, arousing all her senses, and briefly, Toni found herself fantasizing. She recalled the way Deja's pussy use to melt in her mouth just like cotton candy on ice. The way it curved to her lips and cupped perfectly underneath her chin, making going down on Deja appear as a piece of sexually explicit artwork that not even some of the most prominent artists of history could portray. Toni savored the moment, not wanting to let go and accept that Deja had moved on without her.

Quiet wasn't a part of Toni's nature, so she had to say what was on her mind, even if Deja wasn't trying to hear it. "What I ever do to you? You won't even give me a fucking chance?" Toni pleaded. She opened her arms out. "I'm good now. I done been to anger management and all that shit, baby girl. Give daddy another chance. I promise I won't do that shit again." Toni was willing to get on one knee and beg if it came down to it. "Don't do me that way, D. That's my pussy right there," Toni pointed to Deja's middle. "My name all over that shit," she said arrogantly.

Deja looked up at the sky. Last night's rain left its imprint, and the breeze that slid up and down her neck assured her she was still alive and that this wasn't a cold day in hell, because for a second there, she thought that's exactly where she was, because Toni was the devil calling in for a favor. She erased her conceptual distractions and faced Toni with a harder truth.

"First of all, you can quit screaming before you wake up my damn neighbors. And second of all, *'my pussy'* will never belong in *'your mouth'* again. So quit claiming it. Now, do yourself a favor and find somebody else to harass." She surfed her mental Rolodex. "And does Ms. Benefield know you're here, violating your probation?" Deja interrogated with a roll of the neck.

Toni picked up her face. "You funny. You real fucking funny these days. You really must think I give a damn about these white folks. And if I wanted to harass your ass, you'd feel it, baby. Believe that. Know that!" Toni held up her hands and backed away from the door. The mention of her PO helped her reconsider the more important things in life, like her freedom. "I'ma let you make it with all that fly shit. You think you too good now 'cause your daddy done moved you out of the ghetto and put you out here with these bougie, nosy motherfuckers?" Toni's head moved up and down as she spoke with much conviction. "Just remember, you can take the girl out of the hood, but you can't take the hood out of the girl." Toni flashed that permanent reminder that Deja must've needed. "This was us right here. All day, every day. Don't you realize by now that I love you, girl?"

Inside Toni's left wrist was a heart with the letters D and T in the center. Toni had used a pencil eraser to trigger the abrasion, persistently rubbing layers of skin away to shape a slightly deformed heart with her and Deja's initials carved inside of it. That heart signified a time in Deja's life when she and death became best friends, and the people around her became her enemies. It was her lowest point. A time when she hated herself for allowing love to weaken her the way that it had. Now, there was nothing that could reduce her to that way of thinking again, not even Toni and her phony lullabies.

"My father moved me out here to get me far away from your sick ass!"

"Listen to you. You're even starting to talk like these motherfuckas." Toni shook her head sadly, a visible frown painted her disappointment. "I had hope for you, girl," she said with a twisted grin. "But you ain't learned shit since I been away."

"Fuck you! Are you finished?" Deja's tempo changed drastically, competing against Toni's. "Take your ass back to the hood and leave me the fuck alone before I call the police on your ass," she hollered, her threat turning into a promise. "I bet you understand *that*, now, don't you?"

"I ain't scared of no law! Like I'm supposed to go run and hide off of a threat?" Toni said, outshouting Deja. She slapped her hands against her jeans. "So, I guess it falls like that now?"

Deja didn't say a word.

Toni tucked in her lower lip. "Fuck it. Save it. I'll roll," she told Deja. She pushed her finger into her chest, taking baby steps backward toward her F150 truck she had parked alongside the curb. "You do this to me?" she asked, shaking her head solemnly. "You can't get rid of me, D! You ain't figured that out by now? I'm in here," Toni said, pointing to her own head. "I'm locked in that motherfucka, and I'm the only one with a key, baby girl." She closed her fist, then blew some steam off into it like a microphone check. "But it's all gravy, baby," she hollered, fanning her bling in the air. "You don't fuck with me no more after all the shit we done been through? Ha-ha. Deja's a brand-new woman now, y'all!" she shouted. "Miss New and Improved got a new attitude!" Toni sang out, mocking Deja. "I'm out, boo. You ain't gotta worry about me no more. That was ya chance right there."

Deja shook her head in pity. In a way, she felt sorry for Toni because she realized that the woman needed all the help she could get. And to think there was a time when she worshiped the ground Toni walked on. Not anymore. Toni was battling something much deeper than Deja had imagined, and for the sake of her own mental stability, she had to withdraw from their toxic relationship before she got hurt worse.

As soon as both of Toni's feet were off the ground and in her truck, Deja slammed the door behind her, throwing herself up against it. She exhaled, thankful that the drama had finally tore its ass. She peeked out of the shutters to see if anyone had come out to see who the idiot was that insisted on airing their dirty laundry publicly. Thankfully, the coast was clear.

Had Deja known that Toni would find her, she would have asked her father to make sure her house was unlisted just as her phone line was. But none of that mattered because Toni was finally out of her hair, once and for all.

Deja couldn't believe how her day had already gotten off to such a bad start. She could only hope that the rest of the day wouldn't pan out like this. Not when she had Erykah Badu hosting Magical Mic night at Club Sandrene's tonight. Here she was dealing with Toni's crazy ass when she had bigger problems to deal with. Number one being her outfit, and number two being her indecisiveness on which poetic piece she would share with the crowd. In just the couple of months that Deja operated Sandrene's, she managed to rake in a substantial crowd of open-mic lovers. She thought that would add flavor to the club's mix, and it did, ten times over. Sandrene's was now one of the hottest spots on Saturday nights. It was a great place to treat your lady to or to simply hang out and mingle.

Deja closed and opened her eyes. Just as the painful recollections of Toni began to ignite her memory, her telephone rang, rescuing her from that involuntary trip back down memory lane.

"Hello."

"Deja! Where have you been? I've been trying to call your butt all night," Nessa went off.

"I was out running errands," Deja lied. She walked over to the refrigerator and dispensed a couple of ice cubes. She had gotten warm, and her mouth was feeling dry. She slid both dripping cubes across her forehead, down the sides of her face, and around her lips. Maybe she set the temperature too high or perhaps Toni really did work up her nerves and shot her levels up just that quickly. "Never mind that," Deja finished. "You are not going to believe who just left here," she promised her friend, still stunned herself that Toni was just on her doorstep, putting all her business on blast. Deja continued explaining the inevitable. "Toni had the nerve to show up over here and—"

"Girl, you ain't hearing me!" Nessa spoke louder, cutting her off. "I've been trying to call you all night because Sand called!"

If nothing else grabbed Deja's attention, *that* did. "Sand called?" Deja felt her heart dancing through her shirt, and everything that had just happened didn't even matter anymore. It was as good as forgotten. Chills shot up her spine, and that humming between her legs was calmed just from hearing Nessa speak Sand's name.

"Just get your butt over here so you can hear this message she left on my machine for you," Nessa said.

Deja didn't ask questions. She'd save them for once she got there. "Just a quick shower and I'll be right over," she said, unsure of where Sand may have been when she called.

"Okay. I'll be here for a while longer; then I'm off to the shop. I have a client coming in at nine."

"I'll be there." Deja hung up the phone and raced for the bathroom. She adjusted the shower temperature to what her body agreed with. Stepping inside, she allowed those raining waters to stroke her skin and dance on the cliff of her nipples. She thought about Sand as she relaxed her shoulders, extending her chest beyond its natural stretch. She begged the waters to gobble her breasts in one greedy swallow as she squeezed her twins and rubbed the bar of soap over them. Even through the lather, her breasts glistened like tiny lightbulbs under the skylight over her walk-in shower. The thick creamy lather slid down her body, and strangely, it reminded her of Sand licking her, tasting her. She was becoming so wet that she could feel her sudsy pussy blowing bubbles. She escorted her hands to where that celebration was taking place.

Why did it always boil down to a desperate moment like this? Moments where she had to rely on a two-finger discount to get her off. She glanced over at the beautiful mounted mirror that covered half the bathroom's stone walls. She observed the way her breasts complemented each other, hand in hand. She envisioned Sand moving between her breasts, her desiring flesh floating to her lips like magnets. It was all so real and so gratifying just knowing what was in store as the water continuously flowed over her temple, drinking up its sweetest temptation.

As time slipped away, Deja seductively pulled at her nipples. Her pussy began administering orders, and she obediently began inching her fingers inside of her. She was wet, too damn wet to be all alone at a time like this. She withdrew her fingers, but the urge to please herself lured them back in. Before Deja could count to three, she was working her middle finger in and out of her juiciness like a mad machine. "Oh yes," she moaned in pleasure, feeling herself being taken to another place. She bit down softly on her bottom lip. *That's right. Fuck me, Sand. Fuck me like I'm yours!*

Between the four walls of her bathroom, Sand was fucking her shitless. Deja couldn't hold on. She was about to come. "Aww, yes," she cried out, pumping herself faster. Suddenly, her phone rang again, interrupting her private session, but Deja refused to let that drive away her nut and prolong her goal. Her hands were playing pitty-pat with her middle. She wasn't stopping. She was already there. Now all she had to do was come.

Ding, ding, ding!

"Fuck!" she yelled. Deja tried tuning everything out of her mind that wasn't involved in the important matter at hand. She controlled her balance. She could feel the waves of her moving climax putting up a Mike Tyson and Evander Holyfield fight.

Her phone rang again. *Ring, ring, ring!*

Then her doorbell. *Ding, ding, ding!*

This couldn't be happening. Deja tried ignoring the phone and doorbell, but it wasn't working. She could feel her nut getting discouraged. *"No no no. Um, right there. Almost there,"* she told it.

Ring, ring, ring!

"Wait!" she yelled. *"Shit! Who in the hell could that be calling me?"* Then she considered the possibilities of it being Nessa, telling her that Sand had called again. She ended her play session, stepped out of the shower, and wrapped herself in a towel. In the fogged mirror, she acknowledged her reflection. Her once-straightened hair was all wet, just as wet as her pussy. The phone rang again. Deja hurried to it. Just as she figured it would, the ringing stopped right before she could lift the receiver from its cradle.

Ding, ding, ding!

She scurried for the door. If it was Toni again God help her because Deja was ready to call the police and have her crazy ass thrown in jail. She wasn't about to put up with her shit again. In a voice so angelic, but clearly upset, "Who is it?" she called out with her ear partially to the door. When no one said anything, Deja stared down the eye of the peephole. She didn't recognize the lady and young man on her porch, but she unchained her lock and cracked the door open anyway.

"May I . . . help . . . you with something?" Deja asked. As she took another hard look, she trusted that her eyes were not deceiving her. She blinked water from them, pulled the hair that clung to her face behind her ears, and swallowed the huge lump forming in her throat. Uncertainty clouded her judgment. "Sand?"

"What's up, Deja? Long time no see," Sand smiled. "Can we, uh, come in for a second?" She shifted the large duffel bag from one hand to the other.

Deja felt light-headed. Faint. Her mind had to have been playing tricks on her, and she couldn't formulate a sentence to save her life. "Um, yeah. I, uh . . . was just getting ready—" She stopped and caught her breath, then exhaled deeply. "Wow. This is a big surprise," she managed.

"I'm Ty, and, ma'am, look here, I have to pee really, really bad. You mind if I use your bathroom?" she rudely interrupted.

"Sure. Come on in." Deja opened the door wider, looking upside Ty's head at the outrageous hairdo, trying her hardest not stare at her black eye and busted lip. "It's right back there to your right." She allowed room for Ty to pass.

"Thaaank you!" Ty walked around Sand and quickly in the direction Deja sent her.

Deja then immediately switched her attention back to Sand who was wearing just a wife beater and jeans. Her small breasts, Deja barely noticed. She faced Sand for the first time in months. Sand's hair was all gone, and she looked different from the images filtered in Deja's memory.

"It's been a long time," Deja started out.

Sand stepped closer to Deja, shutting the door behind them.

"I thought you were—"

"Ssshhh." Sand silenced Deja with her finger. "I just want to look at you for a moment." Sand felt the vibe. It was so strong she could only shake her head.

"What? What is it?" Deja asked, gazing into Sand's hazel-brown eyes.

"This reminds me of something." Sand stopped. "Us, right here, right now."

"What?" Deja asked, her eyes begging for Sand to spit it out.

Sand took in Deja's body from head to toe. She was so damn tempted to unwrap the towel and set her body free. "You and I."

Deja wasn't following.

Sand pulled Deja into her. She kissed her forehead, then her nose.

"Please, don't do this to me again," Deja moaned.

Sand whispered in her ear, "This feels like déjà vu."

Deja smiled, lifting her head slightly. Water drizzled down her neck and back. "And what if it is déjà vu?" she asked. "What are you going to do with it?"

Sand brought her lips to Deja's. Kept them there for all of sixty seconds. They only stopped because they heard the toilet flushing, and then Ty screaming at the top of her lungs as if somebody was killing her. Soon after, she emerged from behind the six-foot-tall grandfather clock.

"Ugh! I'm allergic to cats," she huffed. She stomped at Whiskers and watched him scamper to the opposite side of the house, more scared of her than she was of him. "Sand, are we chilling here for a minute?" Ty asked.

"We've been rolling around all morning, and I ain't had nobody's sleep," she complained.

Sand looked back at Deja. Deja's eyes gave her the answer.

"Just for a little bit; then we have to be out," Sand told Ty.

"I'll go grab some extra pillows and a blanket. You can stay here for however long you need. You know that," Deja assured Sand.

Sand smiled because she did know that.

When Deja returned, Ty was already stretched out on the sofa, making herself at home. Sand, on the other hand, was standing, awaiting Deja's next request. Deja placed the pillows and blanket beside Ty. "There's more if you need them," she told her. Ty wrapped herself up and closed her eyes.

Deja turned to face her old lover. "There's room in the guest room if you'd prefer."

Sand smirked as she curled her lips. "Oh yeah?"

"Yeah. I mean, unless you're more comfortable in here, with your friend?" Deja asked cautiously. She didn't know the situation, and she was never one to make assumptions.

Sand chuckled. "I only have one *friend*." She smiled, correcting what Deja had implied.

Stepping closer, "Oh really? And who might that be?" Deja asked with a sinister smile plastered on her face.

Sand looked over at Ty who was knocked out. She then glanced over at the clock. There was still a schedule to keep. Deja had backed her into a corner, and the longer Sand stood there, the harder it was for her to walk away. "You're my friend," she said finally, gazing into Deja's beautiful coffee-brown eyes. "You're the only friend I have right now. Ain't nobody else out here for me.

Nobody I can trust. I thought I had that a long time ago, but I was wrong. And I'm just not trying to get caught up no more," Sand vented.

Deja saw the hurt and disappointment in her face, and she wanted to be the one to take it all away.

Sand put her arms around Deja's body to console her, or maybe to console herself.

Standing between a yesterday and a tomorrow, Deja's mind rested on the right now. She needed Sand, wanted Sand, and was not afraid to tell her so. "Sand, I love you."

Sand looked at Deja with a fresh pair of eyes. "You love me?"

Deja's words came out so sincere. "Yeah, I do."

They hadn't even known each other that long, but yet, Deja had developed strong feelings for her. Feelings that she had surely mistaken for love. Sand tried to disguise her shock. "How much? How much do you think you love me?"

Deja could taste Sand's breath every time she opened her mouth to speak. That sweet cigar smell lingered between them. Insecurity stirred emotions in Deja that caused her to doubt herself. Her bottom lip began to quiver. *Does Sand really need an answer to that?* Immediately, flashbacks of Sand and her together reassured those feelings she'd had from day one. There was nothing more to think about because the answer was already there. Sand just didn't see it. Deja vowed she'd never fall in love again. But this feeling she had right now, this crave—was worth giving love another try.

"I love you a lot," Deja declared. "I think about you all day and all night. When I go to sleep, and when I wake up. I can't stop thinking about you." She tried to control her emotions. "It's like," she sniffed, "you and I are supposed to be," she proclaimed. "Every part of me wants to be in your life. I feel something special when I'm with you."

Deja hesitated as she went on. "And since that night," even if Sand couldn't remember that passion-filled night they shared, Deja wanted her to know that it existed, "I have been a wreck around here. You consume my thoughts, my prayers, and when I go to sleep, you're there, in my dreams."

Sand dipped her fingers into Deja's dimples. She felt it too. There was a chemistry between them, and like Deja, she also thought about her morning, noon, and night. It was scary in some ways because the one woman Sand loved deeply and shared everything with had betrayed her. Now she had reached a point where she believed true love would never exist. But here was Deja, standing before her, spilling out those powerful words, "I love you." Those words changed things. Gave you another way of examining what was staring you right in the face.

Standing toe-to-toe, lip-to-lip, Sand felt that radiating surge of energy trigger her most sensitive spots. "Show me how much you love me then," she challenged Deja.

Deja waited for that last response to register. She traced Sand's mouth, then her chin. Her manicured fingernail tip glided so softly over what was destined to be hers. She took the towel that she'd wrapped herself in and untucked it to expose her nakedness. "I can definitely show you better than I can tell you," she smiled. She led the way to her room with Sand following closely behind. The doors closed, the heat returned, their bodies unified, and once again, everything that Deja so badly wanted to happen took place again, again, and again.

12

"*Thank God for 24-hour Walmarts and corner stores,*" Illusion thought as she pulled into the parking lot. She grabbed the Walmart bag that had her new change of clothes in it. A pair of khaki straight-legged slacks and a toasted-beige cropped cardigan pulled over a white tank. It was the cheapest ensemble she could throw together for less than thirty bucks. She even found a sexy pair of chocolate pumps with a four-inch heel, which, compared to what she's used to wearing, felt like flats underneath her feet.

"Haaa chooo!" Illusion sneezed for the fifth time. She just knew it. Her ass was catching a cold, but she had something for that too. She popped another Air-Borne just after taking three less than an hour before.

Illusion turned off the engine and walked inside the store. Her dress was still somewhat damp, and she'd bet anything that this was one time she actually looked like a hooker. "Where's your restroom?" she asked the Arabian guy standing behind the register wearing a turban.

The clerk stared Illusion up and down, prejudging her the second she entered the store. "The restrooms are in the back," he said, glancing down at the plastic bag in her hand.

Illusion made her way toward the back of the store.

"*Awww, sookie, sookie, now.*"

Illusion turned around to see who the baritone voice belonged to.

"What that'll run me?" the man asked, not cutting any corners. He zipped his fly, running his hands over his graying mustache. He gave Illusion a roguish, devil-eyed stare, placing her in a categorical spot in his mind. The man's work jeans were just as filthy as his black, steel-toe boots, plus he smelled like he'd been hauling garbage.

Illusion read the white embroidered name and logo on his company's shirt. She suppressed the remarks she felt getting ready to leap off her tongue and instead, tried to sustain the horrid smell blowing in her direction. "I take it you were talking to me?" she smiled, batting her lashes a time or two.

"You the only one standing here, right?" The man tugged at the instantaneous erection she'd given him.

Illusion only stared at him, glancing feverishly at the rising lump in his pants.

The clerk behind the register watched Illusion in the store's surveillance camera. "No soliciting in my store," he hollered.

Illusion batted her lengthy lashes again. The looks they exchanged said more than what needed to be heard. She glided her tongue across her lips in a slow and sexy manner, then pulled it back in. "Look, let me use the ladies' room, and then we can talk some more. Is that all right with you?"

Watching Illusion half-naked in that dress had the man counting down. He wanted her services badly. "All right. That'll work. You can find me over there." He pointed to his big rig that was parked across the street. "I got a bed and everything for you," he told her, rolling the toothpick in his mouth around as he sucked on his tongue.

"I'll meet you in your office, then," Illusion whispered seductively as she turned her back and walked into the bathroom. She was already calculating how much she would charge his ass.

Before Illusion slipped off her dress, she checked to see if there were any paper towels, but there were none in sight. She raised the flap on the tissue dispenser, and it too was empty. Then she snatched open the door and yelled to the attendant. "Excuse me, where do you keep your bathroom supplies?" After not getting a response, Illusion ran over to the aisle and snatched up a roll of tissue and baby wipes. She freshened up, brushed her teeth, and then jumped into her change of clothes. She raked her tousled hair with her fingertips, braiding it into a long braid that hung down her back. After that, she powdered her nose, rubbed on some blush, puckered her lips, and with the tip of her pinky finger, applied a strawberry-flavored lip balm. She massaged them together, readying them for their next paying project.

Illusion opened the restroom door, heading to pay for the wipes she'd taken when a fine gentleman, standing in line, caught her eye. She headed in his direction and took her place in line right behind him.

"Can I get ten on pump two, my man?" she heard him ask the clerk.

"I'm sorry, but that pump isn't working," the clerk told him. "I'll put the money on the other one."

"Not a problem." He slid the clerk a fifty-dollar bill. The handsome stranger had all Illusion's attention, especially his midnight skin, broad shoulders, and coal-black waves in his hair. And to top it all off, he smelled like money. "Excuse me, baby," he apologized after backing into Illusion and barely missing her toes.

His gray eyes caught her way off guard. She just stood there, soaking in his fineness. She stepped out of his way. He smiled back at her, nodded, then walked off. Illusion watched him waltz right out the door. Without making eye contact with the clerk, she said, "Here, I took some wipes off your shelf," and handed him a five-dollar bill.

She watched *him* climb into his Infiniti and reverse his way to the other available pump.

The clerk looked over his glasses at Illusion. "And a roll of Charmin," he chimed in, including an additional $2.99 plus tax to her total.

Illusion looked at the clerk like he had lost his mind. "I'm not paying for that. It should have already been in there. How you expect people to wipe their ass?" She tapped at the counter, motioning for her change.

"Miss, that's not my problem. There were napkins on the sink."

"Napkins? I wasn't gon' wipe my . . ." There was movement in her third eye. Illusion glanced back out the door, still admiring Mr. Fine on the third pump. He blended in so well with his car that any darker and you'd need a flashlight to find him. The awakening sun bounced off his body like a spotlight, showcasing all of what the rest of the world was missing out on.

The clerk shot Illusion a disapproving look, frowning as though he had a bad taste mingling in his mouth that would not subside. "Look, lady. I charge you for the tissue you took."

"Here. Take it!" Illusion slapped a dollar on the counter and walked off.

She stepped outside and strutted over to the borrowed BMW she was pushing for the time being. The alarm chirped, and she hopped right in. She pulled up to the opposite side of the fourth pump that wasn't being used, got out, lifted the nozzle, and pretended to pump gas into the tank. She waited for *him* to speak first. When he didn't, she said, "Excuse me," and blushed from ear to ear. "Did anyone ever tell you that you have the sexiest eyes they'd ever seen?" She lowered the handle and placed the nozzle back onto its hook. Then she walked around to where this guy stood, catching a glimpse of his license plate in the process. It was a Florida plate. *Oooh, an out-of-towner,* she presumed.

"No. I don't think I've heard that one before," he lied, finding humor in her steadfast approach.

"Well, I find that hard to believe because a man as fine as you," she paused, smiling, "deserves to be told a lot of things. I think you know where I'm going with this," she smiled, then licked her lips. "Let me show you around Dallas sometime."

Illusion held his attention. She was the most attractive woman he'd ever seen in his life, but he knew he'd be a fool to admit that kind of truth. As if considering, "Oh yeah? Humph. So, what can you show me that I might not already know about the D?" He crossed his arms and leaned against his car while waiting for her to enlighten him.

Illusion took two steps closer and whispered in his ear the way she hoped he'd let her do later. "I can make you forget all about that woman back in Florida," she assured him, without a doubt. The look on her face was nothing short of a woman with determination that went after what she wanted, when she wanted it.

He lowered his eyes and drew his neck back. "Word?" he chuckled.

Illusion stood with no shame in her game and all confidence. She could fuck his world up and have him worshiping her pussy before night's end. But right now, she wanted to know exactly what was so damned funny. She slid her hands across her hips, making sure he took full notice of the package. "I didn't realize I was so funny before," she said finally.

"I'm sorry. I don't mean to laugh. It's just that," he stopped, held his thoughts for a second. "Damn, y'all Dallas women sure do get straight to the point, don't cha?

Y'all don't even give a brotha a life jacket. You just throw him in the pool and let him figure out how to swim all on his own, huh?"

Illusion shrugged her shoulders. Maybe that was true for some, but she wasn't concerned about any other ho except for the ho in her that was dying to get to know him a little better and on a much more personal note. She studied him closely, digesting the idea of what his dick must taste like.

"Whoo. I don't mean to come off ugly or ill-mannered in no kind of way, so do excuse me in advance. But," he scratched his head, "I really don't think I'm what you're looking for in a man," he admitted. Seeing where the conversation was heading, he pulled out of it prematurely. There wasn't room for distractions like this one. He came too far. He was on a mission, and he predicted this woman before him would make him lose focus of the reason he was back in a place he vowed to never return to. He turned his back to Illusion and walked over to his side of the car, opened his car door, and hopped in.

"How you know what I'm looking for?" Illusion called out to him. "You don't know anything about me. I could be the best thing that ever happened to you," she insisted. "You know what I'm worth out here?" She considered throwing some numbers his way, just so he'd know he was in the presence of the real deal, but decided against it.

"Look, I'm not sure what you're used to around here, but me personally, I don't expect a woman to have sex with me when she doesn't even know me. You too damn pretty for that, and I couldn't live with myself knowing I cheated you out of what should be more than what you make in a day's pay." He smiled, allowing himself to stay in the game but ahead in the race. Had it been a few years ago, he knew he would have taken the pussy coupon, hit it, and quit it. But that was then. "Besides, you wouldn't be interested in a guy of my caliber," he told her flatly.

Illusion just looked at him. Was she being turned down? "And why wouldn't I be interested in a guy like you?" Her menacing stare should have bore holes through his grape-colored skin. When he dropped, then lifted his head back up, his diamond solitaires glistened in her face.

He collected himself. Did she really want the answer to that? "Well, first off, I'm no trick." He looked around, cranking his engine. They were holding up apparently the only two other good pumps since pump two was broken and pump one had a line forming.

"So, you know my type? Or you *think* you do?" she challenged. A trick to her was just another spot to fill in her little black book and a reliable stream of income. Her regulars never let her down. They'd make permanent room to see her. After all, she was their bonus prize they'd busted overtime for all week. But did that mean those were her type? Hell, no. Illusion crossed her arms, feeling somewhat insulted.

"No, I don't know your type. I just know me." He held up his finger, mouthing apologies to the people that waited impatiently in their vehicles.

Illusion was astounded. Not even Denzel Washington could play a better role than the one he was playing. She had never had to work so hard to convince a man of anything. The bit of dialogue they shared, she found it to be interesting enough to still bless him with her full attention.

"But I do happen to be on a special quest; otherwise, I'd enjoy talking with you some more," he continued. He reached for his designer shades hanging off the visor and placed them over his face. Then he watched Illusion lose the thrill in her eyes. But it was his loss, not hers.

Illusion ignored the honking of car horns behind them. "Special quest? Okay, well, I don't wanna hold you up," she said, as she sneaked a quick scan of his car. She blocked the sun out of her eyes and just when she decided to let the man move on about his business, she almost gave herself whiplash. There was a gold cross hanging on the neck of his rearview mirror, but that wasn't the reason her mouth flew open and her eyes began to strain. She tried to make out the girl who was posed in the picture wearing a red, white, and blue cheerleader uniform. She stepped closer until her breasts were nearly rubbing up against his ride. It had to be her. There was no doubt about it. Illusion broke out in chills, although she was standing directly in the morning sunlight. Gesturing to the picture, "Who's the girl?" she asked. She had to take a second and third look. "She's pretty."

"Oh, this?" He took the wallet-sized portrait down and kissed it.

Illusion's nose flared up, and the butterflies in her stomach began to swarm around.

His voice weakened. "This my baby sister, Tylesha," he said, staring closely at the wallet portrait. "This here was her junior year in high school." He inhaled deeply. "I drove all the way from Florida for this girl right here, and I promised my mother that I ain't leaving until I find her."Illusion remained paralyzed in complete and suffocating shock. *"Look, lady, can you move your car!"* a black guy yelled out of his window at her.

"Don't you see me talking, rude ass?" Illusion snapped back. She turned back to Ty's brother.

"Speaking of that, that's my mission for being out this early 'cause a brother normally don't crack a peek until at least ten in the morning," he laughed. *Beep! Beep!* "Well, I better get out of these folks' way. Thanks for the compliment," he smiled.

"Huh? What?" Illusion had spaced out for a moment.

"My eyes, remember? Being sexy and all," he grinned, showing a beautiful set of straight white teeth.

"Oh yeah." Illusion rubbed her forehead. She wanted to tell him. She tried to tell him, but the words wouldn't come out fast enough. "I," she inhaled. "Um . . . I think I can help you find your sister." She dropped her head and faced him again.

He muted the stereo volume so that he could hear her better. "What was that?" he asked her.

Illusion struggled with a way to tell him. She bit down on her bottom lip.

"Fuck you!" the irate guy yelled, whipping his truck around and reversing to the lane with the longer line. Illusion held up her middle finger without looking in his direction. "I know her. We. Humph. Look, I know your sister, okay? Let me just help you find her."

He looked baffled, but the seriousness in Illusion's face and voice said it all. She knew something. She had information. He removed his shades as if doing so would give him a better understanding of what she was telling him.

Illusion felt faint, and the burden that rested on her heart was all too unbearable. It was that exact same feeling she felt oftentimes when she thought about her baby. She wished she hadn't run into him today. She wished she could walk away and pretend that Ty was better off in the streets, even if she knew it wasn't true. Instead of feeling what she felt, she wished she was across the street, inside that truck, making her wages by the nut.

"Are you telling me you know where my sister might be?"

"Yeah," Illusion nodded. She was almost too ashamed to admit that she had that kind of information now. "I do. But I just hope you're ready to find out," she told him sadly.

"You stealing my gas! Come back! I not charge correctly!" the short Arabian clerk yelled from the front door at everyone who zoomed past in their cars, scurrying across the parking lot in different directions. He had a pen and paper in hand trying to record the license plates but couldn't write them down fast enough.

Illusion looked around, then at the pump's display. It was blinking. The clerk had turned them all off. "Follow me!" She circled the pump and hopped in the BMW. She drove it about half a block up from the service station, then she pulled into an empty driveway, just as if it were her own, and jumped out of the car lugging her belongings. She activated the alarm on the car, then slid the keys into her purse and quickly hopped inside the waiting Infiniti. She hoped this man wouldn't ask her any questions about the car she just jumped out of, the house they were driving away from, and the bag of clothes she just pushed between her feet.

"So back to my sister, where is she?"

Illusion looked on in silence as he navigated his way through the South Dallas neighborhood. She finally looked up at Ty's brother. "I'll tell you where to find your sister," she said. "And when you do, the best thing you can do for her is get her out of Texas. That's if you want to keep her alive," she said seriously.

Trent looked from her, then back to the road. He gripped the wheel tighter. A million things ran through his mind. He could only think the worst of what this woman was trying to tell him, but luckily, he came to Dallas prepared for anything.

"By the way, you never told me your name," Illusion said, reaching for the sunglasses that rested in his lap.

"You never asked," he smiled slyly, making a right and merging on to the I-30 freeway. "I'm Trent," he said, scoping Illusion out in the corner of his eye as she placed his shades over her face.

"Trent?" she repeated. She turned to face him. "Well, Trent, I'm Illeshia."

"Nice to meet you, Illeshia."

"Pleasure's all mines," she smiled. Illusion took another look around her. She was just as afraid now of being spotted as she was earlier. She leaned farther back in her seat. As long as she was wanted by Chyna, she could never get comfortable.

Ever.

13

Fantasy's head moved feverishly between Chyna's succulent thighs. She kissed and drove her pretty pink tongue repeatedly over her lover and pimp's smooth, erotic flesh until all Chyna could do was moan in pure ecstasy and spit orgasm after orgasm into her mouth. She pulled her in closer, gyrating her own hips while her wife's tongue twirled the tip of her clit. It felt so good, but Chyna wanted more. She flipped Fantasy on her backside and played out the scene from all the times before.

"Make me come," Fantasy called out.

Chyna was right behind her. She rocked her harder, faster. She was in control. Fantasy's head fell back, and her breasts stole the show. Chyna moved her hands over Fantasy's bouncing breasts, cupping them in her palm as she massaged her nipples between her fingers.

"Oh shit!" Fantasy cried out, her radiator overheating. She felt the rush of her orgasm bombard all her senses. She made the entire bed shake as if a herd of cows jumped in with them. Chyna looked down at her own wet stomach and satin sheets. She uncrossed her legs and eased off her bitch. "If my phone rings, answer it," she said. "I'm expecting a drop today."

Fantasy nodded her head obediently. "Okay," she yawned. This was why she felt special. Chyna wasn't fucking and spending time with the other girls like she did with her. She was her token, and it would always be that way if she had anything to do with it.

Three hours had passed before Chyna picked up the phone to call one of her runners. "I need to talk to P," she said.

"Yeah, this him. What up wit'cha?" P answered groggily.

"What's up with me? Nigga, where the fuck is my shit?" Chyna lashed out into the receiver.

"The drop? Man, you better get outta here with that shit, Chyna. That's been done. Ya boy made that happen for us last night. Shit, you got your days twisted up or something? You got your dough."

Chyna gripped the phone tighter. "If I had it, motherfucker, I wouldn't be calling you, now, would I?" She glanced at her watch. She was already behind schedule.

"Man, catch this," P said in his morning voice. "We did what you told us to. It was that new mark-ass cop friend of yours and whoever the fuck those other cats are you get down with," P said, rambling off names. "We dropped half a mil last night on ya boy. Him and Aaron counted that shit, gave us our keys, and caught ghost. So all that shit you talkin' in my ear right now ain't what's up, ma."

Chyna got quiet. This couldn't be happening.

Fantasy made her way back from the bathroom. She recognized the heated look in Chyna's face.

"Look, my business is done here in Dallas. *Adiós* this shit," P said before hanging up in her face.

Chyna stared at the phone in her hand.

"What's going on?" Fantasy asked.

Chyna didn't say a word. She tried calling James, but every call went straight to voice mail. She was furious. She punched in Aaron's number, a veteran officer on the force, and her inside connect.

"You've reached Aaron. Leave me ya number and a message, and I'll hit you back."

Chyna didn't want to talk to no damn answering machine! The anger that filled her made her hurl the phone clean across the room. She dragged her fingernails through her hair, nearly peeling the skin off her scalp. "Goddammit!" she yelled. She finally raised her head and saw Fantasy standing in a corner, afraid to make a move. "Call Fletch!" she ordered.

Fantasy knew by the look in Chyna's eyes that it could only mean trouble. She picked up Chyna's phone and punched in Fletch's digits as Chyna paced the room. She waited after a few rings, then handed her the phone.

"Hello," the raspy voice on the other end of the telephone line called out.

"Let me talk to Fletch," Chyna demanded.

"Who's this?" the woman questioned, unaware that she was speaking to Fletch's boss.

"Bitch, just put him on the motherfucking phone!"

"Bitch?" The woman directed her anger at Fletch. *"I'm tired of your bitches calling. You need to check your hoes—"*

"Didn't nobody tell your ass to answer my phone anyway," Fletch fired back. "Who the fuck is this?" he asked, still half-asleep.

"So, I have to be one of your bitches now?"

Fletch's eyes popped open, and the bass in his voice vanished once he realized it was Chyna. He double-checked the number on the phone. "Chyna? I, uh, was, uh, just about to call you," he said, trying to get his lie together. "Man, I looked all night for Illusion's ass. She must have—"

Chyna cut him off and saved him the embarrassment of getting bitched out in front of his woman. "Look," she exhaled, "I got crossed last night, and I need you to help me track my package."

Fletch was almost unsure if the woman on the phone was really Chyna, sounding as desperate as she was sounding right now. "What kind of package?" he asked warily.

Chyna knew that she was about to give Fletch more information than he needed to know, but she didn't feel like she had much of a choice. All she wanted was her fucking money. She cleared her throat. "Half a million dollars."

Those last few words had his full attention. He wiped the matter out of his eyes and hopped out of the bed and took a walk down the hall, away from the woman whose name had completely escaped him. He rested on the love seat, lit up the leftover blunt in the ashtray, and concentrated on his next question. He had to consider what was in it for him, but Chyna quickly eased his concerns.

"Fifty grand!" she blurted, reading his mind.

That was more than Fletch could ask for. He quickly agreed to do it. "Let me round up my boys and get some shit crackalacking," he said with confidence. Fletch knew the streets like nobody's business, so he was certain that somebody was gonna slip up.

Chyna made a mental deduction of what she had just promised Fletch. That fifty grand dropped to twenty-five hundred immediately. He was crazy if he thought for one second that she didn't know he was fucking Ty behind her back, but now was not the time to bring it to the table. "You do that," she told him. "In the meantime, Illusion is still a priority."

Fletch rolled his eyes as he inhaled his morning herb.

Chyna rattled off her instructions. "I'll call you in about an hour. Until then, I think you need to check Ms. Mouth over there. She needs to recognize a superior when she's speaking to one." With that, she disconnected the call. Chyna played everything out in her mind. She knew she could only count on Fletch to a certain extent, but right now, he was her only hope, so all she could do was believe that everything would pan out nice and smoothly. She took another look at Fantasy. "Go round up the girls. I want everybody to hear this."

Fantasy stood to her feet and headed in the direction of upstairs.

Chyna had a lot on her plate, but that wasn't anything new. She closed her eyes, exhaled a sigh, and balled her fists at her side. She didn't have time for this shit today. She checked the time again. She had runs to make, appointments to clear, and dope to distribute.

All the girls stumbled in one by one, a few looking as though they were about to rip the runway, and the others still draped in whatever they slept in. Chyna glanced around the room, eyeballing every last one of them. She was two short of twelve girls.

"What's going on? We having a meeting or something?" Peaches asked everybody. All the other women stared at her bug-eyed.

The room was quiet, and Chyna had all ears tuned into what she had to say. "I normally don't like to waste my time having to do this, but I will because I wanted y'all to get the news from me first." She looked around the room and locked eyes with her moneymakers. There was complete silence as everyone held on to their breath.

"I've just been informed that," Chyna braced herself for the lie she was about to feed them, "Illusion was murdered last night."

Every single mouth in the room flew open. A few of the women fell into a huddle and started crying while many of the others showed no remorse, aside from Peaches who stood in shock. She and Illusion had gotten real tight in the two months they lived in that house. She did not want to believe her friend was dead. She covered her face with her hands, and her own eyes began to mist. Several of the girls cried on each other's shoulders while the few that were jealous of Illusion batted their lashes and conversed among themselves. The news was devastating but not enough to throw them off focus. They all dismissed themselves, and Peaches fell in line behind the others. She couldn't wait until this was all over. She closed the door to her room. Without Illusion and Ty being there, her rooming mates, Peaches was all alone. She pulled out her cell and sent an anonymous text message. Seconds later, she had a reply.

Chyna and Fantasy stood beside each other, knowing the women couldn't wait to get on their cell phones and spread the news like wildfire. Chyna had just put out an APB on Illusion just that quickly, so wherever she was hiding, Chyna knew that it wouldn't be for long.

"Call Parkland and see what's taking Sand and Ty so long," she told Fantasy. "They should have been back by now." She closed and locked her room door, then walked into the bathroom. She wasn't in there for ten minutes before she came back out with five bricks of cocaine that were hidden in the ceiling. She lined the packages on the bed, then began placing them in a padded combination briefcase.

Fantasy walked around the bed and took a seat on the chaise. "Dallas, Texas," she began, seconds after dialing the number for information. "I need the number to Parkland Hospital." It only took a second before the number was being called off to her. "Yes, transfer me."

"Parkland Emergency, Shaniah speaking."

"Yes, ma'am," Fantasy went from hood to proper. "I just found out that my sister was rushed to the emergency room." She paused for dramatic effect. "I would just like to know how she's doing or if she's being admitted so that I can go see her." The lie rolled off her tongue with ease.

"What's your sister's name?" the woman asked.

"Her name is Tylesha Marshall. T-Y-L-E-S-H-A."

"And when did she come in?"

"Last night. Well, early this morning, I believe." Fantasy could hear the woman pecking away at her computer.

"*As of right now, I don't show we have her in the computer. But it could be that our systems haven't been updated, so you may want to try back in about an hour or so, just to be sure.*"

"Okay. I'll do that." Fantasy hung up.

"What they say?" Chyna asked, securing the briefcase.

"That I need to call back in an hour. The computers aren't updated."

Chyna took a mad breath, then finally walked over to Fantasy. She reached for her hand. The time had come to find out if Fantasy was truly worth everything she had put into her. Before her uncle D'Troy went down, he sat her down the same way she was about to do Fantasy.

"Let me holla at you right quick," Chyna said.

Fantasy took a seat beside her pimp. "What's up, bae?"

Chyna stared deeply into her eyes. "If anything was to happen to me, I need to know that I can trust you."

Fantasy studied Chyna's face. She couldn't bear the thought of losing her. Chyna was all she had.

"I have to know right now that you're all the way down for me," Chyna continued.

With a weakened stare, Fantasy caressed the side of Chyna's face and assured her of what she should have already known. She had proven herself over and over again. "Chyna, I'm not going anywhere. Whatever you need from me, I got you."

That was all Chyna needed to hear. "Good. Because I have your first assignment."

14

"Mama, are we there yet?" Jo Jo asked again for the umpteenth time. The mini-Afros all the boys had should have been a health hazard, but right now, Jo Jo was the only one whining. He could feel the oil sheen frying his scalp underneath all that thick hair. It was at least eighty degrees outside, but with the Texas humidity, it felt more like 100 degrees, not to mention the Buick didn't have air-conditioning.

"Here." Shun retrieved a baby wipe from her Louis Vuitton knockoff. "Cool down with this." She made a quick left and whipped into the parking lot of Town East Mall. The mall was already packed, and it was barely noon. Everyone apparently out Christmas shopping. The cars behind Shun began circling around and heading toward the overflow section, which seemed like it was two miles away from the mall's entrance.

Rene leaned forward, hoping to spot someone pulling out. She watched a young couple holding hands heading toward their car. "Right there. I think they're leaving," she pointed out to Shun.

As Shun was about to reverse and go after the free space, another car quickly pulled behind. "Motherfuckas! I know y'all saw me with my lights on," she cursed, throwing her hands in the air.

"Shun! Quit that cussing." Rene looked back in the seat at the four boys who were all just as irritated. She should have never let Shun talk her out of taking her own car.

At least they would've had cool air. She rolled her eyes and shook her head. This was absolutely ridiculous.

"Aha! Found us one."

Rene turned to face forward. A blue sign with the bold white outline of a wheelchair was posted in clear view for even someone who was color blind to see. "Shun, you're in handicap parking," Rene said.

"Yeah, I know. That's why I came prepared." Shun hung a miniature version of the sign in front of them, on her rearview mirror. "Now, this is what you call VIP," she laughed.

Rene shook her head in embarrassment but was too hot to even argue with her. She wanted nothing more but to get out of that hot-ass car. As soon as the kids stepped foot inside the mall, they spotted the Pet Depot to their left. They ran over, huddling around the rabbit bin.

"Look, Mama. Oooh, look, Auntie," they pointed out in excitement. Rene and Shun exchanged knowing looks, following after them.

"So, are you and the boys spending Christmas out of town this year? I heard you tell Jo Jo's daddy that y'all were going to New York," Rene said, admitting to over-hearing Shun's phone call earlier that morning. "Since when do you have family up there?"

"Yeah, I did tell him that, didn't I?" Shun giggled.

Rene didn't even have to guess to know that her friend had lied.

"Girl, he been bugging me about wanting to take Jo Jo with him for Christmas this year, but you think I'm about to let my baby go anywhere with his dawg ass? Here it is eight years later, and all of a sudden, he wants to play daddy." She pursed her lips and shook her head. "I'm not putting my son through that. He doesn't even know his ass, and out of the blue, he wanna call and spend time?" Shun ranted. "I told him to fuck himself and send me my damn child support check on time for a change."

Rene was sorry she invited the conversation. She was more interested in the black-and-white Shih Tzus and their little circus act they were putting on. She tapped on the glass trying to get their attention. "Aww. You see that?" she asked Shun, smiling. "They smiled at me."

"Oookaayy. Time to go." Shun called out for Jo Jo, who rounded up the other three that weren't trailing too far behind.

"Mama! We found Puff Daddy and Lil' Kim," Jo Jo told his mother, pointing in the direction of the guinea pigs.

"Baby, those are not *the* Puff Daddys and Lil' Kims we have. They just happen to look like them."

"Who's Puff Daddy and Lil' Kim?" Rene asked curiously, still tapping on the tank.

"Girl, the rats," Shun whispered. "Let's go." Shun grabbed the younger ones by their hands and marched them out the door.

"Rats? You got rats in your house?" As the question left her mouth, Rene knew she'd be looking around for her own place.

The mall scenery was a refreshing one. Rene and Shun shopped until they couldn't shop anymore, and that's because they had nearly exhausted all their funds. Shun had gotten so carried away that she lost track of time over an hour ago, and Rene just didn't care because this was the best she'd felt in months. When Shun counted the bags in her hands and finally realized that she spent over three grand in less than two hours, she knew it was time to get the hell up out of there. But she had to admit that she and the kids were definitely going to be styling and profiling for the holidays.

Thirty minutes later, she found herself in Dillard's at the fragrance counter. She walked from counter to counter collecting samples of all the latest perfumes. The long, black, twisted weave ponytail slid on and off her shoulder every time she lifted her wrist to her nose. Rene had chosen the drawstring accessory as a temporary solution until they could strip the curl from Shun's hair completely. The entire ensemble Shun rocked today was all fashionably selected by Rene. Shun couldn't help taking notice of how her once full-figured shapeless body now looked slimming and curvaceous in a pair of black, wide-legged trousers and a black, silver, and gray retro tunic. Her makeup was flattering with just enough foundation and blush, and her usual overdone cherry jubilee lipstick had been replaced with MAC's Spite and a touch of chestnut, which outlined her full lips. Shun's long, curled lashes were no longer invisible, and the neglected piercings in her ears were paired with silver, dangling butterflies. The only complaint Shun had was that her girdle fit too damned tight. She tried to cope with why her jiggle shouldn't wiggle but could never come to terms with it. She dreaded the thing, but she had to admit, her rump was sitting tight.

"Excuse me, miss, you dropped these."

The man walking toward them had to have been signed, sealed, and delivered straight to Shun. She stopped in her footsteps. So many things ran through her mind, but she had to remember she was a Christian woman, and as a Christian woman, she knew she shouldn't be thinking the way she was thinking, but this brother was fine as hell. Her mouth watered, and she tried her best to act civilized. Instead of being her usual down-to-earth self, Shun pretended she was a nice, classy sister with so much going on that she needed a personal assistant to help lift her up onto her high horse. But then she remembered what, for her, was a reality check. She had four crumb snatchers. What fine and available man in his right mind would want a woman with that many kids?

She depressingly slid off her horse and fell on her ass on the way down. Shun exhaled when she realized the man was only waving her car keys.

"Can't get far without these, now, can we?" the man said, placing the keys into Shun's left hand.

Shun stared at the gentleman before her as though she had never seen a man in such a form before. She cleared her throat. "Thank you. I'm not sure how these got away from me," she laughed at herself, dropping them in the deep pockets of her new tote.

"So, uh, do these handsome young men belong to you?" the tall, salt-and-pepper-haired specimen asked her.

Shun was too caught up in how good looking he was to have heard what he said, let alone comprehend it. She just nodded her head slowly. *Lawd, please don't let him be married*. She searched his left hand until she came across a flashing red light. It was every single woman's envy—a wedding band. She snapped out of her dream world and flushed those last-minute hopes down the toilet.

"Yes, these are my handsome young boys," she stated proudly. She took a look at her children who were on their best behavior because they'd been forewarned that if they embarrassed her at the mall, they could kiss their dreams of a PlayStation 3 good-bye.

"Well, that one there," the man pointed to the tallest of the four, "has NBA written all over him."

"You think so? That's the same thing his coach says. I hope he does make his mama proud." Shun gave Jo Jo another look. Every time she looked at her son, she saw his father. But even if she could go back in time, she'd do it all over again. She didn't regret any of her children, only the stupid bastards that fathered them. "Now that you mention it, I think I do see a little M J in there trying to come out," she laughed, and Jo Jo nodded his head.

He really did want to be an NBA baller when he grew up. Just like Mike.

The stranger chuckled. "Yes, indeed. He's going to make you guys very proud. Well, I guess I better head back over here to—"

Shun finished the sentence for him. "Your wife."

He drew his neck back. Then it dawned on him. He removed the gold wedding band from his finger just as his sister was walking up.

"Carl, where you run off to? I need Dad's ring so the clerk can engrave it. Ain't gon' do no good while it's on your finger," his sister fussed at him.

Carl handed her the ring. "Sorry 'bout that. I just saw this beautiful woman walking past the counter," he gestured to Shun, never removing his eyes from hers, "and I just couldn't help myself. I guess I was staring a little too hard because before you knew it, she had dropped her keys." Carl looked Shun straight in the face, his earnest smile so believing.

His sister took the ring out of his hand. She smiled and extended a warm handshake to Shun. "Hi. I'm his baby sister, Darlene."

"Ooohh, don't give my age away," Carl joked.

"And my brother is single, smart, handsome, and, did I mention *single?*" Darlene laughed. "I need somebody to get him out of my hair," she teased, elbowing Carl in the arm.

Shun liked Darlene right off. She returned the smile. She watched her boys out of the corner of her eyes, and they were still behaving well. She almost couldn't believe it.

"Go on, woman. Get outta here," Carl told his sister as he playfully shoved her away.

Shun waved good-bye to Darlene and fixated her eyes back on Carl. He had 101 percent of her attention.

"Well, I know right now probably isn't the best time to be asking you if you're involved with anyone, but I've learned a long time ago that you never know if you don't ask," Carl said.

Shun relieved him of the pressure and volunteered her availability status. "I'm single. But if the right man comes along, I hope I will no longer have to be," she replied. She spoke the truth the only way she knew it.

Carl nodded in agreement. Everything about her felt right.

Rene felt a vibration shoot from the inside of her purse. Her heart nearly stopped when she pulled it out to answer it. "This is Rene."

"We need to meet again."

Rene recognized the voice right way. Nervously, she asked, "Can I talk to Sand?"

"Last time I checked, she didn't want to talk to you, Rene," Chyna said firmly, hoping to fuel the fire between the two.

Rene felt like she had just been stabbed in the heart. "Please, tell her I really need to talk to her," she begged, tears tingling her eyes. She wanted to hear Sand's voice again. She wanted to tell her that she was sorry, that she loved her. And after she got all that out, she was going to ask her about the woman that had allegedly been killed in their apartment.

So many questions flooded Rene, and all she hoped for were answers. She wanted to hear Sand's side of the story first because at the moment, she wasn't sure what to believe, or who to believe anymore. Rene wanted Sand to know that she was still there and that she would do anything to make things right between them. That included working for Chyna.

"I'll see if I can convince her to call you," Chyna told Rene. "But before I do that, you and I have some loose ends to tie up first."

Rene exhaled. "What do you want me to do?"

Chyna longed to hear those words. "I have a job that I need completed, and one of my partners is under the weather," she said, referring to Illusion. "I'm prepared to throw in an additional five grand on top of what I've already given you," she said casually as if she were offering Rene a million-dollar deal she couldn't refuse. "That should compensate for the last-minute trouble."

Rene's stomach started to turn.

"And since we're on the subject," she added, "Albery is on the books for Christmas Eve."

"Christmas Eve?" Rene hesitated.

"Is that a problem?" Chyna asked.

At first, Rene was quiet. "No," she said finally.

"That's a good girl. I'll call you in the next hour on where to meet me," Chyna said. "Oh, and, Rene, you should really consider the more prized options in life. Those that could afford you a better lifestyle than the one you have." She let those last few words marinate. "Just call me when you're ready to make some *real* money," she concluded.

Rene wasn't interested in shit else Chyna had to say. She was just ready for all of this to be over with. "I'll think about it," she lied, ending their call.

Rene tried wiping the pain out of her eyes before heading over to the Pet Depot to meet Shun and the boys. She still hadn't told Shun everything, and if she and Shun were friends at all, she knew it wouldn't be long before more questions followed.

"Are you guys ready?" Rene asked, overloaded with department store bags that she could barely carry without shifting from one arm to the other.

"Whooo . . . I know I am." Shun's open-toe heels were the reason she was ready to jet. They were only three inches high, and she thought she'd pass out from walking around the mall for so long in them. Nevertheless, she still roamed and sashayed from one store to the other, feeling incredible. It was the first time in quite awhile that she actually felt confident about herself. "Girl, I think I lost about fifteen pounds walking around this mall," Shun told Rene. "I tell you, these shoes are murdering a sister. Where you find these damn things at?" she asked, limping in the direction of the exit.

Rene didn't respond. She couldn't. There were already too many other things crowding her mind.

"So where we headed to now? Wanna catch a movie or something?" Shun unlocked the car doors, and the boys all climbed in the backseat.

Rene placed all the shopping bags in the trunk, then got in the car. "Can't do a movie. I have to meet up with someone tonight," she told Shun dryly.

Shun didn't remember Rene mentioning having other plans, but she let it go. "Oh, okay. Well," her face instantly lit up with glee remembering her latest encounter at the mall, "let me tell you about Carl," she smiled widely.

"Mama gotta new boyfriend," one of the boys snickered from the backseat.

Shun looked in her mirror to see which of the four made the remark. She knew it had to be one of the youngest. She gave them a "don't make me pull this car over and beat your ass" look that they understood all too well. They quickly straightened their act and turned down the volume on their ears like they were trained to do when adults were speaking.

Shun drove the Buick down Town East Boulevard, heading for the freeway. She pulled onto the 635 ramp, losing herself in the traffic of holiday shoppers and angry drivers with road rage who tested her sanity. For a second, Carl crossed her mind. She found herself weighing the possibilities, and she couldn't stop smiling.

Rene was still in her own world. That little bit of excitement and bubbly momentum she had earlier today had crawled back in its shell. She was back to a reality that she had become quite familiar with—being alone.

Shun caught Rene gazing out of her window, clearly in deep thought. She decided to keep her exciting news to herself for the time being because the most important thing right now was finding out what was wrong with her friend. Everything else could wait.

15

"Are you okay," Deja asked Sand, who was staring up at the rotating ceiling fan as if it were some cool new invention she had never seen before. She looked so good to Deja lying there in just a wife beater and boxer shorts, but Deja would not be distracted. She wasn't going for the silent treatment this time. Sand had gotten away with that once before, but not today, not if she could help it.

"Yeah, I'm cool," Sand lied. She was still trying to wrap her mind around the fact that she might have been wanted for murder. If anything Chyna told her about Jasmine being in her and Rene's apartment *that day* was true, then she knew, without a doubt, that she was a prime suspect. Chyna told Sand that if she had not shown up at her door before Rene that day, Jasmine would have executed her plans to tell Rene who she was and how she and Sand had been together. What Sand had once believed to be a lie was now starting to feel like the truth. Maybe Chyna did prevent her from being found out. Maybe she did take care of her problem for her. But none of it mattered anymore because she and Rene were done.

While Sand was forced to fathom the inevitable, there was nothing that could deny her the reminder of the current situation that had escalated from all of this. She was hauling around half a million dollars that she was sure belonged to Chyna. And that was the least of her worries because no matter how hard she tried, Rene still managed to squeeze into her mental space, pushing aside all of the above, and provoking those ill thoughts Sand found herself having of her. Like at this moment, she wanted to find Rene, strangle the hell out of her, and demand to know if she meant to hurt her the way she had. That's all she wanted, all she felt she deserved—a fucking explanation.

Sand would have taken a bullet for Rene at the drop of a dime. She would have done just about anything to keep her out of harm's way. With all that security and protection she was providing for Rene, she should have been making sure her own shit was guarded because now she was the one feeling like she'd been shot in the heart. And once again, Deja was ready to save her.

Sand should have felt bad for messing around with Deja, but the truth was, she didn't. Instead, she wanted to believe that she was getting even, especially after what Rene had done to her. But deep down, Sand knew that she was only fooling herself. Rene had not only cheated on her with a man, but she had gotten pregnant by dude, and there wasn't shit she could do that would top that level of betrayal.

"So you're cool?" Deja asked, repeating what Sand had just told her. She twisted her mouth. She knew Sand was lying when she answered so quickly. She wasn't cool, not at all. There was something bothering her since the moment she walked through her door, and Deja could see it all over her face. "Sand, I want to ask you something, and it's up to you if you want to answer," Deja said, turning fully over and onto her right side. The flannel sheets were pulled close to her chest, the smell of their sex still clinging to them.

Sand nodded, then turned only her head to face Deja. "Shoot for it, ma."

Deja was nervous all over again, but she had to fight it. This was the moment she'd been waiting for. She tried not to think about it, but it kept tugging at her, pulling her away from what she knew was the truth. Sand was innocent. But she needed to validate that by hearing it from her own mouth. She readied herself for what she was about to say. Her voice fell hoarse before she could get the words to come out. She cleared her throat. "Have you killed anybody?"

Sand's heart stopped. She didn't see that one coming. "Come on now, Deja." She reached for her hand. "I know you really don't know a *whole* lot about me," she said, seeing how Deja's eyes lost their attention, and then eventually found their way back, "but trust me, I'm not a killer." She sensed a whirlwind of doubt from Deja. "I'm telling you the truth." She used her index finger to gently lift Deja's chin. "You gotta believe me, ma. I didn't kill that girl." She took another breather. "Please don't tell me you think I did that shit!"

With watering eyes, Deja said, "I want to believe you. I've just been hearing things, and then that day I went and picked you up from that bar . . . and the cops pulling us over . . . I mean, what was that all about?"

Sand had to think back to months ago. "Deja, those weren't cops. I mean, they weren't real cops."

Deja gave Sand a mixed expression. "What do you mean? I saw them. They were right there," she began easing her hands back down to her side.

Sand raised completely up. "You saw them put me in a car and drive the hell away. If they were *real* cops, do you think I'd be sitting here beside you right now? Naw, 'cause I'd be in somebody's jail cell vomiting molded bologna and stale-ass bread!"

Deja shook her head. She knew what she saw, and she saw it with her own two eyes.

"Look, ma. I'm telling you that I was set up." Sand stood to her feet and started getting dressed.

"Set up? By who?" Deja was trying her best to grasp every bit of information she was hearing.

Sand sat back down on the edge of the bed, lifting the bag that would explain all this shit in a way that she couldn't. She was about to prove to Deja exactly what type of people she was really dealing with, along with the danger they were capable of causing. She began unzipping the bag.

Deja waited expressionless for Sand to show her whatever it was she needed to see. Suddenly, Sand looked nauseated. Deja didn't know what was wrong, but she knew judging by the look on Sand's face that something was definitely wrong.

Sand broke out in a sweat as she pulled out the blanket Deja had given Ty to sleep with, along with the marble orbs that decorated Deja's bar and cocktail table. There was also a short scribbled note from Ty.

I can't go back to that house. I'm sorry, Sand. I need this money to get out of town. Nothing personal.

Ty

Sand crumbled the letter into her hand, snatched open the guest room door, and found exactly what she knew she'd find—an empty room.

Deja chased behind her, dragging the sheet along with her. "What's going on? Where did your friend go?"

"Fuck!" Sand yelled, ready to put a hole in the wall. "I can't believe this shit! That bitch just ran off with all the fucking money."

"What money?" Deja asked, clueless.

Sand ignored her. Her head was spinning. "I'm good as dead," she mumbled to herself but loud enough for Deja to hear.

"What have you gotten yourself into?"

"How the fuck am I gonna replace half a million dollars?" Sand spat.

Deja's mouth hung open, and her fixated eyes bucked in disbelief. "What were you doing with that kind of money? Wait, is that the *only* reason you came here?"

"Not right now, Deja. Now ain't the time," Sand warned.

Ty had waited until she could hear Sand and Deja in the midst of making love. Then she tiptoed into the bedroom, undetected. She eased the heavy bag from right under their noses, and then silently eased out of the doorway, cracking the door just a little. She tiptoed back into the living room, over by the couch and quietly unzipped the bag. It was all there. Safe and sound. She pulled the pillowcase off the pillow and loaded all the money into it. Then she took the letter she'd written, folded it, and laid it at the bottom of the bag for them to find later—much later. Long after she was gone.

Ty had wrapped every single orb and statue that she spotted, including the six that decorated the bar, inside of the blanket to add weight to the bag. Then just the way she had before, she glided back into the room and placed the bag in its exact spot. She walked out the front door with half a million dollars in a floral pink and green pillowcase. She walked until she came to a Laundromat, then went right inside, took a seat on one of the benches, and contemplated her next move. She observed everyone and everything surrounding her. Nothing appeared out of the ordinary. After a few minutes, she walked over to the pay phone and pressed o for an operator, with the packed pillowcase right beside her.

"I need to make a collect call."

"Yes, and your name?"

"Tylesha."

"The number you would like to place the call to?"

Ty rattled off the phone number.

"Hold please."

Ty waited patiently.

"Ma'am your call has been accepted. You have a good day."

"Hello! Hello! Tylesha, baby, is that you?" It was her mother on the other end of the line.

Ty's hands shook nervously. She hadn't spoken to her mother in months. "It's me, Mama," Ty answered painfully.

"Are you all right? Where are you, baby? Please let me come and get you," her mother pleaded.

"I can't tell you that right now. But I wanted you to know that I'm okay. I just needed some time away, that's all," Ty spoke softly into the phone.

"Baby, whatever's going on with you, we can get through together. I just want you to come back home. It's been three months," her mother cried. "I can't . . . oh, God. Just please come home." She knew why her daughter ran away. She always knew. She just didn't want to accept it. "I believed you," she admitted finally. The pain in her voice was still present. "I confronted him about it, and he left." She stopped to catch her breath. She couldn't even say her husband's name right now. "But he doesn't matter because all I want is my baby back home," she said through the tears that flowed down her cheeks.

Ty sniffed. "Mama, don't cry. Please." The tears pooling in her eyes began to sting. She tried blinking them away only to encourage their stay. "Mama, don't."

"Tylesha, just please come home. I'm begging you. Your brother has been driving up and down the streets all time of night and morning looking for you. None of us knew where you were. You've got us all worried sick, including Mama. And you know how your grandmother's congestive heart condition is."

Ty was still frozen in disbelief. "Trent's here?" she managed to ask.

Her mother choked back her tears before she could resume. "He was worried to death about you, Tylesha. You could have been in danger, for all we knew. You could have been dead. Anything."

"Does he know about Mason?" Ty asked. She was afraid that if her big brother knew, it would only make the situation worse.

"No. He doesn't know. I don't think we should—"

Ty finished for her. "We won't tell him." There was a silent agreement between them. Ty struggled to keep a dry face because she didn't want to attract any attention. "I'm coming home, Mama. Let me just work out a couple of things first," she promised her mother, sadness floating in her voice.

"All right, baby." She sniffed. "Mama loves you."

"I love you too." Seconds later, the call was disconnected, and all Ty could hear was a dial tone. She flung the bag back over her shoulder and walked right out of the laundromat. She had to figure out a way to get out of this mess, and she only knew one person that could help her. She just hoped like hell she hadn't already screwed up.

"This shit is getting crazy!" Sand yelled. "I was chilling in my own little world before all of this drama took over."

Deja watched Sand pace back and forth. She didn't know what to do to get her to stop, so she just sat on the edge of the sofa and waited for the storm to pass. Her head fell into her hands. After listening to Sand fill her in on all that was going on, she didn't know what else there was to say or do. All she knew was that she needed to say something.

"What if we called her and explained to her what happened?" No sooner than Deja finished that sentence did she realize what she had suggested.

"Call? Explain?" Sand drew her entire body back. "Ain't no calling and explaining to this bitch. I don't think you following me, Deja. When I say Chyna is bad news—she bad news! This ho got the whole damn city on payroll," she enlightened. "I already told you how she set me up. Now she blackmailing me. I make the wrong move, and my ass going down for murder. Ain't no talking out of this shit. The only talking she gon' wanna do is with one of these." She flashed the gun that she had discreetly tucked under her shirt.

"I'm going to help you get out of this. Just calm down and let's think for a second." Deja pointed beside her. "Sit. And please don't show me that gun again. I'm terrified of those things," she admitted.

Sand was furious. She had it in her right mind to hop in any one of those cars in the driveway and go after Ty. She didn't know what she would do once she laid eyes on her, but she knew it wasn't going to be anything pretty. She never should have trusted her. Ty had been gaming her all along. She should have dropped her ass off at the emergency room and rolled out like she started to do in the first place, then none of this would be happening.

Sand finally sat down and tried to calm her nerves. Deja placed her hand on top of Sand's and began to rub her ever so softly.

"It's all going to be okay. I promise we'll get through this together," Deja reassured.

Sand listened to her comforting words closely. Deja had included herself in her drama. She pulled her arm away. "No. Listen to me." She lifted Deja's chin. "I need you to keep holding down my club. You the only one I know I can count on to do that," she told her.

Earlier, right after their first round of sex, Deja brought Sand up to speed about everything that had happened since they last saw each other. She told her how she had been overseeing Sandrene's and how she tried finding Rene so that she could have Sand's car towed to the address on her insurance card. But when she went over there to the apartment, the new tenant who lived there informed her that no one had lived there by that name. So Deja had the car towed to her place. She told Sand about the two instances she had seen Rene. Once at the barbershop, and then at the gym. She purposely left out the times she had followed Rene. Just like last night when she had seen Rene with a woman. The two of them were standing on a railroad track so close that they were only inches from kissing. Deja realized then that Rene was having an affair. But she couldn't bring herself to deliver more bad news. Sand was dealing with enough.

"Whatever you need me to do, I'll do," Deja offered.

"How much you say you put up for me?"

"Almost sixty grand," Deja answered.

"Damn," Sand practically whispered. The idea she had was blown out of the water. Sixty Gs was a long way off from half a mil. "I'm fucked. Man, ain't no other way up outta this shit." She stood to her feet. "Look, I gotta go. I ain't gon' figure shit out sitting 'round here."

Deja jumped up. "Wait. Where you going? What are you gon' do?" Sand brushed past her, nearly knocking her back on her ass. She watched Sand head for the door, then turn around one last time.

"Look, I'll call you when I can. Right now, I gotta bounce. Just handle that business for me." Sand twisted on her baseball cap.

"How are you gonna call? You don't even have my number," Deja shot out.

"That's why you gon' give it to me." Sand patted down her jeans while Deja scurried around the living room, searching for pen and paper. Sand double-checked for her wallet. "If all else fails, I know Nessa knows how to get in touch with you."

Deja power-walked over to where Sand stood. "Here. No need for that. Don't lose this."

Sand accepted the piece of paper into her hands along with a gold house key. "What's this for?"

Deja stared up at her and the warmth hovering around them made her feel something special. "Just in case you need to come back. For anything," she added.

Sand folded the paper around the key and slipped it into her pocket. She'd battle those questions later.

"Sand, I really do—"

Ding, ding, ding.

She looked Deja over. "You expectin' somebody?" Her guard immediately went up, and she placed her hands over her piece.

Deja quietly shook her head, but her face said otherwise. She rushed to the door, hoping like hell it wasn't Toni again. If it was, how was she going to explain the unexplainable? She hesitantly tiptoed to the peephole and zoomed in on her visitor. When she got a good look at the blue-blond spiked hair, black eye, and a figure not far from anorexic, she unlocked and swung open her door. Sand, right behind her, came lunging forward.

"So you think you can fuckin' play me, ho?" Sand barked. Her hand went straight for Ty's left jaw, but she weaved in record time.

Deja pulled Sand back with all her might, but Sand was way too strong for her 147 pounds to compete with. Sand got up close and personal with Ty.

"What? You wanna hit me? I brought the shit back!" Ty yelled. She pushed the pillowcase of money into Sand's chest. "It's all there. Count it if you want to."

Sand snatched the bag, lowering it to her side. She stepped a foot closer to Ty so that the shit she was about to let loose didn't get mistaken. "I ain't fucking with you! If any of this money gone . . ."

Deja switched her eyes from Ty, then back to Sand. She could see her nosy neighbors peeking out of their blinds from across the street. "Let's go back in the house, y'all. You can talk it out in here." She opened her door wider, but neither of them budged.

"Naw. Ain't nothing to talk about." Sand gave Ty a hard up stare, daring her to give her a reason to knock the shit out of her ass. "I gotta get this shit back to Chyna before it get back to her that a drop was made last night while *I* had her car. Knowing her, she already looking for the shit.""What makes you think she ain't looking for me too? You forgot who was with you last night?" Ty said. "It's not just you; it's both of our heads."

Deja rolled her eyes at Ty. She didn't know when to quit. She stared up at Sand with saddened eyes. "All right. I guess we can stick with our original plan. Sandrene's, tonight at eleven." She searched for assurance in Sand's face, but it wasn't there. Deja sensed there were no guarantees, but Sand had given her word, and that's exactly what she was going to hold on to. Her showing up was going to be the only way that she would know that Sand was okay.

As Sand turned to leave, Ty stormed right behind her. "You can't just leave me out here, in the middle of nowhere." She looked around her.

"Humph, watch me." Sand rounded the Lexus, opened the trunk, then hid the pillowcase full of Chyna's money under the trunk board where the spare tire used to be. She pushed the duffel bag back in the center, closed the trunk, and got in the car.

"Sand!"

Sand started the engine, ignoring Ty. Then she backed out of the driveway.

"Sand! I said I was sorry," Ty yelled, chasing after her. She did indeed try to apologize, but when she saw how quickly Sand's fist was coming toward her face once Deja opened that door, the words never quite left her lips.

Sand was halfway down the street before she slammed on the brakes. She had to think with some sense. Ty knew all Chyna's spots, at least those she frequented on a regular basis. Sand knew Ty had information that could assist her with carrying out her plan. "Get in the damn car!" she shouted.

Ty ran for the car and hopped in.

"You see this?" Sand flashed her chrome 9 mm. "I ain't playin' games with you no more."

Ty was petrified, and if she never took anybody seriously, in that moment, she knew to take Sand *very* seriously.

Sand controlled the wheel. Her entire demeanor had changed. She felt like a different person now, and that raging adrenaline that pumped through her veins and knotted her stomach said no different. She punched her foot to the floor and swallowed that reminder. She was doing all of this to protect a woman, a woman she vowed to hate for the rest of her life. And when it was all over and done, Rene would be nothing more than just a hateful memory.

16

Illusion and Trent sat in a smoke-filled room at the opposite end of Applebee's entrance. She was busy trying to digest the steak and potatoes, right along with everything else Trent had just told her. She could hardly believe she was having lunch with a real man of service, a man that was in the military. She didn't know not one black person who could say they even thought about fighting for our country, let alone dying for it. But this man—wow; she just couldn't stop smiling. He was brave. And maybe that's exactly what she needed in her corner . . . a man like him who was fearless. While he could take on an entire country's battle and allow its troubles to rest upon his shoulders, behind him needed to be a woman who he could surrender his tears to. Illusion wished for a second that that woman was her. She wondered if a good man like Trent could ever see himself with someone like her.

She tried not to stare Trent down, but it was so hard, so she diverted her eyes to the attention of men who propositioned her right from in their seats. Some of them with their significant others nearby. On another day, any other day beside today, Illusion would walk right on over and introduce herself. She was bold when it came to moves like that. However, instead of allowing her money-hungry intuition to intervene, she pulled out a cigarette, fondled the tip with her lips, and put her light to it. She sucked out the nicotine as if it would be the last thing she'd ever do. She exhaled a mouthful of smoke rings.

"So, soldier boy, why don't you like being in Dallas? I mean, this is where your family is," she questioned, feeling Trent out.

Trent studied Illusion closely. There was an undeniable mystique about her. "It's not that I don't like Dallas. There's just nothing else here for me."

"And there is in Florida?" she asked, pursing her lips to the side for the smoke to seep out.

"Humph," Trent shook his head. Some things women just didn't understand. Or maybe didn't want to understand. "I moved away because I needed a change. I was so caught up in the street life when I was here that it wasn't even funny. Every choice I *had* to make was a bad one." He referred to the days he posted up in the cut, competing for business. Doing whatever he had to do to take care of his mother and baby sister since their biological father had walked out on them. "So I moved to get away from things that would have landed me either in jail or in the grave." He watched Illusion's expression change.

"But you walked out on the only family you had—" As soon as Illusion said it, she wanted to take it back. Isn't that what she had done to her baby? She shook her head, stared upward, and then sighed. "You know what? Forget I said that just now." A burning sensation moved through her nose. She looked away from him, and the ash developing around her cigarette dropped in her lap.

"You a'ight?" Trent asked, watching her eyes water.

Illusion placed her cigarette into the ashtray. "I need to go to the ladies' room." She slid out of the booth, grabbing her purse.

The moment Illusion stepped inside the stall, she broke down in tears. She leaned her head back against the door and a fury of silent regrets swept across her face.

She missed her baby so much, and there wasn't a second that went by that she didn't think about her. The aches in her belly felt like tiny kicks of life. She rubbed at them, only to be reminded that she'd given that life away.

Illusion relieved herself, then walked to the sink and turned on the faucet. She dipped her fingers under the stream. She couldn't even stand to look at herself as she bent over and scooped cold water into her mouth, only to spit it back out. She pulled out a stick of gum and stuck it into her mouth.

Walking back to the booth where Trent was no longer sitting, Illusion began looking around, almost hysterical. The waitress that waited on their table was passing her by, carrying a full tray of food and drinks. Illusion stopped her. "Hey, did you see where that guy went that I was sitting with?"

The young woman nodded, then pointed to the front of the restaurant where people were both leaving and entering.

Illusion excused herself as she passed those coming toward her. She spotted Trent and walked straight over to where he stood. He was on the phone. Illusion could hear a woman crying in the background.

"Mama, calm down. I'll find her. I promise you. She gon' be all right." Trent's mother was still pouring out her soul over the phone.

Illusion stepped back, giving him his privacy.

When Trent finally looked up, Illusion was standing there, watching him. He walked over to her. "That was my mother." He took a deep breath. "Ty called," he continued. He was visibly worried. "She sounded like she might be in some kind of trouble." He looked Illusion in the eye and placed his hands over hers. "Look, I gotta find my sister. And I gotta find her tonight." Trent had to be sure Illusion knew how important this was. Right now, nothing else mattered to him.

"And we're going to find her," Illusion promised him. "But you have to know what you're about to get yourself involved in."

Trent stared at Illusion incredulously. Hadn't she figured it out? He wasn't scared of shit out here in these streets. These streets are what made him who he was today. A hard-ass nigga with nothing to lose. If anything, it would be a family reunion.

"I don't care. Ain't nothin' gettin' in my way."

"We'll find her. Don't worry." But with the update they just got, even Illusion was starting to have doubts. Because the more time passed, the slimmer their chances of finding Ty were.

17

Chyna rolled up and down the strip in her midnight-black Jaguar five times, hoping to catch Illusion slipping. It was Saturday, and her stable of hoes had their regulars, but Chyna had to pop in on her street interns. They would work the stroll and recruit fresh meat. They were her cover-ups to conceal what was really going down and were put in place to protect the higher-risk clients like the corporate players, mayors, city councilmen, pastors, judges, bank execs, etc., that would regularly partake in her business offerings. So at every turn, Chyna's money train was rolling.

Though only a handful of girls had Chyna's name tattooed on their bodies, it was evident with the clothes they wore, the shoes they rocked, and the cost to have it all—that they were Chyna's livestock. She charged her customers accordingly. And everything she had done was organized and calculated to prevent the slightest mishap, which is why her latest little misfire was going to be handled personally.

While she already knew the money she was expected to make tonight, the fact of the matter was that she was still out five hundred large. Just that single thought made her choke on her own breath. With rage silently coursing through her veins, she vowed that whoever had her money may as well slit their own throat because they were as good as dead.

That took her thoughts back to Albery. She knew where the man rested his head, who cooked his meals, the soap he used when he showered, and the flavor of his toothpaste. She knew Albery like the back of her right hand, and the very thing that she celebrated most happened to be his weakness—beautiful women. It was why he and his wife were now separated. It was why he chose to retire from his own company. It was why he moved from the city and to the quietness of the suburbs. It was also why he would pay thousands to keep his alternative lifestyle private. Chyna used those who were close to him, and those who knew him, to get what she needed to bring him down, because killing him flat-out was too easy. She wanted Albery to die a slow and painful death. And one that wouldn't be missed.

So when Chyna earned Albery's business, she knew it was only a matter of time before she took back every penny her uncle ever put in his broke pockets—plus interest. But there was always the betrayal factor. Her uncle was serving three concurrent life sentences in the federal prison because his lawyer failed to deliver. So as the months went by, Chyna counted down the last days of Albery's life in exchange for D'Troy's. Then her uncle could carry out his sentence knowing that the person who helped put him there was dead.

Chyna picked up her phone and dialed Fletch to see if he had any updates. Waiting for him to answer, she continued surfing the strip, daring to see one of her girls off the clock.

"Dis dat nigga," Fletch answered lively.

"What you find out?" Chyna pressed.

Fletch let out a long and exasperated sigh. "Shit. I mean, I been calling niggas and shit, trying to find out if anybody talking, and everybody playing dumb right now. Don't nobody know nothin'."

Chyna meshed her lips together, tightening her jaws. That was the last thing she wanted to hear. "Well, if nobody's talking, then you must not be giving them a reason to. Somebody knows where the fuck my money is! And I'm paying your ass to find that out!" Chyna was fuming inside. "This shit is making me look bad. Somebody rolling around this motherfucka laughing at me and you!" She wanted Fletch to understand that by him being her right hand, he was getting played too. She told him all kinds of things, psyching him up and playing him like one of her bitches. She needed him to have beef with whoever was behind this, as if it was his own money he got ran down for.

"I'm gon' find them niggas, Chyna. You ain't gotta worry about that shit. 'Cause ain't no motherfucka gon' make Fletch look bad. I don't give a fuck who that nigga is, how he roll, or what he roll!" he boasted, getting crunk off his own hype. He kissed the lips of his Beretta. "Pump fifteen in the nigga's chest and make him feel blessed like a movie star. 'Cause he playing mighty nigga hero right now." He laughed. Fletch thought that was funny. But when you were as high as he was, everything was funny. Even life in itself was a joke.

Fletch was rolling heavy tonight. The Beretta in his lap wasn't the only company he had tagging along. His boy Nike, who he often called on when it was time to put in work, was on his right, getting crunk off the same shit he was on.

Nike bobbed his head to the lyrics of Foxx A Million as the twelves Fletch had shaking in the back brought out his thug persona. He dished out the gutter rap flow as fluent as a Sunday School Bible verse. Nike couldn't contain himself. He was ready to get his feet wet again, and he didn't give a damn about going back to jail because with the lick he was about to hit, his girl and his baby mama were going to be set for a while, at least until he finished his bid. "Yeah, we gon' merk one of these niggas tonight," Nike said, cocking his gun.

Fletch relaxed in his seat, circling the steering wheel with the heel of his palm. "I'll get back with you in like an hour," he told Chyna, taking another pull off his Philly.

Chyna checked her phone. It was a few minutes past the hour. "You do that," she said before hanging up.

Rene sat waiting in the exact spot Chyna asked her to be in. She had gotten there by cab. This time, thank goodness, Chyna didn't ask her to meet her on a railroad track like before. She waited just outside the Starbucks on Northwest Highway, reserving a small, round, brass table while watching the partygoers make their rounds through the crowded parking lot and over to the night-club next door. The fellas that strolled past her like a car show clique, shortcutting through the coffee shop's lot, tooted their horns as their spinning wheels competed for her attention. A few opted to stop, hoping to score a few pointers by spitting their preschool game as they showed off shining grills and bulky neck chains. Their twenty-inch tires were sitting as big as their egos.

Chyna lowered her passenger window halfway, just enough so she could see Rene and Rene could see her. She sucked up every last bit of the image before pressing firmly on her horn.

Rene looked up the second the horn blew, straining her eyes to be sure it was Chyna. She stood from her seat, slid her purse over her shoulder, and walked over to the black Jaguar. She got right in without having to be told.

Chyna greeted her with a smile. "So, are we ready to have a little fun and make some more money?" she asked with a devilish grin.

Rene pulled the seat belt around her. "I'm ready to do whatever I need to do so that Sand and I can move on from this," she answered truthfully. She braced herself for the worst that could happen tonight.

Chyna's smile vanished. She had hoped for a much different response. Maybe one where Rene admitted that she liked the kind of money she was making and that she'd do whatever she needed to keep it coming. Even if it meant cancelling out her ex.

Chyna sped out of the parking lot and in the direction of the Radisson Hotel. Almost an hour later, she and Rene were entering one of the beautiful suites she had reserved.

Rene followed only a few steps behind Chyna who had immediately made her way over to the mahogany table. Chyna placed the guitar case on the floor, right side up, and the other briefcase she carried she laid on the table and unsnapped it right away.

Rene's eyes didn't miss a beat as she watched Chyna pull out a beautiful black negligee. "This is what you're wearing tonight," Chyna informed her.

Rene could only imagine why. She eyed Chyna peculiarly, wondering so many things about the woman.

"My client is very *particular* of what he wants to happen." Chyna directed her eyes to Rene. "I'm sure you understand what I mean by that." She smiled and pulled out a robe, slippers, oil, and condoms. "He likes to eat pussy more than he likes to fuck. So you'll get a break from time to time," Chyna continued. "Before his climax, he likes for you to shove two fingers in his ass." She watched Rene's face turn sour. "Last, but not least, he will finish off in your mouth."

Rene couldn't stomach what she was hearing. The very thought going through her head was that Chyna was insane.

Chyna strutted her long legs in Rene's direction. "You're in good hands," she said, sounding like a protective guardian. "As long as I'm here, nothing will happen to you." Chyna slid her finger gently down the left side of Rene's face. She pulled back as Rene turned her head sideways, resisting her touch. Chyna's hand then fell to her side. She handed Rene the briefcase. "The bathroom's on the left," she said, walking back over to the table.

Rene quickly retreated to the bathroom, closed the door, and locked it. For that brief moment, she was alone. As she eased her clothes off, the unbearable guilt soaring through her entire body almost made her lose her balance. She balled her fists tightly as she stared at her naked silhouette. Tonight, her body no longer belonged to her.

Once Rene stepped out in her costume, Chyna circled her for a full inspection from head to toe. She poured scented oil into her hands and began massaging it into Rene's arms, thighs, ass, and legs. She was gentle with her touch. "Put this on," she said, handing Rene a tube of lipstick. "It's his favorite."

Watching Rene carefully glide the bloody red color over her lips made Chyna's pussy tremble. She shifted a little, never taking her eyes off what was in front of her.

Rene handed the lipstick back to Chyna. She could sense that Chyna was getting turned on by all of this and that was enough to warrant the nausea floating from her gut.

With a sinister grin on her face, Chyna instructed, "Now, turn around."

Hesitantly, Rene turned slowly.

"Centerfold perfect. He's going to fall head over heels for your sexy ass!" Chyna said. "Now this here's a key to the room." Chyna passed Rene a plastic key card. "When you're done, come back and wait for me here."

Rene just stared into thin air.

"Bitch, are you listening to me?"

That got Rene's attention. She nodded profusely, tears rushing her face.

"Now, I'm gon' run this shit by you, play by play, one more time. And I'm warning you right now, you better not fuck this up."

A moment later, Chyna led Rene out the door and ushered her down the hall to the last door on their left. The entire floor belonged to Chyna. Every Friday and Saturday night, she rented every suite on the twelfth floor so that she knew exactly who was where, at what time, and who they were with. These were her high-dollar clients that paid big money to sleep with her girls, so she made sure they got their money's worth.

Chyna knocked twice on the door and was greeted by one of her favorite clients. He was tall and handsome with deep brown eyes and curly black hair. The scanty specs of gray were deceivingly hidden—this time.

"Zirafelli," Chyna smiled seductively as she spoke his name.

He pulled the door open farther, and Chyna and Rene stepped inside. He took one look at Rene and smiled delightfully in approval. Chyna had done right by him, like always. "So, is this the infamous Illusion you've been telling me about?" He leaned forward and gave Chyna a peck on the cheek.

"You knew I'd take good care of you," Chyna said. She glanced over at Rene, then back at her client. "But be gentle with this one, okay?" She lifted one brow at him. "She's my shiny little keepsake."

Zirafelli worked up a laugh. "Aren't they all?" he guffawed, taking a sip of his bourbon.

Rene looked away at Chyna's comment. Her arms felt like dead weight, and her legs like weak sticks that were only seconds away from collapsing beneath her. She resented everything that she knew was getting ready to take place. But in her mind, her heart, and deep down within her soul, she knew she didn't have a choice. Her and Sand's lives depended on the outcome of tonight.

Chyna removed the hat from her head and a full length of body curls cascaded over her shoulders. "All right, I say we get down to business," she suggested to both of them, Zirafelli primarily. Chyna unlatched the guitar case, opened it, and revealed the twelve pounds of cocaine she had placed inside. Zirafelli reached in for one of the bundles, sniffing as hard as he could through the undetectable wrapping. "If you need a taste test, she's right here," Chyna reminded him. She knew how he preferred his high. That's why she packed along his own little prescribed dosage. She slipped Zirafelli a glass vial containing at least two grams of coke. It was a token of her appreciation for remaining such a dedicated customer.

"You sure know how to treat an old man," Zirafelli said with eyes that wouldn't stop roaming Rene's body. "My guy is in the lobby. The same one I always bring," he informed her. He downed the rest of his drink in one swallow.

"Well, I guess I'll leave you two alone then." Chyna gave Zirafelli a departing kiss on the cheek, then glanced over at Rene who was as stiff as a board. "Relax," she whispered in Rene's ear. "It will only hurt as much as you think that it will," she enlightened, hoping that Rene took heed to her earlier warning.

Rene didn't reply, but her icy cold glare spoke volumes.

"Time for me to handle up." Chyna was now ready to transact the additional related business and collect the remainder of her payment. She saw herself out of the room and made her way to the hotel's lobby, leaving Rene and Zirafelli alone to get better acquainted.

***

She could feel his sperm swimming in her mouth, but Rene tried her hardest not to gag. When Zirafelli's final jerks softened and his swollen dick went limp, she slid her mouth from around his penis tip, leaving her with a saltwater taste tempting her to vomit all over his midsection. She could not and would not adhere to his request to swallow, and instead, sent the contents in her mouth erupting down her chin. Without another thought to spare, she jumped to her feet, staggering toward the end of the bed. She quickly gathered the gown and robe, then rushed to the bathroom, gargling what was left of the slimelike residue to keep it from flushing down her windpipe. She held up the lid on the toilet with her free hand, then began throwing up her insides.

Afterward, Rene leaned into the sink, bending over just enough so the cold water could run into her mouth and overflow. She did that repeatedly. When she was satisfied, she walked back into the room, now covered in the hooded, oversized black robe, only to find Zirafelli getting high off the remaining lines of cocaine he hadn't finished snorting off her ass. She watched unbelievingly, her eyes wide and blank, as the powder disappeared into the rolled one hundred-dollar bill.

Zirafelli leaned his head back and held his nose together, trying to relieve himself of the burn. Spotting Rene out of the corner of his eye, he grew shameful for neglecting his manners. He then lifted his imitation straw in her direction. "Care to join me?"

Rene shook her head. "Are we done here?" she asked, ready to get the hell up out of there. This was more than what she cared to see right now. She'd done the deed she was threatened to do, and now it was time to go.

Zirafelli grunted loudly as the tingling sensation traveled up his nose. He looked up. "Not unless you want more of where that came from, sweet cakes! My little blue pill was built to last," he responded with powder the color of snow clinging to his untrimmed nose hairs.

Rene could barely keep it together. She was disgusted at the mere sight of him, let alone the smell and taste of him. She didn't offer a reply, just turned her back and left the room.

She made her way back down the hall and used her key to unlock the door. Finally, she was all alone. She broke down into tears and rushed for the shower. No matter how hard she scrubbed or how hot she raised the temperature, she could never escape the filth clinging to her conscience.

An hour had passed, and Chyna still hadn't returned to the room. Impatient, nervous, and scared out of her mind, Rene decided to go look for her. She headed down the corridor and to the main floor. She did her best to conceal the recurring nightmare playing itself out in her life right now. She returned a weak smile to the elderly white woman shuffling past her and to the clerk who fell in her line of vision in that same moment. It was painful to look happy. Painful to pretend that she was okay.

"Looking for me?" a woman's voice called from behind.

Rene turned to the voice, clearly startled; however, this was nothing new. Chyna had undoubtedly placed a horrifying fear inside of her.

"Yeah. I'm, uh, finished. Zirafelli's still up there . . . if . . . you need . . . to see him."

Chyna moved her lips, but only to chew on her gum as she assessed Rene. She started not to give her a single dime considering how much of a stuck-up little bitch she was. She was burning unnecessary energy on Rene, but she had a much more strategic agenda in progress, and she still needed the girl's help in her plot to kill Albery.

She handed Rene an envelope similar to the one she'd given her before. Rene nervously looked around them, completely on guard. She peeked inside.

"It's all there," Chyna said. "As agreed."

Rene didn't quite know how to react. Everything about this was wrong. She kept reminding herself that it would all be over soon. And then she and Sand could reclaim their lives together. Things could go back to the way they used to be—before all of the lies and secrets. She allowed her emotions to retreat.

"Am I done?"

Chyna tucked her smile. "For now."

18

Fletch knew he was tripping like a motherfucka, but something was telling him that he wasn't. He sped up, moving in on the vehicle in front of him.

Sand took a second look in the rearview mirror before asking Ty to check out the car behind them.

"Oh shit!" Ty cursed, ducking her head.

"What?"

"We got a problem." Ty turned back around in her seat. "What is this nigga doing?" she hissed through clenched teeth.

Sand looked behind them at the Hummer that was riding their taillights. "What? Who is it? You know the nigga or something?" Sand was frantic, and she could barely get the words out as her head moved up and down, back and forth, from the rearview mirror to the road.

"That's Fletch," Ty said as if Sand should have already known. "Chyna's wannabe bodyguard/dealer—just somebody you don't want following you. And if he knows what's up, we're fucked!"

"Well, I'll be damned if I'm stopping this car." Sand floored the accelerator, picking up speed. She was going fifty miles per hour in a thirty-mile zone.

"We ain't got no choice but to stop and see what's up or else this nigga really gone think we up to something. You forget who car we rollin'," Ty reminded her. "Just don't be acting all suspicious and shit. Let me see what's up," she said. She blew out a couple of breaths. "Trust me. I got this nigga," she said confidently.

Fletch wasn't as fucked up as he thought. He recognized the bitch in the passenger seat, and he could smell her pussy blowing in the wind. It was definitely Ty. He pulled along the driver side to see who in the hell this nigga was pushing Chyna's whip, because it sure as hell wasn't somebody he was familiar with.

Nike sat up straighter. He was high, but that didn't alter his concentration or his ability to check out what was popping because his mind was set on one thing: hitting a lick. "Nigga, what the fuck is you doing? You tryna holla at some hoes when we s'posed to be chasing this gwap?" Nike lashed out at Fletch.

Fletch passed the blunt to Nike. "Nigga, holds the fuck up right quick! Something's up." Fletch let down Nike's side of the window. The cool air made room in between them. "S'up? Pull over!" he yelled out to the driver.

Sand, with both her hands glued to the wheel, took one look at Fletch and knew automatically that he wasn't on toy cop security patrol. He had a Suge Knight build with a suave, clean-shaven baby face. And when he opened his mouth, she spotted his heavy metal iced-out grill. "S'up?" he yelled to her again over the thugged-out passenger riding shotgun.

"Just pull over. I got you," Ty whispered to Sand.

Giving in, Sand veered to the right and pulled into a Family Dollar parking lot at the corner of St. Augustine and Scyene. It was dark out, and the red glowing sign offered minimal lighting.

"Just be cool," Ty warned her. She quickly pulled off her jacket and tightened her shirt by knotting it in the back. She ripped it slightly up top so that her usually unnoticeable cleavage, could be seen. Then she flipped down the visor to get a glimpse at exactly what it was she was working with. When a horrifying image of herself materialized in the overhead mirror, she almost freaked out. She had forgotten all about her fresh bruises and scars—until now. Ty returned the mirror back to its closed position.

Fletch hopped out of the Hummer and paced his steps as he walked around to Ty's side, checking back and forth at the driver with an unfriendly mug plastered across his face.

Sand watched as the shadow lurking behind them grew bigger. She took in the atmosphere. Saw how the man that walked around to the passenger door silently called her out from a distance. That's why she cradled her chin and faced ahead, knowing that her protection was only a short reach away.

"Who the fuck is this motherfucka?" Fletch shot to Ty, folding his arms. His eyes bounced back and forth from Ty to her chauffeur.

Ty rolled her window down more. "Heyyy," she said, easing the door open. She tried to play the whole thing off. "Fletch, lemme holla at you for a second, baby." She closed the door, scooped his arm in hers, and walked nearly five feet away from the car.

Fletch tagged beside her, glancing at Sand as often as he felt.

"I got a hustle going right now," Ty began, pulling out the first lie that came to mind. She stuffed her hands in her back pockets. "Man, this bitch got mad dough, and Chyna asked me to run her down and scope her out. She think she pushing weight in her hood." Ty looked Fletch directly in the face, hoping her lie would stand the test.

"Word?"

Ty bounced her head. "Yep. I let her drive 'cause she say she know the hood better than I do." Ty started looking around as if she was lost. "As a matter of fact, where the hell are we?"

"PG. Quit acting dumb," Fletch said, not buying anything she was telling him.

"For real. I ain't never been over here," she lied.

Fletch uncrossed his arms. "Well, I'ma call Chyna right now 'cause she ain't even mention this shit to me." He reached for the cell phone hanging off his hip.

Ty grabbed his hand. "Oh, so you ain't believin' what the fuck I say now?" she frowned, rolling her neck. She threw her hands over her small hips and stretched her titties in his face. "I ain't never gave you a reason to doubt me. All the shit I've done on the DL for you, nigga, and you got the nerve to doubt me over some bullshit that don't even matter? Okay, I see how quick you switch it up when you need your dick sucked again. Better yet, when you need some pussy." Ty knew bringing up the free pussy would cause him to reconsider, especially if he planned on ever hitting it again.

Fletch lowered his hand. "A'ight, if you say so."

"Nigga, I *know* so," Ty boasted. Her head moved along with every word. She stepped closer, lowered her volume. "Let me play this bitch like I know how, make my paper, and catch you on the rebound." She reached out for his dick but instead gripped all jeans.

Fletch licked his lips and squinted his glazed-over eyes. "Yeah, I'm with that shit," he nodded. "Call me as soon as you done with that trick."

"Fo sho. You know how we get down," she grinned, winking one eye. She stuck her salty finger in her mouth. "I'll get these lips all ready," she teased, "because I'm gon' need a real dick by the time I'm done with her ass."

Fletch stirred his tongue around in his mouth. Just thinking about getting some head had his eyes and his mouth watering. Even his jimmy was starting to attack his boxers as he contemplated what positions he would flip Ty's fine ass in later. He didn't care anything about her face being busted in. He just wanted a piece. His cell started to vibrate like crazy. He looked down, recognizing the number. He held up one finger to Ty, answering it before it could go to voice mail. "What up, motherfucka?"

"Nigga, you call me more than my bitches do. What the fuck is up with that shit?"

Ty moved her lips slowly. "We're leaving," she mouthed to Fletch. She backed away, holding her hand up to her left ear. "I'll call you," she whispered. She turned her back and headed for the car where Sand waited impatiently with the engine still running.

"Wait a minute!" he hollered back out to Ty. He was going to ask her what time to meet up. He laughed at his boy. "Fuck you, man. I was calling 'cause Chyna say her eagle didn't drop last night. Know anything about that? 'Cause me and Nike ready to put in some overtime," he said, talking in code. Although he spoke on a burn-out phone that was supposedly impossible to trace due to the chip that was inside of it, he still didn't trust it.

"What you mean she didn't get her payment?" K.C. balked. "I was with Aaron and James when they dropped that shit. Aaron made sure that everybody on payroll got paid last night, and the rest of that shit we dropped off, like always."

"So where the fuck y'all drop it, nigga, 'cause evidently, it ain't where it need to be, or I wouldn't be blowing you up, Einstein-ass nigga," he said sarcastically.

Ty walked back over to where Fletch was, shifting her weight from one side to the other. She began biting down on her lip and rocking her legs. Fletch reached for her hand so that she could feel what she had done to him. His dick had swollen solid and was inches from detonating in his pants. He'd let her suck him off right there, behind that building, if she wasn't so pressed for time.

Ty unzipped Fletch's jeans and stuck her hand inside, massaging his shriveled up balls until he turned red in the face. She made room for herself in his leather coat.

Ty knew that at the rate she was going, it'd only be a matter of minutes before it was all over because she was working the head of his dick like crazy.

"Y'all killing me with this miscommunication shit," K.C. told Fletch. *"We put that shit inside Chyna's trunk. Matter fact, two hoes were in the car. A dyke-looking broad and a ho with some peacock-looking, blue-ass hair. I'm guessing they were the new runners. But Aaron checked that shit out and gave us the green light."*

Fletch was listening to K.C. but concentrated more on the nut filling up Ty's hand. "Yeah, a'ight, then. Let me hit you back," he grunted.

Ty slipped her hands out, grinning from ear to ear. She rubbed the cream in her hands together like lotion, then she slyly glanced back at Sand who was pointing to her wrist, reminding her that they needed to get a move on. "Fletch, we have to go. She has some, uh, customers waiting for her," Ty said.

Fletch pushed his dick back into his boxer shorts. "Really?"

The look Ty received from him was far from the same convinced look he held earlier. She wondered if that had been Chyna on the phone. Wondered if they had been found out.

Fletch reached for Ty's throat. "Bitch, do I look like a motherfuckin' fool to you?" his booming voice echoed.

Ty struggled to breathe. When Sand looked up and saw what was going on, she reached for her strap, but the gun in her face urged her to reconsider. Nike held Fletch's Beretta in one hand and his own 9 mm in the other. "Bitch, get out of the motherfuckin' car!"

Fletch's hands weren't releasing their grip. "Where's the fuckin' money, Ty?"

Ty couldn't talk and could barely breathe. All she could do was nod her head and blink her eyes.

Nike's face lit up when he heard the word money. This was it. He walked Sand around the car, closer to where Fletch and Ty stood.

"Where the money!" Fletch yelled again, ready to rip Ty's head clean off her shoulders.

"Look, I'll give you the money. Just ease the fuck up off her, man. She ain't do shit," Sand spoke up in Ty's defense.

Nike was so excited he could barely hold the Glock straight.

Fletch turned Ty loose, sending her into a choking fit. He wouldn't care if the bitch was dying. He was unaffected as he watched her bent over fighting for air.

Ty palmed her throat and bobbed her head up and down in gasping motions. She hurled out a glob of spit. When she finally regained composure, she stood up straight and cautiously walked directly in front of Fletch as Sand guided them to the trunk of the car.

"It's back here," Sand told them.

Nike waved the nine in her direction as he yelled, "Well, open it, bitch! What you standing there looking at me for?" Nike had both guns trained on Sand at all times, ready to spray.

Sand walked around the car and popped the trunk release. She stepped around toward the back, lifting the trunk slowly. She pulled out the black gym bag and let it drop to the ground.

Nike's eyes flashed dollar signs. This grinding shit was so simple for grimy goon niggas like him. It was in his blood. He kicked the bag closer to him, already feeling his come-up. "Let these hoes roll out," he said.

Fletch looked at him as if he was crazy. "Nah. Chyna gon' hear about this shit." He flipped his phone open.

Nike suddenly positioned one of the guns on Fletch, his beady eyes red as fireballs. His gold teeth were pressed firmly into his bottom lip as he showed off a side of him that only came out when it was time to go after that presidential express train. "Nigga, I said let the hoes roll out. We'll work this shit out ourselves," Nike told Fletch directly.

Fletch felt like a loose cannon. Nike was on some more shit, and he wasn't feeling it one bit.

Sand and Ty took that as their opportunity to bounce before anything major went down like they knew it would. Ty jetted for the car. Sand got in, pushed the gear into *Drive,* and sped off, disappearing into the foggy night.

With both guns aimed in his direction, Fletch didn't have to think like a rocket scientist to know what was about to jump off next. "So this what the fuck you been waiting on, nigga?" Fletch held out his hands, walking up to Nike. "A fucking jack move? You gon' rob me now, nigga? All the cake I put you down with? All the money I put on you?" He pointed to the clothes Nike wore. "I'm the reason these bitches even look at you twice! I'm yo' motherfuckin' come-up, flake-ass nigga! So what? I'm supposed to be scared or some shit?"

Nike was quiet. Fletch should have known the drill by now. He hated to be the one to do it, but it was a fucked-up circumstance. Fletch was his boy, but Nike was hurting for money, and all he needed was an opportunity like this to get him back on his feet. The money he made off jobs Fletch gave him wasn't enough. He even tried to go legit at one point, but nobody wanted to hire an ex-con. So this is what it was, and all that it was going to be—work.

"So you the shit now, Nike? The man with the master plan?" Fletch said with fake enthusiasm. He started clapping. "Bravo, motherfucka. Now you can buy that bitch of yours a bus pass." Fletch faced Nike straight up. He wasn't backing down from this ho-ass nigga, and he wasn't afraid of catching a bullet, again. So with that pistol waving back and forth in his face, he hoped for Nike's sake that he planned on killing him with it.

Nike leveled the Beretta between Fletch's eyes, the shadow of death disguising the pain promised to come. "See ya when I see ya, my nigga."

Fletch rushed him.

Suddenly, Fletch's body dropped to the ground as an orchestra of gunshots rang out into the night. *Bang! Bang! Bang!* A gush of blood spewed from Fletch's neck, chest, and stomach. There was no coming back as his life began to expire with every delayed breath he took. Finally, Fletch surrendered. He closed his eyes and slowly drifted off to an eternal sleep.

Nike waited until Fletch was no longer convulsing and the white cloud of moisture coming from his mouth evaporated into thin air. He then snatched up the bag of money and jumped in the Hummer. He slammed on the accelerator, making a mad dash out of the parking lot and back on St. Augustine. He was trying to get to his girl's house who didn't live far from the murder scene. He made a right on Bruton Road, ran red lights, and side-swiped the orange cones and white construction barrels in the middle of the road. Quickly, he pulled out his cell and started dialing numbers. "Queesha, baby, wake up. It's me," Nike said when she moaned in his ear.

Queesha was half-asleep, but she knew Nike's voice from anywhere. "Where you been at, nigga? It's eleven fucking o'clock," she said, shooting her eyes up at the red numbers on the digital clock. "I thought you said you were coming right back? And that was what—two days ago!" she hollered into the phone. "You was with yo' baby mama, weren't you?" she accused before giving him a chance to get a word in. When he didn't respond quick enough, she said, "I'm tired of your shit, Nike," she yelled. "I can't keep doing this shit! If you want that bitch, you can have her skank ass. I ain't 'bout to let you keep taking me through hoops." She sat up as now she was wide awake.

"If you just listen to me and calm all that shit down, I'll tell you where the fuck I been at, girl! Damn." He chilled, waiting to see if she was going to shut her trap up. "Yo' nigga been out here hustling, making moves," Nike bragged, proud of his recent accomplishment.

"Umm-hmm," Queesha sighed, still not believing anything he had to say.

"For real, doe. I just came up on some fat boy paper, baby."

Queesha's lips curled upward. "Motherfucka, quit lying!"

"A'ight. Don't believe me then. I'm like two minutes from your crib, so be looking out for a nigga," Nike told her. "Your mama woke?"

"Nah. She back there asleep."

Nike got happy. For him, that meant playtime. "I want some bomb-ass head for this shit right here," he told her. He crossed over Buckner and made the first right onto her street. Her porch lights were on, and she was waiting for him at the door, peeking through the ripped screen.

Queesha swapped the telephone from one ear to the other. "Who Hummer you driving?" she asked out of curiosity the instant Nike flashed the headlights in her face.

"Don't worry 'bout all dat. You just get ready to count this cheese yo' nigga done made. And like I said," he reaffirmed, "I want some killer head for this. Nah, scratch that. I want the works. Ass, titties, and all."

As Nike pulled into Queesha's driveway, he hardly gave the car time to come to a complete stop before slamming it into *Park* and snatching the keys out of the ignition.

He grabbed the bag alongside of him, then walked across the frosted grass until he made his way to the three steps guiding the porch.

Queesha wrapped her arms around Nike the moment he stepped in the door, surrendering a dry kiss to his mouth. She sniffed out his collar and his neck for just a hint of another bitch's scent. But all she got was a nose full of weed.

Nike laughed. "You won't take a nigga word for shit, will you?" He shook his head. "Wanna smell him too?" he laughed, leaning back a little bit so that his hard-on could get noticed.

"Fuck you, Nike. Your ass gon' slip up one day," Queesha said.

"Kill all that noise, girl. Huh," Nike handed the heavy bag to her while he walked right past her and straight toward her back room. He threw himself across the triple-stacked mattresses that Queesha claimed for a bed and stretched out like he paid rent there. He waited for her to pour out all his hard work. The blood on his white tee, pants, and shoes didn't matter right now.

Queesha began to unzip the bag, only to pull out a blanket and several marble orbs and miniature statues. She wanted to kick the shit out of Nike. She threw the bag at him as hard as she could. "Motherfucka! You woke me up out my sleep for *this* shit?" she asked with one of the orbs in her hand.

Nike jumped up. He flipped the bag over, but nothing else came out. His head felt tight, and he could feel a strong pressure rise in his chest, strangling him.

"Bitches!" he cursed out loud.

It wasn't a second after he spit the word out that he could hear the wail of sirens in the distance. He stood in a trance as the piercing sound got closer and closer.

Suddenly, there were pounding knocks at the front door. Everybody in the house, including Queesha's mom, jumped out of bed and ran toward the front to see what was going on.

"Dallas Police! Open up!"

Queesha eased the door open, and a swarm of policemen, all dressed in black, barged inside. "He's back there!" she yelled out, moving out of the way. She was just as afraid as the others.

Minutes later, Nike was being read his Miranda rights and escorted out of the house and into the first of the three waiting police cars. All he could say was, "It wasn't me. You got the wrong nigga. Queesha, call my lawyer!"

Queesha and her mom just stood in stunned silence as the officers hauled Nike away.

19

Illusion started to get restless as she and Trent waited in the car for nearly two hours in hopes of spotting one of Chyna's girls. As her eyes moved up and down the polluted strip, she witnessed the exchange of goods and services, all in the name of making a quick dollar. It was nobody's secret what went on inside of the vehicles that lined the industrious boulevard so late in the hour. But it was always business. Illusion checked the time again. It was thirteen past eleven and still no luck.

"Are you sure this is where my sister hangs out?" Trent asked, now a little on the impatient side.

Illusion looked around again. "I'm positive." She could tell Trent was getting ready to blow. "Look, if we don't see nobody in the next ten minutes we can leave, but this is the post," she said.

Trent tried to keep cool. After all, this was his baby sister they were looking for. But the whole idea of Ty on the streets and selling herself didn't sit well with him. Of all things, he would have never guessed she'd be involved in something this extreme. He partly blamed himself, convinced that he never should have left her and went off in the military.

"Back there. Go over there," Illusion pointed.

Trent started the car and made a full U-turn in the middle of the street. He pulled up closer to the curb, lowering Illusion's side of the window.

"Peaches!" Illusion yelled, waving her in their direction.

Peaches spun around on her heels, trying to make out the female that was screaming her name. She walked slowly in her rusty-gold, skintight dress, toward the woman's voice. She pulled several of the tiny microbraids that fell in her face behind her ear, and then popped her eyes wider when she recognized who the woman was. She sprinted toward the car. "Illusion?" she asked in disbelief.

Illusion removed Trent's shades from her eyes and placed them in her lap. She watched her friend's mouth drop and her face unfold as if she were staring at a ghost.

"Hey, ho," Illusion joked, giving Peaches an eyeful. Like always, Peaches's double D cleavage was pushed up in a bra that intentionally exposed the upper half of her tattoo with Chyna's name in a green scripted font. Through her tight, necktie dress, you could see impressions of both her nipple rings. "I'm looking for Ty. Have you seen her?" Illusion asked. She knew that if anybody had the lowdown, it was Peaches.

Peaches leaned her entire body inside the car and threw her arms around Illusion tightly.

"Hey, girly. What's up? What's the matter?" Illusion asked, nearly suffocating from the strong embrace.

When Peaches finally let up, "What the fuck is going on?" she asked Illusion, waving her purse with every word.

"What do you mean what's going on?" Illusion asked, dumbfounded.

Trent sat quietly, staring ahead but with his ears tuned in to their conversation.

"Chyna told us you got did in. That you were dead!" Peaches exclaimed.

"What! Why the fuck would she make up some bullshit like that?" Illusion asked with her face drawn up.

"I don't know. But what I do know is that your ass better disappear before somebody sees you." Peaches began looking around her cautiously.

For a moment Illusion was quiet, trying to put her finger on why Chyna would lay out something like that on her.

"Bitch, you are wanted. Since you're alive, that means Chyna, Fletch, and no telling who else is out here looking for yo' ass." Peaches met eyes with the guy in the driver's seat but didn't bother asking who he was. She really didn't care either because just by looking at him, she sensed that he was a trick that Illusion stumbled upon and was possibly shopping for another female to join their party.

Illusion leaned more into Peaches. "All right, look. You never saw me tonight, okay?" Peaches was nodding her head before Illusion could even get all the words out. "Oh, one other thing," she said, remembering the purpose for being on the strip. "Where is Ty dancing at tonight or does Chyna have her working a party?"

"Ty? Humph, I don't know where that bitch at, but I can tell you this," Peaches volunteered quickly. "She got her ass whooped somethin' serious last night. That ho probably on house arrest. No telling. You know she keep shit stirred up anyway."

Trent raised forward in his seat. "Where can we find her?" he interrupted.

Peaches looked over Illusion's shoulder. Before she could say anything out of line, Illusion did the honors. "Peaches, this is Trent, Ty's brother."

Peaches pulled her neck back and took another look. "Okay, am I missing something?" She stared Trent up and down. He was finer than a motherfucka but related to Ty. Peaches just didn't see the resemblance.

"Look, I'm just trying to find Tylesha," Trent informed her.

Peaches frowned sourly at Ty's government name. "Tylesha?"

"Yes, Tylesha. Now where might I do that?" he asked, adjusting his disposition so that she could understand the urgency.

Peaches looked around again. "Look, I'm not down with that, all right? You might wanna keep riding up the strip," she said loudly.

Illusion could read in between the lines. Peaches began making strange gestures with her eyes. When Illusion looked behind them, she spotted two of Chyna's girls stepping out of a stretch limo. They began walking toward Peaches.

Illusion slipped the shades back over her face.

"Peaches!" one of the voices called out.

Peaches backed away from the Infiniti, mouthing to Illusion to catch up to her later. She turned around and headed toward the duo. "What's up?"

"We been looking for you," one of them said. The girls followed the car with their eyes. "Damn, was that a trick and his woman?"

Peaches relaxed, realizing they hadn't spotted Illusion. It was a close call. "Yeah, he wanted me to fuck his wife while he watched," she lied.

"Well, ho, why you still standing here?" the two joked, high-fiving each other. "That's double pay," one calculated.

Peaches dropped her head. "It's personal." She walked away and left them standing not far from the curb.

"You think they saw you?" Trent asked Illusion, who was fidgeting in her seat. She kept looking behind her, on the side of her, and behind again.

She wasn't sure if they spotted her, and she sure as hell wasn't about to go back to find out. "Look, Trent, I can't do this. I mean, I'm wanted right now. My life is on the line here."

Trent pulled the car into an empty parking lot. "Illeshia, I'm not trying to get sidetracked right now. I have to find my sister. Now if you want me to take you home, I can do that. But I really could use your help on this."

As the quiet moment won Illusion over, she asked him, "And where does that leave me, Trent, huh? I help you, everybody's happy. Everybody gets to fucking sleep. But where does that leave *me?*" she asked him again. "Dead? Laid up in a freezer until somebody comes to identify me? I mean, shit, Ty got her own self in this mess! You think you can just appear out of nowhere and make demands? You don't know this woman. Ty sold herself out the day she got involved with Chyna." The picture she painted of Chyna was a vivid one. She didn't cut any corners, and she refused to spare him the truth. Those resentful tears she fought back betrayed her and began marching down her face. "So why waste your time? Ty made the choice, and now she has to live with it."

Trent found it hard to discern if Illusion was still speaking of Ty, or if maybe she was speaking through Ty. He took it as her telling him why it was that she felt trapped and why she saw no way out. He wrapped his arm around her. "It's okay," he said. "I'm here." He began rubbing her back. "I'm right here."

Illusion lay her head on his shoulder. She allowed the tears that wet her face to drip on his shirt. She took two of her fingers and slid them under her eyes, not believing that she was actually sitting there dropping tears in front of a man that she hadn't even known twenty-four hours. She got herself together and straightened in her seat.

"Look here," Trent held Illusion's chin in his hand, "do you believe in fate, or do you think it was just some weird-ass coincidence the way we met today?"

Illusion was taken by surprise at his question. She nodded her head slowly. "I guess I believe," she answered softly. His warm touch enveloped her and made her feel whole.

"Well, trust and believe this," Trent said. He leaned into Illusion and placed his lips against hers. He wanted to hold her and never let go.

When Illusion finally opened her eyes, everything looked and felt different. Because tonight, for the first time ever, she would trust a man—with her life.

20

Deja and Nessa sat in Sandrene's at a round dining table that was elegantly draped in a golden orange tablecloth and adorned with a black and gold glowing S and R centerpiece, ignited by a single tea light. The sexy ensemble added something special to the ambiance of the room.

The pair stuck out like two green apples in a barrel of candy-coated red ones. Nessa dressed in a backless shimmering silver top, black bottoms, and two-inch heels. Her bulky jewelry received compliments from afar along with the updo ponytail that hung symmetrically down the center of her back. Her makeup was applied lightly, and her smooth, flawless skin was spritzed in Dior. Deja, caught up in the moment, looked equally flattering in a wool, cranberry-red peasant dress, and a pair of heart-shaped diamond studs. Her neck was naked except for the very many hickeys that she attempted to hide with makeup, and resting on her hips was a silver chain belt, matching the eloquent design in the heel of her shoes.

The two continuously relished the incredible poet that was now making his way off the stage. Everybody in the club began clapping and snapping their fingers in the air. While Nessa could hardly understand Deja's rationale for taking it upon herself to oversee the club in Sand's absence, she had to give it to her; it was definitely an upgrade of taste. Everybody was in the house, including South Dallas's own, Erykah Badu. Admiring the scenery,

Nessa took another healthy sip from a glass of blackberry Merlot.

Deja looked around. She was hoping Sand would be there by now, but she wasn't. Once again, Sand was making her feel like a fool. She let out a sigh of disappointment and prepared for the hostess to announce her name.

When Erykah graced the stage, the snaps grew louder, and the whistling from the brothers just wouldn't quit. Ms. Badu picked up the microphone and began clapping with it in her hands. As always, she looked so exotic in a sleeveless, olive-green bell-bottom one-piece, and her hair tucked away in a matching green head wrap. She moved her lips closer to the mic. "Ladies and Gentlemen, let's give Mr. Michael Guinn another round of applause." The few men sprinkled about started barking. It was their way of showing appreciation for the piece Michael had just put down. He recited everything most of them wished they could say to their woman out loud, but only half of them would dare to take it there.

"Now, if that's not spoken word, I don't know what is," Erykah responded to the crowd. Everyone who agreed with her was now up on their feet, waving and fanning the air. "Yeah, y'all feeling that, ain't ya? I see Michael left a lasting impression with some of y'all down there," Erykah joked. The women jeered in agreement. "Well, it doesn't end there," she paused. "Because for our next performance, we have a young lady that I'm sure all of you are familiar with. She's also a very good friend of mine. So Sandrene's, get your snaps together, and show some love for my girl, Deja." Erykah stepped back, and Deja made her way to the center of the stage. The two women embraced in a soft sisterly squeeze.

Deja spoke softly. "Thank you, thank you." The whites of everyone's eyes were fixated on her. "I'm glad you all could make it out tonight. I know this weather has been something else. I tell ya, one minute it's hot and sunny, the next minute we're ruining eighty-dollar hairdos," she chuckled.

"*Say it, girl,*" someone yelled out.

She laughed. "Well, again, I'm very thankful to have had this opportunity to be a part of such a strong movement in our community. I want to thank the Sandrene's staff that has some of the greatest people I know and the easiest to work with on- and offline. And most importantly, I want to thank you. Because you are the sole reasoning why Sandrene's isn't just some ordinary club on the corner. You've dedicated yourselves to us, and we thank you. Our wonderful poets and open-mic artists, thank you. Sand thanks you." Deja took a minute to engage the crowd. "It's been a long time since I've done something like this." She chuckled again, this time more to herself. She held a folded blank sheet of paper in her hands. "*It's all right, girl,*" a woman dressed in all-white yelled from the crowd. Deja met eyes with her supporter. "You're too sweet." She looked around a final time, still no Sand. She swallowed hard, hoping she could get herself through this one. "I'd like to call this piece . . . 'Déjà Vu.'"

The crowd was all ears, and the room fell completely silent. The attendant at the bar had taken a seat, and the waitresses that roamed about stopped what they were doing and faced Deja. Nessa waved at her friend, encouraging her from their front-row table as she upturned her drink. When she turned around, trying her best to see just how many people had shown up tonight, she spotted Sand in the far right corner. She was standing near the entryway of the club, dressed in a solid black wife beater and jeans with her chiseled arms folded over each other. Sand's shoulder-length cornrows were missing, but Nessa would recognize that face and those hazel-brown eyes in a pitch-dark bat cave. She started to get up from her seat and drag Sand over, knowing Deja would turn flips across the stage once she saw her, especially after hearing the message Sand had left for her the night before. As Nessa played back the recording over and over for Deja, she saw the way her eyes lit up every time Sand said, "*I was just lying here thinking about some things. I know this might sound funny, but you were on my mind.*" Deja must have replayed the message ten more times after that.

Nessa swung her legs from under the table and was about to head over to Sand but quickly decided against it when she noticed a light-skinned female with hideous blue-spiked hair standing closely at her side. She couldn't believe the nerve of Sand. Nessa turned her head back around, unnoticed, contemplating if she should even involve herself. She was convinced that it wasn't even worth it. Not when she had warned Deja time and time again. But with Deja so bent on finding love and happiness, Nessa knew that what she had to say wouldn't have mattered one bit. She took another long swallow from her glass and saved her friend the embarrassment.

The vibrating sound of a saxophone invaded the airwaves, and everyone began swaying their heads to the rich melodic interplay of instruments that escaped the wall-mounted speakers hanging throughout the club.

Deja took a deep breath, preparing to freestyle her unique piece, all from the heart. One last time, she searched for her inspiration around the room, and still, it wasn't there. Her body tightened, but she had to get it out. She held the paper loosely at her left side and choked the mic with her free hand. She engaged the crowd—all lovers of spoken word—lost herself in their collective misery, their hopes, their desires. She wondered if any of them really cared to hear what she had to say as she

opened her mouth and got ready to spit them a new
perspective. She allowed her words to float over the
harmonic chords of her introduction and just like that . . .
She was in the zone.

Déjà Vu
Your beauty I dare to compare,
for it's déjà vu
your eyes are so binding and
soul catching as a spider's web,
your fingers are as gentle to my
face as a fly-away leaf.
Why does this feel like déjà vu?

Your inner essence has the
strength of the greatest pine
and to compare your qualities to
nature gives me the ability to love
you.

Have I said this to you before?
Because it feels like
déjà vu.

Your caresses during our
lovemaking turn me into a
developing flower,
an exposed bud surrounded by generous
amounts of dew.
Damn, this feels like déjà vu.

The scent of your overflowing
fountain is that of the morning
rain.
The sound of your most intimate
moan, hmmmm, did I mistake your

pleasure . . . for pain?
As the base
in your voice was as powerful as a
thunderstorm, but on the contrary
your orgasmic song was as sincere
as the tweet of a baby bird.

I am captivated by you, and I
possess a twinkle in my smile for
you,
brighter than that of any star.
You are loved.

I love you,
and I am willing to be yours
faithfully
 if you invite me, I
will accept . . . and submit to only
you
and again, I will inhale
you, and taste you, and devour
you
because before we ever met, I
confessed my love for
you.
That's why this shit feels
so much
like
Déjà Vu.

Deja exited the stage with a roar of applause following
her. She wasn't quite sure where the energy had come
from, but it mysteriously came from somewhere because
she even felt like she did a fantastic job. She walked
confidently back to the table and joined Nessa who was
standing and clapping with a mile-wide smile.

"You were great up there," Nessa said. She witnessed the sadness building in Deja's eyes.

Deja pulled her chair out and sat down. "Thanks."

Nessa watched Deja's hopeful eyes continue to roam around the club until she couldn't take it anymore. "She ain't coming," Nessa said, refusing to tell her that she'd seen Sand only a few minutes ago.

Deja brought her attention back to Nessa after her eyes surfed until she grew dizzy. "What?"

"Sand. That's who you keep looking around for, isn't it?"

Deja lifted her glass, trying to control her desperately seeking eyes. She let the wine mingle in her mouth, tantalizing her tongue, then ease down like a river in her throat. "No." She shifted in her seat, crossing her legs. "I'm not looking for nobody," she lied with a straight face.

Nessa didn't believe her friend. She rolled her eyes upward and mumbled, "Yeah, right."

"I'm just checking out the crowd tonight," Deja said. "It's quite a turnout. I guess the radio advertising was a good idea after all." She dodged the Sand subject. She simply did not feel like going there with Nessa, not right now.

As Erykah Badu's "Danger" filtrated through the speakers, the crowd invited themselves to sing along. *"Because they got the block on lock . . ."* A few took to the dance floor, while others rocked in their seats and enjoyed every dime they'd paid to get inside the club.

Nessa raised her glass in the air. The wine was slowly starting to escalate her levels. "We need to make a toast," she said sluggishly out of nowhere, snapping Deja out of her out-of-mind-and-body coma.

Deja relaxed her hands on the table. "To what?" Her mood had changed drastically, and suddenly, she was ready to go home. Her asking Sand to come was a mistake.

Expecting Sand to come was just a hopeful waste of breath. She should have known better, but yet, she still allowed this woman she hardly even knew to magically reenter the picture after months of no sign she'd be returning—to sex her, fuck her, and then leave, again. Deja felt like a pawn. How could she not see this coming? She cursed herself for being so stupid and so naïve. As she twirled her tongue ring between her teeth, she refamiliarized herself with what Sand's essence tasted like against her lips, then instantly drowned the idea for good that introduced itself out of her imagination. It was over. That was over. She refused to put herself through agony and heartache all over again like she had done with Toni. Deja made a stern commitment to herself that from this moment on, if Sand didn't want to take those extra steps with her, then she would move on. Let it all go and never look back. She would push Sand out of her mind—for good.

Nessa was still holding her glass in the air, waiting for Deja to lift hers. She began shaking it some, blinking her eyes at the same time to redirect Deja's attention. When Deja did finally snap out of it, she raised her glass as well. "To true friendship."

Deja started smiling. "Now, I can drink to that."

They tapped their glasses together, and that resonating response placed them both on the same page of life.

21

"She must really cut for you," Ty said, pulling Sand out of her thoughts after a long drive of dead silence.

Sand had been thinking the exact same thing. She enjoyed the poem, appreciated Deja for all the things she'd done, but Sand knew that Deja was wearing her heart on her sleeve. While she cared for Deja deeply, the facts remained the same. Sand was too involved right now to take things to new heights, and she knew Deja would never accept or settle for that brutal honesty.

Sand didn't respond to what Ty was saying and instead, asked her, "Are you sure you know the code to get in?"

"Positive."

"A'ight, then. Let's do this." Sand pulled up to the security gate and punched in from memory every digit Ty called out. Immediately after entering the last number, the gates began to open slowly. Sand drove through and headed toward the mansion. A few lights were on, but not many. At this time of night, Sand expected no one to be inside, except for one person, and that was Fantasy. All the other girls were more than likely at work.

Sand parked the car directly in front of the house, just as she and Ty had plotted. "Okay, it's all you," she told Ty.

Ty nodded. She was ready to do this, readier than she'd ever be. She unlocked her door, got out, and strutted toward the walkway. Instead of ringing the doorbell, she pounded the wooden door with her fist. Suddenly, she could hear footsteps approaching from the inside.

"Who is it?" Fantasy yelled, squinting through the peephole.

"It's me!" Ty hollered between the fake tears she forced on so quickly.

Fantasy began unchaining every lock in place. "You better have a damn good reason for not calling . . ." Her words trailed off because before she could get the rest of her sentence out, a tall figure sprinted from out of nowhere with a ski mask over his face.

Fantasy jumped, completely caught off guard. Terrified, she backpedaled away from the door and quickly put her hands in the air, shaking her head. "Please, don't shoot," she called out to the intruder. She had no doubt in her mind that he came to rob them.

Sand shoved Ty closer to where Fantasy stood. "Both of y'all turn the fuck around!" she yelled.

Fantasy and Ty did as told. Fantasy glanced over at Ty who had her eyes closed tightly and was breathing like she was having a seizure. Fantasy considered running for her gun but knew she wouldn't get very far without risking several holes being blown into her back. So she waited, hoping this would be quick and painless for all of them.

Sand closed the door behind her and rechained every lock and deadbolt.

Ty kept putting on her Academy Award–winning performance.

With her white and silver fingernails still lifted in the air, Fantasy asked bravely, "What do you want from us?" Her voice was as calm as it could be.

"Did I ask you to talk?" Sand yelled in Fantasy's ear through the mask. Fantasy shook her head and sucked in her dry lips.

"Then don't!"

"But I . . . I . . . I gotta pee . . ." Ty butted in while wiggling around and practically hopping on one leg. For a second, the way things were going, she almost believed it was real, but then remembered it was all a part of the plan—Sand's plan.

"Anybody else in the house?" Sand asked Fantasy.

Fantasy shook her head no.

Sand walked backward toward the living area, never taking her eyes off the two women. She blindly snatched the phone cord from the wall jack, tossing it to Ty. "You wanna go to the bathroom, then I'm going with you. Tie her up."

Ty nervously walked behind Fantasy, reaching for both her arms. She began wrapping the cord tightly around both her wrists, looping it as she went along. When she finally ran out of excess cord, she began making double knots. "There, she's tied," she hollered to Sand. Before she could look up, Sand was throwing a curtain tieback her way that she'd pulled from the draperies.

"Now do her ankles," Sand instructed.

Ty's brows folded in. She pulled a chair from the dining table, sat Fantasy down in it, and commenced to tying her legs from behind. "Just please, please, don't hurt us," she carried on.

Before all of this, Fantasy was in the downstairs bathroom, disrobing and prepping for a warm soak in the tub. Now she stood wearing just a spaghetti tank and thong underwear with her hands tied behind her back, and her ankles shackled with curtain straps. But even still she wasn't afraid of the perpetrator behind the mask. Not only because of who she believed it to be, but because she had been in situations like this before, a million times. And even with a gun in her face, Fantasy managed to maintain her cool.

Sand grabbed Ty by the arm and forced her to lead the way to Chyna's main domain—her bedroom. They ran over to the dressers, throwing clothes out, lifting mattresses—the whole nine. Sand focused on the boxes, the cabinets, whatever appeared to be a stashing ground. After tearing up the room from top to bottom, they both came up empty.

"I don't see it," Ty whispered. "Maybe she got rid of it or something 'cause it ain't in here, and we need to go before somebody shows up."

"Look, I can't go to jail for some shit I didn't do. I have to find that tape."

Ty sighed as she placed her hand over her forehead. "All right, all right. I'll keep looking."

They frantically searched the room but found no tape.

Sand collected herself. She placed the hot mask back over her face. "Come on."

Ty got back into character. She walked obediently back out in front of Sand, her hands closely at her sides.

Sand moved in front of Fantasy. "Peaches, which room does she sleep in?"

Fantasy shot Sand the evil eye. "Y'all can quit with y'all's so-called routine already, and while you're at it, why don't you take that thing off your face? Humph, I mean, we both know you aren't fooling anybody, Sand." Fantasy stared Sand down straight through her mask as a sinister grimace washed over her face.

Sand gave it some consideration, then yanked the mask from over her head. She got so close up in Fantasy's face that she could almost taste her every breath and feel her thumping pulse. "Is *this* a good look for you?" she asked. "Now, I'm going to ask you one more time—"

"Upstairs. Last door on the left," Fantasy shot. Her eyes never left Sand's. "You don't intimidate me. I've chewed and spit out bitches like you."

Slap!

Sand didn't even brace herself for the backhand she sent flying to Fantasy's jaw. "Watch her," Sand ordered Ty, not taking her eyes off Fantasy. She handed Ty the pistol. "If she even blinks the wrong way, you send her pretty little ass on her way." Sand took off for the stairs, climbing them two at a time.

"So, I see we have Dumber and Dumbest," Fantasy mused.

"Shut the hell up!"

"Ty, come on. What do you think you're doing, huh? Do you *really* believe that Chyna's just going to let y'all waltz up in here and get away with this? You must be outta your mind."

Ty stood quietly with the gun aimed at Fantasy's torso.

"I never had the chance to tell you, but you know you were my favorite. I treated you like a sister, Ty," Fantasy lied. "I don't know what the hell Sand calls herself doing, but if you wanna play a part of it, Chyna will know that you participated every step of the way, and I won't be able to save you then."

Ty listened, pretending to think it over. "Oh, really? So you'll just tell Chyna I sat and watched you get yo' ass whooped too then, huh?" she smirked.

Fantasy shook her head. Ty was making this more difficult than it had to be. "Chyna doesn't let anyone run up in her spots and not get dealt with. I'm your only hope to save yourself. Fuck Sand! She's dead after this shit. I can guarantee it," Fantasy spoke with assurance. "Just untie me, Ty. You don't even have to stay to watch what happens."

Ty wasn't falling for it. She grabbed Fantasy by the hair.

"Aggghh!" Fantasy winced.

Ty's left fist gripped every strand of the weave that was sewn in her head. "Chyna fucked up my life! Do you see my face? Take a real good goddamn look!"

Fantasy could barely keep her eyes open with the amount of pressure Ty applied to her scalp. It felt like Ty was squeezing her brain. Fantasy pulled away, but still within Ty's grasp.

"All y'all in this motherfucka can go to hell!" Ty roared. "She made a goddamn whore out of me!" She pushed Fantasy's head back and watched her almost flip over in the chair. Ty was tired of talking, tired of explaining. She aimed the gun back in Fantasy's direction, this time at her face.

Fantasy's heart didn't miss a beat. She flung her hair back. "I remember the day you first stepped foot in this house. Up all night from bad dreams of your stepfather raping you," Fantasy teased, "and your mama not believing you 'cause she knew her daughter was a whore! You seduced him, didn't you?" Fantasy smirked.

Tears flooded Ty's face. That bit of information Ty confided in Fantasy had come back to haunt her.

"You wanted it, didn't you? Just admit it, Ty. You wanted to fuck your mama's husband."

Ty shook her head. "You don't know what you're talking about."

"Say it, Ty. You liked it when he ripped off your panties, stuffed his dick inside of you, and fucked you like you were his woman, his pussy, his ho! Didn't you, Ty?"

"Stop it," Ty panted.

Fantasy went on. "We helped you. We restored you, and we supplied you with a fucking roof over your head. You owe Chyna your life!" she proclaimed. "If you were still on those streets, out there all by yourself, you'd be in the grave by now pushing up weeds and daffodils." Fantasy let the words sit before she went on. "Chyna took a chance on you because she felt sorry for your ass. You were already ho'ing, Ty," Fantasy reminded her. "She just made you better at it!"

Ty realized that she was shaking, and the gun she held tightly became unsteady. Then as if her fingers had a mind of their own, they began sliding over the trigger.

"There's no going back, Ty. We are what we are—so *deal* with it!" Fantasy fumed.

Ty wanted to shut Fantasy up. She wanted to disfigure her beautiful face the same way hers was now. She closed her eyes, not wanting to watch. It'd be too unbearable. Suddenly, she could hear the creeping echo from Fantasy's heartbeat, but the longer she listened, the faster it pounded through her own chest. The images of her stepfather climbing on top of her, breaking through her innocence, began to bombard her final memories of those days back at home. She could feel the tip of her index finger pressing into the belly of that gun. She inhaled, ready to release the pressure of destruction.

"I'll be taking this back now," Sand said, clawing the gun from Ty's grip.

Ty opened her eyes. The whole room was spinning.

Fantasy was quiet. She swallowed hard, visualizing her life flashing before her eyes.

"Are you okay?" Sand asked her.

Ty hesitated before answering. "Yeah. I guess so." She was still trying to shake off what almost happened. "Find it?" she asked.

"Nah, but I found these." Sand tossed a pair of jeans into Fantasy's lap. "There."

"What you expect me to do with these?" Fantasy snapped.

"Put 'em on. You taking a ride with us."

"I'm not going nowhere!"

"Oh, you ain't?"

Sand gave Ty a look. Ty was ahead of the game. She stormed for the kitchen, returning with a box of matches.

She walked over to the windows and pushed back the curtains.

Sand looked at Fantasy, and then around the house.

Fantasy rolled her eyes. "You won't get away with this!"

Sand bent down and began untying the curtain tie-backs around Fantasy's ankles. When she was done, she eased the pants over Fantasy's legs. Standing her to her feet, she guided Fantasy out of the house and into the passenger seat of Chyna's Lexus.

Ty stayed behind for a few additional minutes before she came sprinting out of the door. "Wait a second," she told Sand once she jumped in the back with Fantasy, nearly out of breath.

All eyes were on the mansion. They waited, and within a few seconds, several of the downstairs windows were clouded with smoke. Flames flickered and danced through the house to make their call for help. Sand sped away with Ty laughing hysterically in the backseat.

"I told them hoes!" Ty shouted. "Now, who the hell laughing?" she celebrated.

"Where are you taking me?" Fantasy asked, worried, as they drove away from Chyna's multimillion-dollar home ablaze.

"Don't worry 'bout it. Just enjoy the ride."

"What do you mean there was a fire at my house? How? And why the fuck y'all just now notifying me?" Chyna drilled the representative on the other end of the line.

"Ma'am, again, we were alerted because the smoke alarm sensors went off, setting off your security system. It's standard protocol for us to send someone out in response to any situation in which the alarm is triggered. Now, the only information that I have for you is what I've already given. You will need to contact your local fire station at the number I've provided if you would like further details on your property. All I can do, and have done, is alert authorities."

Chyna didn't want to hear any more. She felt like snatching the insensitive bitch through the phone line. She ended the call and quickly phoned her house. Once the voice mail came on, she hung up. For a second she thought about Fantasy and wondered if she got out okay. But Fantasy wasn't as important as the millions of dollars stashed in her bathroom ceiling, nor the bricks of cocaine hidden in the hardwood planks of her bedroom closet.

The operator had mentioned that the response time was fairly quick, which Chyna hoped may have prevented any major damage. On top of that, the mansion was equipped with ceiling sprinklers throughout in the event of a fire. But even that wasn't enough insurance to bank on.

Chyna finally pulled alongside the curb of Rene's friend's house and unlocked the passenger door. She had worked her enough for the night. She'd let her rest another day before she used her for what she really employed her for.

Rene reached for the door handle until she felt Chyna's hand touch her shoulder. She turned back around to face her.

"I know you may not think much of me, but Sand really is a lucky woman," Chyna said.

Rene felt uneasy. She hardly knew how to respond to that. She pushed open the door and slid out her feet. She let the door close behind her as she took baby steps toward Shun's front porch. When she looked back over her shoulder, Chyna was still watching her. Rene headed back toward the car. "Where is she?" she asked. "Please."

Chyna licked her lips, tilted her head, and looked over her right shoulder. "Where's who?"

"Sand! I want to see her. Now. Tonight. I . . . I . . . I can't do this shit anymore," Rene said, stammering over her words.

Chyna shook her head. "You can't quit just like—"

"If Sand wants me to trick for money and do all this nasty shit you got me doing, then maybe I'm not so damn lucky after all," she said, raising her voice some. "Why is she using me like I'm some ho?" Rene stopped, breathed life into those words. "Is *that* what I am to her now?" she asked Chyna, hoping she would give her something to go on. Rene felt light on her feet. If the wind blew any harder, she'd be whisked away.

Chyna didn't utter a peep. She just sat and watched Rene take herself in circles.

Clearly frustrated, Rene took the envelope of money from her purse and held it out in front of her. "Here's the money back you gave me. Just take me to her. I'm begging you."

Chyna looked condescendingly at the woman.

Rene shook the envelope. "Here. Take it. I don't want anything to do with it."

"Rene, you earned that," Chyna finally said.

"I said I don't want it!" Rene backhanded her tears away. Now was not the time to lose her composure.

Chyna shrugged. "Humph. All right. Suit yourself."

Rene jumped back in the car, strapping herself in.

Chyna took off down the dark street, heading to her place. About a mile away, her phone rang again. This time, it wasn't Fletch or one of her hoes clocking in. This number she didn't recognize.

"All you need to know right now," Sand said firmly into the receiver the second she could hear life breathing into the other end of the line, "is that I got your bitch." She put the phone to Fantasy's mouth.

Fantasy tried screaming through the duct tape over her mouth.

Sand pulled the phone back to her own ear. "Now, I'm gon' make this real short and sweet. I got your money too. And if you want it all back, you better be hearing what the fuck I'm 'bout to say!"

Chyna couldn't believe how Sand had the nerve, the audacity, and the balls to pull a stunt like the one she was pulling now. "I'm listening," she said quietly, occasionally glancing over at Rene who was looking in the mirror, trying to fix her hair and face. Sand called out the location while Chyna made a mental note. "I'll be there. Just be cool, and we'll settle things like two grown women."

"Nah, fuck that! We gon' handle this shit your way. Like two niggas off the street," Sand said. "So don't come at me sideways if you wanna ever see this ho again."

"Where did I go wrong with you?" Chyna asked. "You used to follow by example, and now, you're just . . . lost."

"Chyna, that sixteen-year-old hustler you knew retired. You talking to me now, baby. Sand. Now get to know *me*."

Chyna licked her lips as she remembered that fight Sand put up. "Humph, have you forgotten? I've *already* gotten to know you."

Sand's heart pumped with anger. "Nah, all you know about me is that I ain't got shit to lose. Because of you, I'm wanted for murder! So, whatever I do right now won't even fuckin' matter. They can add the shit to my rap sheet."

"Maybe you should watch how you talk to me. I don't take lightly to threats."

"You're confusing me again," Sand pointed out. "I don't make threats."

Click.

Chyna flipped her phone closed. Sand was threatening her with the two most precious and important things in her life—her bitch and her money. She had to think strategically because right now, she was worried about her paper more than anything. She could have made a call easily, but there was no need for added involvement because things would only get messier than they already were. She was going to handle this one alone.

When Chyna started this, it was all business. She had employed Sand to work out of a Super 8 Motel, moving money back and forth between her accounts every time a wire would hit, which was daily, sometimes hourly. She did this for two-and-a-half months without giving her any problems for only one reason—she didn't want Chyna to lay a finger on Rene like she worried that she would. But it was too late. Chyna had her own intentions the moment she discovered Rene was a former employee of Albery Johnson's law firm. The man she had been hunting down since she was eighteen years old.

"If someone stole half a million dollars from you, what would you do?" Chyna asked Rene out of nowhere.

"Who? Me? It depends," Rene said.

"And on what might that be?" Chyna wanted to know.

There was a brief pause as she eyed Chyna curiously. "On the reason they stole it," Rene offered, clearing her throat.

"So there has to be a reason?" Chyna chuckled to herself. "Well, I guess I'm one ruthless bitch, because you know what I'd do?" She looked over at Rene, and her glossy eyes had every bit of Chyna's attention. "I'd kill 'em. No questions asked."

Rene quickly turned her head to face forward. "Where'd you say Sand was staying?"

Ignoring the question, Chyna reduced her speed and pulled into the parking garage. Immediately a pungent smell hit their noses at the entrance. Chyna circled around and around until she came to the twelfth level, all while thinking how clever Sand had been for suggesting such a place to meet.

Rene leaned forward, trying to read the parking garage posters on the expanse of the cement walls. As she took in her surroundings, she noted there were no other vehicles present. "Where are we?" she asked.

Chyna slammed her brakes and pushed the car in *Park*. "We're in the middle of nowhere," she spat with attitude. With swift movements, she reached underneath her seat, then opened her car door. She hopped out and circled around the front of the car, her silver heels echoing off the rooftop. Chyna took a look down over the edge, examining exactly how high they were up from ground level. Then she took a deep breath and walked around to Rene's side of the car and swung her door open.

"I'd rather wait here while you go get her," Rene said, not feeling the situation one bit. She could sense that something was wrong, especially now with the way Chyna stared down at her. Her tight eyes were frightening and revealed sheer anger. Rene tried to keep cool and ignore the fear and anxiety building up. She folded her arms across her chest, her lips pulled tight. Suddenly, she heard voices and began to panic. Her chest rose and fell. "I think you should just take me back to my friend's house. I'm not up for this tonight," she told Chyna.

Chyna unwrapped her hands from behind her back, revealing a rose pink and chrome caliber pistol. She aimed the gun directly at Rene, watching her flinch from the sight of it. Silently, she cocked the gun. "Let's go."

22

Sand sat watching Fantasy squirm helplessly on the cold pavement with her hands tied behind her back and the duct tape trapping her screams for help. She didn't want to have to do this to her, but she had to. It was the only way out of this mess. She glanced at her watch and estimated the time from when she made the phone call to Chyna. That was over half an hour ago, and she still hadn't shown up. Sand considered whether she should make one last call. Maybe one pressuring Chyna to let her know her time was running down.

She started to make the call but stopped when she heard the sound of footsteps approaching. Someone was there with them. She hurried over to Fantasy and brought her to her feet, gun drawn. Sand tried counting the steps as they grew closer and closer with every passing second. She could tell by the echo of heels that whoever it was knew exactly where to find them. But that person hadn't come alone.

Sand wrapped her arm around Fantasy's neck in a choke hold. She only allowed enough room for her to breathe comfortably. With her other arm, she raised the gun and aimed it directly at Fantasy's head. Both Sand and Fantasy watched four legs move in their direction. The muffled screams coming from Fantasy kept everyone on guard.

Chyna was right on Rene's heels as she walked closely behind her, a gun rubbing persistently against her spine. As they moved in closer, Rene broke down in tears.

Sand strained her eyes and hoped that she was losing it. Because every angle and curve of the body moving in on them, she recognized. It couldn't be, but it was. Rene was standing only a few feet away from her with tears plummeting down her face. Sand started to breathe heavily.

"I see we're all here like one big happy family," Chyna grinned, hoping to prove to Sand that she wasn't the least bit afraid of this little scare tactic she called herself pulling.

Sand never had so much hate for one person in her life. She gave Chyna a hard up, fuck-you stare.

"I think you have something of mines," Chyna said, glancing down at the loaded pillowcase near Sand's foot.

Sand was still stuck on the fact that Rene was standing only a few feet away with the bitch that she wanted to make a history lesson out of. "If you so much as breathed on her wrong—" Sand relayed strongly to Chyna.

"Sand, cut the bullshit. You're wasting my time! If you want to keep this precious jewel of yours," Chyna said as she slid the gun over Rene's ass, then again to her back, "I suggest you make no mistakes here tonight."

Sand pushed Fantasy's head back farther. "I will shoot this bitch!"

Chyna let out a laugh. "You are so fucking predictable," she smirked. "But I'll tell you what. Untie my woman, give her the bag, and we'll call all this even. I'll even let you make it out of here walking."

Sand's mean mug was comfortable on her face. Chyna must have thought she was running this show. "Now, are you finished making demands that you aren't going to see happen tonight?" Sand had everyone's attention. She tried not to look at Rene because she no longer saw that innocent, angelic face she once fell in love with. All she saw now staring up at her was a stranger.

"I'll give you half of your money now and the other half when I've reached my destination." Sand lifted the bag in the air with one hand. It was a lot lighter than it had been. "Sand, why do you insist on making this harder than it has to be? I want my money. And I want *all* of it. *Now!*"

Sand smiled. She was playing the same manipulative game Chyna was known for playing. "You're desperate right now. You need this money, and if you're as smart as you look, I know you don't take me for a fool or a coward!" Sand began untying Fantasy. Her wrists fell free.

Fantasy quickly snatched the tape off her mouth. She maintained her position, knowing what was at stake. She dared not make a false move. But she looked Sand dead in the eye. She could smell the fear all over her.

Sand read Fantasy's thoughts and knew that Fantasy would have killed her if she had the chance. She turned her attention back to Chyna. "I'll call you on where you can pick up the rest."

Chyna bit down on her lip. This shit was not happening the way it was supposed to. Hesitantly, she nodded her head and swirled her tongue around her gritted teeth. "You'll regret this," she told Sand in all honesty.

Sand handed the bag to Fantasy, motioning with the gun for her to take that trip.

Chyna followed Sand's lead. "Walk," she whispered in Rene's ear. "And I'm certain that you will keep our little business agreements private. Confidentiality is very important as far as my clients are concerned—*all* of them," she added.

Rene nodded slowly. Chyna had definitely gotten her point across. As Rene placed one foot in front of the other, she could sense the gun being aimed directly at the back of her head. She was scared to death, and she could feel Chyna pulling the trigger with every step she made. She hurried past Fantasy, avoiding eye contact. When she finally made it to Sand, face-to-face, she inhaled deeply as tears came crashing down her face.

Sand looked at Rene, then rolled her eyes upward. She couldn't do this right now, not in this frame of mind. Not with this gun in her hand portraying her to be somebody she wasn't. She suppressed that confrontational chip on her shoulder and let her thoughts get back on track. She watched closely as Chyna opened the bag, eyeballed the money, and closed it back again.

"When will I get the rest of my money?" she asked angrily.

Sand saw the desperation that was still planted in Chyna's face. "I'll call you. You'll get it." She never took her eyes off the two women as they hurriedly disappeared down the ramp. Once they were out of sight, she put her gun away. "What the fuck was you doing with her tonight?" she lashed out at Rene. "You know what?" She looked Rene up and down, "I don't even think I want the answer to that."

Rene shook her head, realizing at that moment that Sand really didn't know about all the things Chyna had her doing. She grew disgusted with herself. Chyna had been playing her all this time. Rene couldn't stomach the thought of it. That would explain why Chyna felt the need to pay her. That was why she asked that she keep their business agreements between them. Rene felt herself getting dizzier by the minute. How would she explain herself? She couldn't. She couldn't let Sand know about all the horrible, degrading shit she had done. "It's nothing," she lied. "I just want to—" she reached for Sand's hand, but Sand snatched it away from her.

"Don't put your hands on me." Sand peered at Rene as though she was contagious. "And you just wanna *what?* Lie to me? Hide money from me? Have another motherfuckin' baby on me?"

Sand's voice echoed in the garage. She was inches away from knocking the shit out of Rene. She began counting backward before her temper got the best of her. She wasn't going to give Rene the benefit of seeing her go off. That would be giving her too much. She couldn't have Rene knowing that she hadn't slept, eaten, or felt right since she'd been gone. Nah, she couldn't do it. She had to hold her ground and take the shit like a man. Rene was safe right now, and that's all that mattered. Now she could move on, knowing that Rene was out of harm's way. They could go their separate ways and never see each other again for all she cared.

"I'm sorry," Rene blurted. Her trembling lips bartered for forgiveness. "I didn't mean to hurt you," she said as the developing tears that rounded her cheeks played freely.

"Fuck you, Rene! I ain't falling for that shit again." Sand recalled the times before when she questioned whether Rene was cheating on her. Thinking back on it now, she should have followed her instincts and maybe this shit wouldn't hurt like it was hurting now.

Rene stopped and wiped her face. "Now you wait a damn minute. I did my dirt, but I sure as hell wasn't alone." Sand looked at her dumbfounded. "You cheated on me too," Rene cried. "The bitch had the nerve to come to our apartment with that shit! Were you fucking her in our house? In our *bed,* Sand?"

Sand's brows folded. Rene didn't need an explanation, and she sure as hell wasn't offering one, even if it did mean telling her the truth and relieving her of those fucked-up accusations she had insulted her with. Rene should have known that she would have never brought another woman into their bed. She had that much respect for her. But as Sand stared down at Rene, the bitter expression matching her own, she didn't give a damn how Rene felt about anything right about now.

Angered by Sand's silence, Rene blurted, "I lost my baby because of your cheating ass!"

Her words were like spitballs of fire. "You know what, Rene? It's over. That shit is done. We're done. Now you can go on with your happy little life. Marry the man of your dreams and have all the babies you want," she glared at Rene. "I'll take you to Shun's and y'all can sit around and talk about how I'm such a bad, heartless person." Sand couldn't contain her emotions any longer. The love, the hate, the pain she bottled inside came tumbling down her cheeks.

Rene stood in a state of shock. "How can you stand here and act like I never meant anything to you? I tried. I'm still trying," she admitted.

Sand shook her head. She didn't want to hear that. "Stop. Just quit already. It ain't gon' never be the same. You know that, and I know that."

Rene reached for Sand's hand. "It doesn't need to be the same. That way didn't work for us," she said. "We can start over. From scratch. No more secrets and no more lies."

Sand didn't refuse her hand this time. She stared into Rene's precious soul. She asked herself if things would be different the next time around, and if she loved this woman unconditionally. A lot had happened. More baggage and drama was brought to their union that was already challenged. But was their relationship salvageable and worth another try?

Rene interrupted her thoughts. "Please. I'm begging you," she whispered through her soft lips. "Give us another chance, and I promise things will be better than before."

Sand swallowed her stubborn guilt. She wanted to believe that she could offer Rene everything her heart desired. "I got one question."

"Anything," Rene said before Sand could get all the words out.

"Did you love him?"

Rene captured Sand's hazel eyes within hers. She stepped closer and pressed her body into Sand's. It was warm there. "I've never loved anyone but you."

Sand leaned down, found Rene's lips, and rested her own there. She inhaled every bit of Rene for as long as she could until a masculine scent swept over her. She smelled a man on Rene's body, in Rene's hair, on Rene's lips. She pretended he wasn't there and that she was only imagining it. She wanted to make Rene hers again. This time, she'd do it right.

"I love you so much," Rene cried out.

Sand rubbed her back. "I love you too, baby. God knows I love you too." She grabbed Rene by the hand. "Come on. I have somebody waiting out front."

"Over there," Ty said to the driver, tapping him on his shoulders. He had fallen asleep from waiting so long. She rolled down her back window. "Sand!" she yelled out.

Sand spotted the Yellow Cab right away. She held Rene tightly by the hand as they ran for the car. Cold air and rain splattered against their faces.

Ty held the back door open, trying to make out the other woman. She wondered who the pretty chick was and where she could have come from.

Rene's wet mane began to curl tightly, all the way up to her roots, ruining hours of hot iron pressing. But at that moment she didn't care half as much about her hair as she did about seeing Sand again.

"Here's a paper towel," Ty offered.

Rene reached for it. "Thank you." She began blotting her face dry. She looked up at Sand, her hair, face, and arms all victims of the rain. She began wiping Sand's face. "I don't need you getting sick on me."

Sand could watch this woman like this for all of eternity. "What if I like the idea of lying up in bed all day so you can wait on me hand and foot?" she asked slyly.

Rene leaned in as close as she could. "You don't have to be sick for me to do that." Rene glided her hands down the sides of Sand's face.

Ty suddenly cleared her throat.

"Oh, my bad," Sand said, catching the hint. "Rene, this is Ty. Ty, this is Rene, my girl."

"Oh, the girlfriend," Ty said, giving Sand an awkward look. But Sand pretended not to notice it. "You are so pretty," Ty added. "Sand definitely knows how to pick 'em," she said, successfully hiding the sarcasm in her comment.

"Thank you. You are too," Rene complimented, impressed by Ty's frankness.

Ty wanted to believe Rene, but she knew the woman was only being polite. She'd seen herself in the mirror, and she knew she was far from being anything close to the pretty she once was, unless being pretty damn scary counted for something.

"Where to, ladies, and, uh, sir?" The cabdriver asked with uncertainty.

Sand looked at the meter. It was pushing eighty dollars. "Ty, we'll take you home first."

"Okay." Ty gave the driver her mother's address.

Rene lay her head on Sand's shoulder. She kept it there the entire ride.

So many things ran through Sand's mind. Chief among them was Deja. She knew that Deja deserved some type of closure. And while Sand hated to have to face her, stripped from the old conditions that were no longer available to her, she knew she had to do it. Deja deserved the truth. Sand could never love her the way she loved Rene. And for that reason, she had to say good-bye.

Ty snuck through her old bedroom window, just like old times. She didn't want her mother to see her like this, in this shape. As her feet touched the hardwood floor, she sighed in relief that she was back home safe. She slid the glass back down and locked it, then she turned around, searching for the lamp in the dark. Sliding a finger over the switch, she turned it on—but was more than surprised to find her mother sitting there, on her perfectly made bed, holding a Bible.

"I left it unlocked for you. I knew you'd come home," her mother said faithfully. "God showed it to me, just as clear as I can see day," she smiled.

"Mama!" Ty ran over to hug her mother. She released all the cries stored inside of her as her mother held and rocked her in her arms like a little girl.

"Thank you, Jesus, for bringing my baby back home to me," her mother cried out to her Savior as she squeezed her daughter tighter. "You don't have to worry about no one hurting you anymore, ever again," Ty's mother told her. "He's gone," she wept. "He's gone, and he ain't ever coming back."

Ty raised her head. "Mama, I'm sorry," she said. Her mother looked her over. Not once did she ask about the scars and bruises that covered Ty's face and arms. And while they nestled in each other's arms, Ty noticed the dark circles and bags underneath her mother's eyes—testimonies to her restless nights. She couldn't even put a meal down her stomach without worrying about if her child had eaten that day. "You don't have to be sorry,

Tylesha. It's not your fault, baby. None of this is your fault. I should have listened to you when you came to me. I blame myself for this." Ty's face was drenched as she rocked with her mother, sharing her pain. She exhaled. It was all over, she told herself. Everything could go back to being normal again, back to when she had a life—a life that belonged to her.

23

Sunday Morning

"We need to talk," Sand whispered to Rene, waking her out of her sleep.

"Umm," Rene moaned. She was exhausted, and she couldn't see how Sand could even be awake so early, considering the long night they had. After they dropped Ty off at her mother's house, they had the cabdriver swing by Shun's so that Rene could grab some clothes. After that, he brought them to the hotel room.

Last night was about all the days they spent away from each other and all the nights they struggled to get through, alone. It was about two people expressing their love, compassion, and desire for one another, their feelings, and their deepest regrets. Last night was about a real commitment to true love.

"Babe, I need you to wake up. I really need to talk to you," Sand said, a little louder this time.

Rene's voice was groggy. "What time is it?"

"Probably around eight."

Rene barely opened one eye. "Are you serious? Because it sure doesn't feel like it's eight anything." She pulled herself up in the bed and quickly noted how Sand had already gotten fully dressed while she remained in her birthday suit. "So what is it that you want to talk about?" she asked with a smile.

Sand sat on the edge of the bed. Rene's pink toenails peeked from underneath the covers.

Rene gauged the look in Sand's eyes. She wasn't getting a good vibe. She changed positions, crawled over the thick bedspread and made her way to the opposite end of the bed. "What's wrong?"

"Rene, I think I'm wanted. But I swear to you, on my mama's grave, that I ain't kill nobody."

Rene just listened, allowed Sand to talk without interruption.

Sand looked her woman straight in the eyes, her morning glow so inviting. "Baby, I cheated on you. More than once. More than twice," she willingly admitted. "I fucked up. Big time. But I didn't kill that damn girl. I didn't," she kept saying. Her pleading eyes wanted more from Rene than what Rene was offering. "Bae, you listening to me?" Sand asked, unsure. "I said I'm wanted for murder."

Rene eased off the bed. She had heard from Sand's mouth all she needed to hear. "Sand, I know all about Jasmine."

Sand was taken aback. "What?"

"I said," Rene allowed that jealousy to hang off her lips, "I know all about her. Y'all's relationship—"

"It wasn't a relationship," Sand corrected.

"The threesome. I know about it all." Rene could barely look at Sand anymore as her attention found its way to the stained carpet. Now she remembered why she hated motels. They were nasty, unkempt, and smelled like cheap potpourri and stale sex. She finally looked up again. "How long, Sand? Were you even going to tell me, or were you going to wait until I had to hear it from somewhere else?"

As Sand sat on the edge of the bed, totally confused, she could only bring herself to ask Rene one question, a question that didn't even matter. "Who told you?"

"Tsk." Rene folded her arms. She wanted to tell Sand about the night Vincent had come over. About June Bug raping her. About the earring the detectives found in their apartment that belonged to the dead woman—but where would she begin? There was so much Sand didn't know about. So much that Rene wished she could just leave it all in the past and never have to hear about it again. "It doesn't matter who told me. Because I trusted you!" Rene pulled back the strands of hair that fell in her face.

"Like I trusted you! So don't flip this around on me when you know damn well you were out there doing the same thing I was! At least I didn't cross the damn line! A *man*, Rene? You know how that shit made me feel? Made me look? So what have I been all this time, huh?" Sand asked seriously, getting everything off her chest. "A lesbian experiment? Something to quench your curiosity until you figured out if you were straight, gay, or bisexual?"

Rene stood up in shock, not believing that Sand could even fix her mouth to say the things she was pushing down her throat. "You know none of that's true. I love you! Yes, you know you were my first, but I've never looked at you as some . . . experiment. I fell hard for *you*. For *you!* I was only trying to make sense of this . . . I never liked being judged or criticized. And I didn't know how to handle all of the pressure, the denial . . . that came with accepting that I was in love with another woman. And the truth is, when I needed you to help me sort through all of those emotions, you weren't there. You were always running around with your friends, always drinking, smoking, partying, and coming in all times of night like you didn't have a woman at home. How do you think *I* felt?" she fired back. "What was *I* supposed to do with people all in my ear about you cheating on me and making me look like a damn fool?"

"I was working on my club and trying to make a living to support both of us! You know that. And fuck Shun!" Sand spat as Rene's comment sank in. She knew those were the people Rene was talking about. "If you didn't keep her in our business all the time, she wouldn't have shit to laugh and gossip about. So I blame that nonsense on *you*."

"But I needed you, Sand. I was going through something that I couldn't fight alone, and you weren't there," Rene said softly as that pent-up anger drenched her cheeks. She wanted Sand to know how trying their relationship had been for her and how she struggled to bring herself to terms with her sexuality. "I didn't know if I was completely delusional or just flat-out insanely in love." She stared Sand deeply in the eyes. "I needed that confirmation from you."

Sand stood up, waiting a few minutes before she said anything. "I'm sorry," she whispered. She moved closer to claim the woman that was meant to be hers. She held out her hands and wiped the tears from her eyes. "I never meant to hurt you," she said. "I know I fucked up. I'm knowing this. And I hate I took you through all that. You didn't deserve that treatment."

Rene nestled her head against Sand's chest.

"Look at me," Sand said. "I'm going to prove to you that this shit we got . . . this right here," she said, pointing her finger between them, "is real. And I swear to you from this moment on, you will never have to worry about me not being there for you again. Because I'm right here, baby." She kissed the top of Rene's left hand, every last one of her fingers, and then the inside of her palm. "And I don't plan on going no-motherfucking-where." She planted the last kiss on her salty, wet lips.

"I love you so much," Rene said, moving her hands to the sides of Sand's face.

Sand just stared at her woman, loving everything about her that there was to love. "Get dressed," she told Rene. "I have somebody I want you to meet." Sand figured now was the time for Rene to see where those long days and nights were being spent.

"Who?" Rene asked. She reached for her jeans which were hanging off the arm of the only chair in their room, but as soon as she did, Sand was taking them out of her hands. "Thought you said you wanted me to get ready?"

"I do," Sand said, pulling her by the waist. "After this." She slid Rene's sherbet-orange thong down slow and easy, caressing her ass along the way. She unwrapped it from around her ankles and tossed it onto the bed.

"What are you doing?" Before Rene knew it, her feet were no longer touching the floor. She held on as tightly as she could as Sand used her upper body strength to lift her above her chest. Both of her legs straddled Sand's shoulders until her ample flesh soon found its way in the warmth of her girlfriend's mouth. She let out a sensual moan. It felt so good having Sand so close to her body, touching her, squeezing her, making her this hot. This wet. The cool breeze slithering up and down her spine made its way to her lower end and between her cheeks as Sand sucked the softness out of her nipples.

"Oh yes . . ." Rene cried out as the heat simmering between them began moving farther below her waist. She couldn't resist what she felt, and she wanted it more than anything in the world. Her pussy was throbbing in agreement and screamed for its lover's comeback as Sand laid her on her back. Rene began rolling her fingers over what used to be a head full of natural brown hair. She invited her lover inside of her, every bit of her that wanted to be there until Sand's tongue began playing along the cliff of her engorged clit. Rene grabbed her own breasts that were bouncing up and down while Sand's tongue maneuvered its way to the middle, the bottom, and then the ceiling of her pussy. She called out Sand's name over and over again. As if her legs had a mind of their own, they fell open even wider.

Sand's fingers continuously surfed along the lips of Rene's crying pussy before finding themselves inside of Rene's own mouth. Rene closed her eyes as she seductively sucked the sweetest coconut milk right off Sand's fingertips. With every lick, she felt herself getting wetter and wetter until she had to open her eyes, look down, and be certain that the housekeeper hadn't come in and thrown a bucket of hot water on them both.

Sand raised up her shirt and lay down, giving Rene the liberty to saddle up. She grabbed one of the very many pillows, then placed it behind her head.

"Ummm," Rene moaned, knowing what time it was. She didn't hesitate as she climbed over Sand's body, straddling her face. Her swelling lips brushed against Sand's chin before Sand could even open her mouth to take it there.

"That's it. Keep it there," Rene panted. "Oh God, it's coming, it's coming," she cheered on until finally, a spill of juices emitted from between her legs and down her lover's throat.

Ty woke to the smell of bacon, eggs, chicken, grits, and buttermilk waffles. She was so happy to be home again, in her own room, her own bed. She tossed the covers back and dragged both feet to the side of the bed, then walked around her room wearing a pair of silk green pajamas from so many winters ago. She felt like she had to piss a river as she made her way to the huge bathroom connected to her room. She was beginning to feel like her old self again. She leaned into the vanity mirror and saw how her scars were darker and more noticeable than they had been two nights ago. Her eye was so swollen she could barely see out of it, and her lip looked like somebody took a chunk out of it. She turned away, not wanting to see herself in such horrible shape. Ty knew that she would never be the same again after living in that house. But if she hadn't learned anything else, she learned that the streets loved no one.

She took a quick piss and slipped off her PJs, then stepped into the shower and buried her head under the warm stream. This was one time she honestly believed that all the bad she'd ever done was being washed away. Ty felt like she was being born again.

Illusion could smell Trent's mother's entire kitchen on her doorstep. She was hesitant about getting out of the car, and now that she had, she started to turn back around, unsure of why she was even there.

"Where you going?" Trent asked, grabbing her by her elbow.

"I can't. If she sees me with you, she's gon' freak out," Illusion explained. "I can't go in there."

"Look, if it wasn't for you, no telling how out of my mind I might be right now. So regardless, you here with me, and we going in. Together. A'ight?"

Illusion wasn't feeling it at all. Maybe Trent didn't know how crazy his sister really was.

"Now, when my mom called me, I told her how you and I both had a long-ass night. Knowing my moms, she probably already cooked up enough food for all of Dallas. So you telling me you gon' let all that good food in there go to waste?"

Illusion took a deep breath, then let out a sigh.

Trent pulled her closer to him, taking her chin in his hand. "I told you, I'm not going to let anything happen to you. I got you. But you have to trust me."

Illusion couldn't resist Trent's smile, his touch. "So now you my bodyguard?" she smiled.

"Yeah. I'm yo' bodyguard," he laughed, flexing his muscles.

Illusion couldn't stop laughing. "Okay. But if she even attempts to come at me, I'm out. I refuse to be disrespected, and I'm not going to bring *our* drama into your *mama's* house."

"Understood. I can live with that." Trent began pushing open the door. He led Illusion through the house by the hand.

Illusion got a glimpse of the framed portraits that hung throughout on a designated half-and-half brown and sage painted wall. Even the few pictures that decorated the mantle caught her eye. She saw both Trent and Ty when they were much younger, some including them together, others with them hogging the camera alone.

"Ma, where you at?" Trent called out to his mother.

"I'm in here, son."

Trent headed for the kitchen. His mother was removing oven mitts from her hands when he walked in. Trent leaned in and kissed her on the cheek. "Mama, this Illeshia, an old friend of Tylesha's," he fibbed.

"How you doing, ma'am? You have a beautiful home," Illusion expressed, extending her hand.

"Why, I thank you. It didn't come by easy, I can tell you that," Trent's mother smiled. "Well, y'all go on and wash up. I know you gotta be starving by now. I'll put your plates out on the table for ya 'cause I need to be getting ready for church. Sister Hal will be here any minute now to pick me up."

"All right, Mama," Trent said, leaning in to kiss his mother again.

"Your sister is in there freshening up," his mother volunteered. "She should be out any minute now. She been in there for hours already," she laughed. "Might need to go in there after her." She turned to Illusion. "And nice meeting you, young lady. I appreciate you helping my son out like you've done."

"It was my pleasure, Mrs.—"

"Just call me Jackie, baby."

Illusion appreciated their mother's generosity and hospitality. "Thanks, Jackie."

Trent showed Illusion down the hall and to the bathroom. When Illusion came back out, he couldn't help stopping just to stare at her.

As Ty put on her clothes, she could hear faint voices coming from the living room. It sounded like her mother's close friend, church buddy, and Avon sales rep, Sister Hal. They would alternate Sunday's driving to church, so this Sunday had to be hers. Ty thought about staying in the room until they left, but it seemed that as the thought entered her brain, Sister Hal and her mom were walking into her room.

"There she is! Give your auntie some sugar, baby," Sister Hal said, limping over to Ty.

Ty frowned her nose up at the terrible brand of perfume and slobber that she could feel on her face.

"Boy, don't we have some catchin' up to do," Sister Hal smiled.

Ty just nodded her head, trying her best to not pass out.

"Let's go, sister. We don't wanna be late. You know we have to get there early if we want a good seat," Ty's mother said. She could read the transparent expression on her daughter's face.

"Well, I'm gon' see you after church," Sister Hal told Ty.

"Okay," Ty answered back, not looking forward to it.

Ty's mother took one last peek inside her room. "Your brother is here," she smiled. "I know you two have a lot of catching up to do, so I'll see you when church lets out."

"Okay, Mama," Ty said before her mother closed the door.

Ty couldn't wait to see Trent. She finished playing in her hair, threw on her footies, and hurried toward the kitchen. When Ty hit the corner, she spotted her brother right away.

Trent looked up.

Illusion looked up and was caught by surprise at Ty's overnight transformation. Her spiked hair was now straightened. Her makeup all gone. Even the clothes she wore made her look different from the Ty she remembered knocking the hell out of.

Ty's face said more than what her mouth could let out. It was like someone was strangling her to death. She scanned the room, looking for Chyna. Her body tensed up, and her breathing became labored as she stared Illusion up and down.

Trent rose from his seat. "What's up, baby sis?" he attempted.

As far as Ty was concerned, Trent was nowhere in the room. It was just her and Illusion.

"Tylesha," Trent said.

Illusion pushed her chair away from her plate. "Trent, I better go."

"Yeah, bitch, you better raise the fuck up outta here!"

"No. You're here with me," Trent said, trying to stop her.

Ty dragged her eyes to her brother's. "Why did you bring her here? You don't know shit about her!" she shot.

She watched Illusion get up from the table and make her way to the door. "That's right, get the hell outta my house!" Ty hollered. "My brother doesn't fuck with tramp bitches like you! You're way out of your league, ho!" Illusion opened the door and walked out.

Trent shook his sister. "Tylesha! Stop it. What the hell has gotten into you? Now you don't know shit about what she's been through these last couple of days. And while you were running around, damn near about to give Mama a heart attack, she was helping me look for your ass. She didn't have to do that!"

"And I didn't ask her to!"

"No, but *I* did! You think I could just sit back and watch my mama cry day and night over you? Not eating. Not sleeping. What the hell is *wrong* with you? Huh?"

Ty remained quiet, her eyes beginning to fill with water. "She'll use you!" she screamed.

Trent didn't want to hear it. "Tylesha, let me worry about that. That's *my* business right there," he said, pointing the other way. "And I don't need *you* in it."

Ty rolled her eyes, and for once, she didn't say another word.

Trent brought himself to calm down. "Look," her brother said, "my main concern is you, Tylesha. I'm just glad you're home safe and sound. Now you don't have to talk to me right this second, but when you are ready, I'll be here to listen." Trent wasn't going to pressure her. He wanted her to come around on her own time. Regardless of how much he already knew from Illusion, he wanted to hear it in Ty's own words. "Now, can big brother get a hug?"

Ty chuckled before giving her brother a tight squeeze. She wiped her eyes.

"Come on around here and get you some of this good cooking," Trent playfully ordered.

Ty walked around the table and reluctantly took a seat. "Now I'm gone go check on her."

He left Ty at the table and headed for the front door to get Illusion. He stepped on the front porch but wasn't surprised to find Illusion already gone.

24

"A'ight, my nigga! Call me if you need anything else. You know I got you, dawg," Sand's stud brother and best friend, Finesse, told her as they gave each other dap.

"Bet that. But I think I'm good to go now," Sand said, checking herself over.

Finesse owned and managed her own hip-hop clothing store. She was Sand's primary source for all the latest hookups. After seeing Sand the way she was today, Finesse knew her homie must've been going through something ill because she had never seen her in such tore up shape. She looked stressed, worried, and just plain worn-the-fuck-out. Her clothes were wrinkled, fade no longer faded, even her kicks looked like they'd been taking a nap. But Finesse tightened her dawg up. She was fresher than fresh in a brown and ivory long-sleeved Ed Hardy sweater and heavily starched jeans. She finished off the outfit with a pair of white and brown Bathing Apes.

Sand waited until Finesse pulled off before she took the key to Deja's house out of her pocket. She pondered over what she was going to say, telling herself that whatever she came up with wasn't going to change anything because after today, Deja would hate her for the rest of her natural-born life.

As she made her way to the porch, Sand looked over her shoulder. Her car was in the same spot, parked beside Deja's. She took a deep breath. She wondered if she should use the key again like she had yesterday when she came back to secure the other $250,000 of

Chyna's money. She wanted it somewhere safe, and Deja's place was the only spot that came to mind. So as Ty waited in the car, marveling over every single house that was extravagantly lit and decorated in the tradition of Christmas, she went in, hid the money, and left. Now, she had come to retrieve both the money and her car.

She pressed the faintly lit doorbell, hoping Deja would answer on the first ring. When she didn't, she pressed it again.

"Gimme a second," Deja called out. She muted her television and made her way to the door, cat in hand. As she got a glimpse of who it was, she began punching her security code into the keypad to deactivate the alarm. She eased the door open. "Good morning," she said. Her greeting was formal, distant, and compared to the other times, weak.

The moment Deja's body was in full view, Sand wanted to close her eyes and wish that the woman didn't look, smell, and taste like she remembered. "Can I come in real quick?" she managed to ask.

Deja hesitated. "I, um, don't see why not." She opened the door wider and made room for Sand to step inside. She tried her hardest to hide her frustration that was still lingering in every crease of her skin. She hadn't forgotten the very reason she was up all night, worrying sick, wishing, hoping, and praying that Sand was all right. And there was no show, no call, nothing to relieve her of that worry. But here Sand was, perfectly fine and still breathing like she prayed she would be.

As Sand made her way into the house, she acknowledged Whiskers by rubbing the top of his head. He purred, stretching his arms out to play. Sand didn't know why, but part of her felt happy to be with Deja while the other part of her wished it was still back at the room with Rene. She had promised Rene that she wouldn't be gone long, giving her enough time to recuperate from the rendezvous that had taken place this morning. In her mind, she held on to that promise.

"Well, first, I just want you to know that I appreciate everything you've done for me these past few months. Because you didn't have to," Sand started.

Deja just looked Sand in her hazel-brown eyes as she lowered Whiskers to the floor. She approached Sand closer, wanting her to feel the pain she was feeling at that very moment. And before Deja knew it, her right hand was giving her the freedom to deliver that message.

Sand didn't even bother to pamper the sting that had the entire left side of her face spasming. "I deserved that," she told Deja, watching the tears in her eyes fall all at once. "This ain't easy for me either," she assured her. "But I can't keep leading you on like this. You deserve more than that, and I—"

"Stop!" Deja said, cutting her off. "I get it. I'm a big girl." She tried laughing back her cry. "It doesn't take all of that for me to understand what you're trying to tell me." She held her head up, swallowing the jittery feeling she felt whisking in her throat. "I get it. I've always gotten it. And still, I'm always the one looking stupid in the end," she mumbled disgustingly at herself. "I knew what I was up against," she admitted shamefully. "And I blame myself, Sand, not you. I shouldn't have gotten caught up in it from the start."

Sand searched her heart for something to say but came up short. "Deja, please," she pleaded. "It's not you."

"Yes, it is. Tell me how it can't be. I try doing everything right. I open my heart. I give, I, I," she stopped. She looked deeply into Sand's eyes. "You know what?" she exhaled. "You don't owe me a damn thing." She shook her head in defeat. How could she lead herself back down this path? She felt so stupid.

"Deja, come on, now." Sand tried to grab her hand, but she yanked it away from her.

"Don't touch me!"

Taken aback by her tone, Sand gave her space. After two full minutes of awkward silence, Sand opened her mouth to say something. "I dropped something off last night. I'll just get it and be out of your way."

Deja was turned completely around. She couldn't bear to look at Sand without feeling like her heart was being yanked out and set on fire. Somehow, she thought Sand would be different—they'd be different—but she was wrong.

As Sand returned from Deja's bedroom with a brief-case in hand, she noticed Deja had not budged. She thought about giving her a good-bye hug, maybe a kiss, but knew that would be against her better judgment. She hated that she felt like shit right now. The mixed feelings she had smothered her in an uncomfortable guilt unlike anything she'd ever felt before. She laid the single gold key on top of the bar, showed herself back to the door, opened it slightly, but not before turning to face Deja one last time. "You know, I really didn't know you could flow like that." Sand let the words sit on her tongue for a second. "And for the record, it was always a pleasure with you, every second of it," she said, referring to Deja's poem. "Just remember that." With that, she turned the doorknob and walked out.

Deja wanted Sand's parting words to mean so much more than she knew they did. As she turned to lock the door, she realized that this was it. But how could she miss her when she never had her in the first place? Sand was walking right out of her life, the same way she had walked into it. Nothing more than a brief, unexpected interruption. The only difference was the shit hurt like hell.

***

Sand pulled out of the driveway, the case of money on the backseat. She pulled out Rene's cell and made a quick call to an old friend. Everything was going exactly as planned.

25

Chyna and Fantasy waited as Aaron walked his two darling little girls and wife to their minivan. Apparently, they were going to church without him. Chyna noticed the girls were wearing matching dresses, white and pink ruffled socks, and white dress shoes. Both their hair had been pulled back in a ponytail, no curls, just their straight natural brown hair, adorned with a single pink lace ribbon that their mother had tied loosely in a bow. They looked like brown-skinned fairies. Their skin wasn't as dark as their father's, but monitoring both of them closely, Chyna could tell they shared his shady bloodline.

Aaron kissed each one of them good-bye, mumbling something that Chyna couldn't make out. She knew it was something enticing enough to make the wife lean back over for a second and third kiss.

Several minutes later, long after the caravan had driven away, Chyna and Fantasy approached Aaron's doorstep. Chyna didn't bother ringing the doorbell, just twisted the handle. As fate would have it, she walked right in. Fantasy followed only a few heels behind her.

Aaron, upstairs in his master bath, was lining up his goatee when he thought he heard the door downstairs open and close. "Juanita?" he called out to his wife. He figured she forgot something like always. He powered off his clippers and placed them back in the portable leather

case. He listened more closely. "Juanita, baby?" There
was still no reply. He walked back into the bedroom, tripping over unwrapped toys and rolls of wrapping paper
in the process. "I'm upstairs, honey!" he yelled a little
louder this time. Still nothing. But he heard footsteps.
He walked over to his bed and lifted up his king mattress.
In a deep pocket inside of his box spring was where his
heater slept. He loaded up, running to the window that
overlooked the yard and cobblestone driveway. When he
saw that his wife's van wasn't there, he took to the stairs.

Chyna took one last puff of her cigarette before smash-
ing it into the red and gold table runner in front of her.
She pursed her lips to the side and let a mouthful of
smoke seep out while timing exactly how long it would
take for Aaron to come down from his cavern.

Aaron checked the front door first. It was closed,
locked, and chained. As he made his way through the
foyer, he noticed a trail of mud leading farther into his
house. Cocking the gun, he followed that trail.

"Officer Fields," Chyna said, spinning herself slowly
around in the swivel chair until she and Aaron were
face-to-face.

"What the fuck are you doing in my house?"

"Ssshhh . . ." Chyna held her index finger to her perfectly lined, strawberry-painted lips. "We wouldn't want
to wake the neighbors, now, would we?"

Aaron's forehead began to perspire, and droplets of
sweat soon began creeping down the sides of his face.
"I'm gon' ask you one more damn time!"

"Oh, I'll be long gone before the wife gets back, if that's
what you're all nervous about. As a matter of fact, she

won't even know I was here," Chyna said. Her pasted smile never left her face.

Aaron held the gun tighter.

"Put the gun down," Chyna urged him. "You're starting to make me feel like you're not so happy to see me."

"What is this shit about, Chyna? You don't come into my motherfucking house unannounced! Are you crazy? And where's James? Does he know about this shit?"

"You don't work for James; you work for *me!*" Chyna clarified for him. "Now, you do realize that I have to clean up this big mess you made?"

Aaron had no idea what the hell Chyna was talking about. "Mess? What mess?"

"The money from the drop!"

"Look, I don't know shit about no money! The only money that rolled through here is what came in from the last shipment we sent off on Friday. And you got that money already."

Chyna stood from the chair. "I trusted James when he brought you in," she said, shaking her head but never taking her eyes off him.

"And you can still trust me. I've kept my word."

Chyna's cold eyes showed no mercy. "Aaron, your services are no longer needed."

"Chyna, come on, baby. I ain't never pulled no dumb shit on you—ever. I make sure everybody get their cut, and when it's done, your piece gets delivered to you. Hell, I even got all these thugs on the block and in the cut paranoid that if they ain't pushin' yo' shit, then they're nothing but Christmas bonuses for my big boys. I've made a name for you!" he said. "And I'm the one doing all the damn work and facing all the time! So don't run up in here like you've done shit but sit on your ass and call shots."

Chyna maintained a straight face. Aaron was right in so many ways, but he wasn't seeing the bigger picture. She thought about writing the shit down in Braille for him. Maybe that would have suited him better. Or maybe he was more comfortable hearing it from somebody else, somebody with a dick much bigger than his.

"Aaron, the exchange you made on Friday," she watched his eyes light up as he waited with baited breath, "did *not* reach its destination."

"What the fuck are you talking about? I was standing right there. I put that shit in there myself," he contested, pointing downward with his gun.

"Did you ever think to look at the driver, because it sure as hell wasn't me or either of my runners?"

Aaron got quiet. He didn't get a good look at the driver, but he swore to himself it was one of her people. Who else would be driving Chyna's car that time of night and at the exact meet-up point? He was only running a few minutes behind schedule. Luckily, he recognized Chyna's car when he did.

"Yeah, I saw the driver," he lied. "And he watched me load that shit up, and after that, we all rolled out. So this ain't on me, Chyna." The fear in Aaron's eyes was unmistakable. He knew Chyna, and he knew what she was capable of.

Staring deeply into her eyes, he tried reading her next move. She was alone, empty-handed, and was never the one to get her hands dirty . . . so he'd been told. The missing piece to his puzzle was solved when he heard what sounded like an echo from a gun being cocked. He slowly turned behind him and stood face-to-face with Fantasy who was dressed in a black trench coat with oversized shades on her face. The gun in Aaron's hand seemed to melt between his fingers as it dropped to the plush white carpeting stretched beneath their feet.

Staring down the barrel of that gun was like staring into hell. Aaron knew he'd be going there. All the people he'd killed, all the money he'd stolen, all the dirt he'd ever done was coming back to haunt him. He mouthed the simplest word, "Please," but knew for himself that would get him nowhere. He turned back around to face Chyna, only to find another .22 automatic aimed in his face. His heart pounded in his chest as he tried calculating his next move. "You gon' kill me? Right here in my home? My kids. My wife," he pleaded, pushing those words past his crusty, trembling lips.

Chyna didn't give a damn about the wife or the kids. The man who murdered her mother didn't, so why should she have heart for a dirty motherfucka who deserved to die? Somebody who wasn't even kin. She pictured her mother pleading those exact words over and over, *"Please. I have a daughter."* But that wasn't enough to save her.

Aaron stood between the two women fearing for his life. One he knew for sure was ready to end it without a second thought about it. He looked over Chyna's shoulders at the two portraits on the wall, his twin daughters smiling back at him. He relaxed his eyes on his wife. Her body he knew he'd never touch, kiss, or be inside of again. Aaron wondered what she would do and how she would make it without him. Then his eyes roamed the brightly lit tree. He wouldn't make it to see his girls open the ton of presents their mother had stashed upstairs in the bedroom. He'd miss their birthdays, their first dates, their weddings. He'd miss it all.

Desperate, he found himself asking, begging, one final time. "Please, don't do this. I can arrange some things," he told Chyna. He spoke fast as a round of tears started down his face. "I have about ten thousand dollars upstairs. I-I . . . can get you more this afternoon.

Lemme just make a phone call. I can get your money back," he said, running out of breath.

Chyna let Aaron go on. Unbeknownst to him, she had already tracked her package, but she needed to make an example out of him. His senseless error could have cost her big time.

"You see how quick I moved on that detective following you?" Aaron continued. "All the shit he had on you—history. So you'll have your money by midnight," he promised her. "With interest. You know I'm good for it, baby. Please. I'm begging you."

Aaron's lips were bargaining with Chyna to reconsider, but she had interpreted them differently. In her mind, they were rushing her to get it over with. She gave Aaron one last chance to say his prayers before rocking him to sleep. A fourth of a second later, she let the hot iron loose into his forehead and watched heartlessly as his body dropped to her feet and blood ooze from the hole in his face. Then she stepped right over his lifeless body.

No mercy. No love.

26

"Okay, we're here," Sand told Rene as she led her by the hand into the warehouse building. She closed the door behind them.

"So, can I open my eyes now?" Rene asked as Sand let her hand drop.

Sand moved swiftly through the club, looking back every now and then at Rene. "Nah, not yet. Keep 'em closed." This was the moment Sand had been looking forward to for the longest, and she couldn't wait to see the look on Rene's face. She darted over to the deejay booth, flipped through the collection of CDs on a nearby table, and popped one in.

Rene, still quiet, eyes twitching and knees trembling, couldn't wait to see what it was that Sand had in store for her. She thought about taking a peek. Just a small peek to see what was up, and when she did, "*I don't remember telling you to open your eyes,*" Sand said, surprising her as she stood directly in front of her. Rene jumped a little as if she had been caught red-handed stealing cookies out of a cookie jar. She let out a mischievous chuckle. "Oh, I thought I heard you say—"

Sand leaned into Rene and kissed her on her lying lips. "Nah, see, 'cause I done already saw ya. So don't try to switch it up now," she said, smiling.

Rene kissed her back, closed her eyes once again, and let Usher speak to them through the surround sound speakers that boomed in every direction. She placed her hands around Sand's neck loosely, allowing the vibe floating between them to seduce her. She wrapped herself up in the moment until she felt Sand's lips slowly departing.

"I wanna show you something." Sand grabbed Rene by the hand again and led her farther into the club. She hit all six light switches and watched Sandrene's light up like New York City's Times Square.

"Where are we?" Rene whispered. With each step they took, her eyes perused over the beautifully decorated tables, bars, dance floor, and stage. She couldn't believe what she was seeing, and the farther they moved through the club, the quicker she began putting the pieces together.

But Sand wasn't finished with her tour. "Hold on, there's more," she said excitedly.

Rene braced herself, and before she knew it, they were stepping into the club's VIP section that she had earlier mistaken for just a mirror. And the way it wrapped around the entire dance floor was why she believed that it was just a backdrop for the dancers to watch themselves in. But only the inside members of VIP could have the advantage and enjoyment of being in two places at one time while those less fortunate benefited from their own show.

"You know all those long nights away from home?" Sand asked, breaking Rene's train of thought.

Rene nodded, waiting to be told that what she was thinking was right.

Sand stared deeply into her girlfriend's beautiful brown eyes. "I was here. Right here."

Rene's eyes roamed continuously up and down, left and right. She couldn't believe all the time and money Sand had invested into the place. And here they stood, celebrating this moment for the first time, together.

"Why didn't you tell me sooner?" Rene asked. "I mean, I knew you were thinking about doing something like this, but I had no idea you were—" She cut herself short. "I'm so proud of you," she let out finally. "You did it, baby." That's what Rene admired about Sand so much: her drive and determination.

"I wanted to tell you sooner, but, let's just say we got off track." Sand swallowed hard, taking a deep breath in the process. "But we're here now."

Rene cupped Sand's chin. "I love you so much. I don't know what I would ever do without you in my life," she confessed deeply. She reached in for a kiss. Their tongues intertwined until they became lost in each other's souls. Rene backed Sand into a corner, up against a wall. She eased her shirt from over her head, feeding it to the floor. The second Sand tried to reverse the hold Rene had on her, Rene grabbed her by both her wrists and pinned them together with one hand. She kissed and licked the hardness of Sand's flat stomach. The red marks that were already there, she didn't question, only escorted her tongue on a new path over her lover's hemisphere.

Sand's head rested against the cold wall as she gripped fistfuls of Rene's hair.

Rene wanted to remember this day just like this. Right here, right now, they were making memories. She unbuckled Sand's pants and let them drop to her ankles. She wanted to taste and get to know every part of Sand that there was to know. But before she could devote herself to that mystery that stared her in the face, she turned to the pair of eyes she felt resting on her back.

"Deja!" Sand jumped, snapping out of her trance. She quickly bent down and pulled her jeans back over her boxers.

Rene stood to her feet, clearing her throat.

"I just came by to drop this off," Deja said, her eyes darting between Sand and Rene. She balled her left fist, brought it to her lips, and closed her eyes as though she was trying to wish the image away. "Why did I have to see this shit?" she asked herself.

Sand accepted the brown folder Deja held in her hand.

"The check is in there. The combos to the safe," Deja inhaled another deep breath. "Everything is in there." She couldn't take it anymore. She smiled at Rene with such sincere hate. She rubbed her hands over her forehead and communicated to Sand with her eyes. The heartfelt passion was still there, and right now, it was making her look like a fool. Deja forced herself to try to understand it. She tossed it around and around, back and forth all morning. She even played with the idea of being *the other woman.* Wondered if she could accept that position and be content with it. She wondered if Sand was worth that much and if her heart was something that could be sacrificed.

Sand remained calm but speechless. All she could think was, *Don't do this. Not here. Not now,* as she felt Deja's mouth preparing itself to speak.

Rene disrupted the ice-cold silence. "Haven't we met before?" she asked Deja, trying to remember where she might have known her.

Deja rolled her eyes mockingly but undetectably. "I believe we may have crossed paths a time or two," she replied dryly.

Sand played the quiet game through the awkwardness.

"Well, it was nice working for you," Deja said, speaking up. "But I guess you won't be needing me anymore."

Sand felt her chest swelling. "I appreciate everything you've done for me and for the club."

Deja just smiled. "Oh, one more thing." She reached in her purse and pulled out her duplicated set of keys. "I won't be needing these." She placed the keys in Sand's hand and then turned away to leave. She wanted to remember Sand just like this.

Once Deja was completely gone, Rene turned to Sand. No words were needed. They embraced in a tight hug, both knowing that some things were better understood when they were left unsaid.

27

Sunday Evening

"Sooooo," Shun started out. Her nose was flared as she exhaled. "I take it y'all are back together?" she asked, coming up from a sit-up.

Rene was glowing, and she knew it. Her rainy days were over, and now she was dancing under the rainbow. She allowed Shun's observation to settle in along with the steak and potatoes she had just stuffed herself with. Hearing someone else acknowledge that she and Sand were an item again meant so much to her.

"Yeah, we've decided that we're going to go ahead and give it another try. We've worked out our differences, and now we can focus more on our future," Rene smiled. She continued to put the last few items in her suitcase, checking everything twice and making sure she wasn't packing up any rodents along with her.

Shun sat up on her mat. "I'm so proud of y'all," she said, nearly out of breath. "I told you y'all were gon' work it out, didn't I?" She started out on her second set.

"Yeah, you did," Rene admitted. She zipped both bags and set them side by side on the floor.

"Now, what are y'all gonna do next?"

Rene watched her friend closely as she struggled coming up, going down, and coming up again. She was sweating profusely, and she knew that in any minute, Shun was going to be crunched over complaining about the burn. "We're going to see about getting an apartment up north somewhere. Addison, Plano . . . I don't know yet. In the meantime, we'll be staying with Sand's best friend Finesse until we can find us a place. She has this big old house her grandmother left her, so she's dying for some company."

Shun just shook her head. "I don't know how much more of this I can take." She was leaning over to the side, clutching her stomach. "Girl, this shit is worse than labor!"

"Umm, um, um." Rene shook her head. "See? Listen to you. I told you your butt couldn't hang. You asked me to show you some stuff, and you can't even handle it," Rene beamed. "I hope this Carl guy is worth all this," she teased, throwing her hand over her hip.

Shun found the words to get her through this madness. "Oh, he is." Suddenly, she had the strength to carry her through. This time, she stood to her feet and began jogging in place. Her red, white, and blue polka-dot bandanna made her feel like she was racing in the Olympics. "I've got to look good for the anniversary ceremony," she said, just putting it all out there. "I want his parents to notice me. Hell, I want the *whole family* to notice me."

Rene worked up a laugh. "All right, then, girlfriend. Press on. And while you're doin' that, I need to use this phone book," she said, reaching into a pile of collected White Pages stacked in a corner. Rene counted at least eight of them.

"Who you looking for?" Shun questioned.

Rene sat on the floor and crossed her legs Indian style. "Hendell Ross," she said, flipping through the residential listing.

"Who in the hell is a Hendell, and what kind of name is that for a black man?"

"Well, this Hendell isn't black." Rene took her finger and went up and down the list of Rosses.

Shun was now pumping her fist in the air and making up moves to add to her workout routine as she lunged forward and pulled back. First the right foot, and then went the left. "Well, I figured that," she told Rene. "Whatcha lookin' for him for?"

"I think it's time for a little family reunion. I know all too well what it's like to not have your biological parents a part of your life, so if my luck is still hot, I think I can convince Sand to reconcile with her father. I mean, she always talked about how much she missed her family, and I think a phone conversation would be a great start."

"Well, look at you being all sentimental and stuff," Shun teased.

Rene scrolled farther down the page. "Found it! I need a phone. Give me a phone; hurry, hurry." She was too excited about the possibility of reuniting Sand and her father for the holiday.

"Here, here," Shun said, rushing over. She shoved the cordless in Rene's hands and watched her dial the numbers with both of her thumbs.

"Hello, may I speak to Mr. Hendell Ross, please?" Rene said as soon as the male voice on the other end of the line answered.

"Who's calling?"

Rene grew nervous. "Hello, sir. My name is Rene Brown." She hesitated for a second. "I'm a very good friend of your daughter." The other end of the line fell silent. Too silent. "Mr. Ross?" Rene said, checking to be sure that they hadn't gotten disconnected.

"Is she dead?"

Rene was caught off guard. She twisted her face. "No, sir, she's not."

Shun walked over to her friend and took a seat beside her, listening in as best she could.

"Well, then, I guess you're interrupting my show."

Click.

Rene just held the phone in her hands. It took Shun pulling it from her grasp for her to realize what had just happened. "He doesn't want anything to do with his own child," Rene said unbelievably.

Shun witnessed the hurt in her eyes. She didn't have an answer for her friend. Not right now and probably not ever.

Sand was nervous as hell, and everything around her looked, smelled, and felt like a setup. The strong stench of urine lit her nose on fire as she waited in a dead-end alley for Chyna to show up for the rest of her money. In the back of Sand's mind, something was telling her to call it off. But she had come too far, and this was the closest she'd ever gotten to getting revenge on Chyna for trying to set her up for Jasmine's murder. It was the only way she saw out of this mess she was in. And now, with her palms sweating and her heart racing, for some strange reason, she felt like a hypocrite.

"I can't do this," she mumbled into the earpiece. "I can't do it. Call it off. Y'all hearing me? Call this shit off. Man, I can't do this like this." She wanted her name cleared of whatever it was they might have had on her, but there was no way in hell she was going to narc.

"Cassandra, it's too late for that," the federal agent said.

She hollered out to who she thought was her friend, but had all along been the undercover after Chyna. "James, you said if I didn't wanna do this shit, that I could pull out. I'm pulling out, goddamn it! Call it."

"You can't, Sand. She's already here."

***

Peaches stuffed whatever she could into a small blue and green bag as she raced from one end of the room to the other. Everything she owned she was taking with her. That meant the clothes on her back, the shoes on her feet, and the personal music collection she'd accumulated over the years. Music was her escape from everything she dealt with on a daily basis. It took her away, and when it was time to come back, it helped her to cope.

She was halfway down the stairs, halfway out of the house and almost on her way to a better life when her phone rang. She knew by the ring tone who it was, and she could sense that something wasn't right. Why would he be calling her this soon? Something had to be wrong. "James?" she answered.

"She didn't show up. Get out of—"

Before she could comprehend what he had just said, a strong kick to her back sent her flying down the flight of stairs, face-first.

Sand was so nervous she could barely stand still. She reached for her piece, and then remembered that it wasn't there. As the long-haired figure moved toward her, she began to feel that feeling again. This was a setup. "Where the fuck is Chyna?"

Fantasy's conniving smile didn't go unnoticed. "Didn't think you'd see me again, did you?" She looked Sand straight in the eye. "Where's the money?"

Sand stepped closer to Fantasy. "I'm not giving you shit until you tell me where the fuck Chyna's at!" she said louder than before, hoping the feds were getting everything.

"Didn't your mother ever tell you not to stick your nose where it doesn't belong?" Fantasy smirked. She stepped even closer. Her nipples rubbed against Sand's chest.

"Tell me to my face that you don't want this pussy. That you never thought about it."

Sand didn't flinch.

"Say it! Tell me the thought never crossed your mind about what it would be like to fuck Chyna's main bitch."

Sand took a few steps back. She gripped the briefcase tighter. "Yeah, I thought about it," she whispered, playing into Fantasy's little mind game. "I thought about how I could eliminate the bitch, just to get closer to you," she lied, looking Fantasy dead in the eye.

"Really?" Fantasy asked. She slid her gun from her purse. "What about now? Do you *still* wanna fuck me, Sand? Do you still want Chyna's bitch?"

"Get that gun outta my face," she warned Fantasy.

Fantasy ignored her. She was running this shit now. She came there to get Chyna's grip and put an end to their problem child. "Give me the motherfucking money!"

Sand thought about making a break for it but knew that if she tried, she wouldn't get very far. Not with the bullets of a Beretta hunting her down.

"It ain't so funny now, huh? Is this a good look for you, Sand?" she asked. "Is this a fucking good look for you?" Fantasy yelled to her face.

Sand took a deep breath. If this was how she had to go, she was ready to accept that destiny. "Shoot me," she whispered. "Get the shit over with!" Suddenly rapid footsteps were coming from all different directions.

"Police! Drop your weapon!"

Fantasy didn't bother turning around. "Chyna sent me here to handle your ass. Fuck the money." She cocked the gun, her finger rubbing against the heart of the trigger. She showed no remorse for what she knew she was prepared to do here tonight. It wouldn't be the first time she'd killed for Chyna.

Sand closed her eyes and dropped the case of money to the ground.

"Don't do it!"

It was too late. One shot rang from Fantasy's gun, and another blast came from behind them. Sand, barely on her feet, caught Fantasy as she fell into her arms. She held on as long as she could, until her own legs gave out.

"We need an ambulance! We've got two down. I repeat, two down." The first officer ran to Sand's aid. He checked her pulse. *"Stay with me."*

Sand struggled to breathe. Her body felt cold as ice as she lay in a puddle of her own blood.

"Get her on the gurney now!"

"Stay with us!" a paramedic said. *"What's her name?"*

"Twenty-two-year-old black female . . . Cassandra Janene Ross."

"What happened?"

"One bullet to the chest . . ."

"We need to notify the family . . ."

"Somebody talk to me . . ."

"Code blue!"

"She's going into cardiac arrest!"

Peaches spit out the blood that filled her mouth. She crawled until another kick lifted her off her stomach and onto her side. Groaning, she rolled onto her back.

"Where the fuck you think you going?" Chyna asked her.

A string of blood dripped from Peaches's nose. "Nowhere," she choked.

Chyna walked closer to Peaches and bent down to where she lay on her back. "It doesn't look like that to me." She picked up the phone that lay beside her, checking the last incoming call. She pressed *Talk*. A familiar voice answered on the first ring.

"Peaches, did you get out of the house?"

Chyna glared at the bitch who she realized had just double-crossed her. She then came to the brutal reality: James wasn't a dirty cop; he was an undercover for the feds. And for the last two years, she had been housing their informant.

28

Rene checked the volume on the phone again. It was still on. As she lifted the receiver, the dial tone greeted her. Tears made waves in her eyes. "I can't believe I fell for it."

Shun reached over to her and held her in her arms.

"She was just lying to me. How could she look me in the face and lie like that?"

"Don't. You quit that right now. Sand loves you! She would never up and leave you like that after all y'all just been through."

"Well, explain why I haven't heard from her since she dropped me off here." Rene waited. Shun said nothing. "I didn't think you could." It had been three days since Rene last talked to Sand, and she was worried sick that something might have happened to her. All she told her was that she had to handle some business and that she'd be right back for her. She never came back. She didn't even call. Rene actually believed that they were getting back together, and now she felt stupid for her wishful thinking. But she needed to hear Sand say that they were over for her to accept that this was the end. She crawled back in bed. She didn't know what to make of all of this. Was Sand in trouble, or was this another one of her disappearing acts? "You and Carl go ahead and enjoy yourselves," she told Shun. "I'll be okay."

Shun kissed her on her forehead. "If you need me for anything, call me. After the ceremony, Carl is going to take us to his ranch out in Forney to spend the holiday, but now, if you need anything, you call me, and I'll come running."

Rene smiled up at her friend. She was so beautiful in the champagne-gold, form-fitting dress that showed off her new figure. Her hair was done in beautiful long curls that draped her shoulders, and her makeup was flawless. For once in her life, Rene was happy to see her friend confident with who she was. "I'll be fine. I promise," Rene said.

"Okay. Now get yourself some sleep, and I'll call you first thing in the morning so that you can hear the boys when they open all those presents you bought for them. Lawd knows you might even hear 'em screaming before I get the call in."

Rene could only force a smile.

"Get you some rest, sweetie," Shun said before closing the door shut.

Rene closed her eyes again and slowly drifted off to sleep.

"Come on, y'all!" Shun yelled at the boys like a drill sergeant the second she turned the corner. They lined up in front of her with their overnight gear in hand. "Now remember," Shun started, "speak when you spoken to, and when you ain't . . ." she waited for them to complete the rest of the sentence.

"Hush our mouths."

It was a full eight hours later when Rene decided to finally get out of bed. She had been completely out of it. She moved through the front room. It was so dark in the house, and the bit of light that she did see was coming from the window. That light immediately vanished.

Seconds later, a vibrating sound was coming from her purse. She walked over to it and reached inside with the intention of throwing it in the trash, but instead, she answered it.

"I'm not doing it, so you can forget about it!" she raged with attitude. She flipped the phone closed and walked into the kitchen. She tossed it in the trash, hoping to never have to hear or see that crazy bitch Chyna again. Minutes later, the doorbell rang, and without hesitation, she went to answer it.

Before Chyna pulled up at the house where Rene had been staying, she had been thinking about her last two projects that she had to knock out before hopping on that plane for Mexico tonight. She had to get out of Dallas. And thanks to Peaches, she now knew about how long the feds had been watching her. Peaches had told Chyna that they were expecting her to show up for the money instead of Fantasy. After hearing that, Chyna wasn't sure if Fantasy was dead or alive. All she was certain of was that she was wanted and that the feds had been waiting for the perfect time to move in on her. But she fixed them all because right after sending a bullet into Peaches's brain, she set fire to her. Dead informants didn't talk.

Chyna now made her own path to the front door. Once Rene opened it, Chyna locked eyes with her. Chyna had only one thing on her mind.

Revenge.

Albery waited in his country lake house for his date to arrive after getting confirmation that she was on schedule. He had just stepped out of the shower and was stepping into his pants when the doorbell rang. He took a chocolate-covered strawberry from the fruit tray and nibbled on it while walking to the door. Then he looked out of the peephole to see two beautiful women standing on his front porch. His dick hardened instantly.

"Albery," Chyna said with a satisfied grin. "I would like for you to meet your date, Illusion."

Rene rolled her eyes. She hated the fuck out of this new name Chyna had been shopping her around with. She pulled the hair out of her face. Underneath the mahogany mink coat Chyna made her wear was nothing but her naked body.

Albery stretched the smile that was already on his face. "Do come in," he sang.

Chyna smiled in his face, and the second she passed him, grimaced with disgust.

Rene brushed against Albery slightly as she walked by him. He grabbed her by the arm. "Illusion, huh? So that's what they call you now?"

Rene's lips didn't offer him anything.

"I always knew underneath that innocent face was just another ho," he smirked. "But this is ten grand I *definitely* don't mind spending. So make it worth every penny."

Rene snatched her arm back. "Oh, I will." She followed behind Chyna, adapting to her new role.

Chyna placed the bag she had brought in with her on the kitchen counter. She reached in for a CD and walked it over to the radio, making herself right at home. She hit *Play*, escalating the volume.

Albery couldn't take his eyes off Rene. She looked exactly how he remembered her. He had spent so many nights masturbating to the thought of fucking her, but now he could have her for as long as he wanted, however he wanted. He was ready to skip the small talk and get right down to business.

Chyna made her way through the house as if she had spent time there before. And she had. Without Albery knowing, she planted the pictures, made the calls, and even wrote the bogus letters that gave his wife the evidence she needed to leave his ass. Chyna had done it all. She wanted to make Albery's life as miserable as she could before his dying days.

She walked into Albery's room and began stripping out of her clothes until she was down to nothing.

"So, to what do I owe this double pleasure?" Albery excitedly licked his lips. He had no idea that he would be getting two for the price of one tonight. It was going to be a nice Christmas after all.

"This one is on me," Rene said out of nowhere, taking Chyna's lead. She eased the coat off of her shoulders and let it drop to the floor. Her naked body had both Albery's and Chyna's attention as she climbed up the two steps to the platform where his bed was. She mounted the bed one leg at a time and rested on her knees as Chyna made the first move.

Albery grabbed a bottle of limited edition Dom Pérignon White Gold Jeroboam that complemented the fruit tray. He commenced to drinking the champagne straight from the bottle. He watched Chyna's hand slide over and around both of Rene's lusciously oiled breasts. He pulled on his dick, knowing that it could only be ignored for so long. Chyna then began massaging and licking her own nipple, right before easing her finger inside of her pussy. She made a moaning sound and then leaned in to kiss Rene.

Rene couldn't bring herself to kiss another woman other than Sand. Getting the hint, Chyna wrapped her lips around Rene's chocolate nipples instead. Chyna raised her head and saw how Albery had gotten completely naked and was now stroking himself to a harder erection.He couldn't hold back. He made his way over to the platform and onto the bed. He kissed Rene on her honey-brown ass.

Rene held her composure. She followed the cues and tried hard to relax, for she knew that in only a matter of minutes, things would change. She turned her body around and forced Albery onto his back, then straddled him. She rubbed her hands over his dick. The harder he got, the tighter it felt against her hands.

"Suck it," he said, smiling up at Rene.

Chyna eased off the bed, walked over to the fruit tray, and slid a fresh piece of kiwi into Albery's mouth.

Albery felt like exploding. "Umm. Give me another one."

Chyna fed him another piece, this time taking a bite from it first.

Albery felt Rene's teeth graze against his head, and oddly, the pain felt good. He saw how sexy she looked in the mirror above his bed. He grabbed her head and forced himself farther down her throat.

Chyna fed him a grape, a strawberry, and then a piece of melon. This was the night she had been waiting for, and she wanted to savor every minute of it. "Where's the whipped cream?" she asked him.

"In the fridge," Albery said, anticipating what was next to come.

Chyna left the room and headed for the kitchen. When she returned, Rene was still teasing him, following the script. "Let me have some of this," Chyna said, shaking the whip cream up and spraying it over Albery's midsection.

Rene made her way to Albery's chest, kissing and seductively licking every inch of his skin.

Chyna placed her hand around Albery's fully matured dick, stroking it faster. She looked back at him and could no longer see the whites of his eyes. That was her cue to do what she came to do. She took the blade from her mouth and in one clean sweep, sliced the thickest vein she felt throbbing against the inside of her hand.

"Awwww!" Albery howled, grabbing for the pain in his dick.

When Rene turned around and saw all that blood, she too began screaming as she quickly jumped out of the bed, tripping over the steps.

"You fuckin' bitch!" Albery screamed at the top of his lungs.

Chyna got up in his face. "Where's the safe?"

Albery screamed in agony as he followed the bloody blade hanging over his throat. He choked on his own spit as he called out for help. But no one would hear him because the nearest neighbor was three miles away.

"I said, where's the fucking safe?" Chyna drilled, viciously twisting his balls with her left hand.

Albery pointed to the wall to the left of them.

Chyna motioned to Rene who had wrapped herself back in the coat. "Open it."

Rene, scared half to death, hurried over to the wall. She removed the painting that Albery had pointed to and began fiddling with the digital combination lock. "What's the combination?" she yelled with shaky hands.

Chyna looked down at Albery who was turning colors. "You heard her!" she said, releasing his dick until more blood came gushing out.

Albery painfully called out the six digits, and Rene punched them in. She waited nervously as the red light turned green. She opened the door, bucking her eyes at the bricks of money that aligned the steel safe from top to bottom. She pulled out one of the bundles and tossed it to Chyna.

Chyna caught the package and then turned back around to face Albery. She was close enough to kiss him. She placed the hundred-thousand-dollar package beside him. "You remember Donald Troy, now, don't you, Albery?"

The tears in Albery's eyes began swimming down his face.

"You remember the money you stole from him? The life conviction you got him?"

Albery winced in pain.

"Say hello to his niece," Chyna said. She lifted her hand above his throat, determined to finish him off when the sound of a gun rang heavily in her ears. She lowered her hand and forced herself to turn around.

Rene was shaking like a leaf as she held tightly in her hands the gun that she had just pulled out of the safe. "Stop! You said we were coming here to take back the money he owed you. You didn't say shit about killing anybody!"

Chyna eased her legs from around Albery's body.

"Don't you fucking move," Rene warned.

Chyna couldn't believe what was happening. "So what you gon' do with that gun, huh? Shoot me?" Rene didn't strike her as the type to hurt a fly, let alone shoot someone. Chyna took in a deep breath. "Rene, do us both a favor and start the fucking car while I finish what I came to do!"

Rene looked from Albery to Chyna. "Nobody's dying here tonight." She walked over to the phone and called 911. "I need an ambulance," she rattled off, "at—" she glanced around the room, hoping to see something with his address on it. She broke out in a sweat. "It's uh, uh . . ."

"Ma'am, I need the address so that I can get someone en route."

"I don't know it!" Rene yelled at the operator in frustration. She began calling out the landmarks that she remembered passing by. "Please, just hurry," she said before hanging up.

Rene walked cautiously around the bed and over to the ice bucket with the gun trained in Chyna's direction the entire time. She pulled out the chilling champagne bottle and tossed it to Chyna. "Put this on him," she said, placing both hands back on the gun.

Chyna caught the bottle before it could hit her face. She roughly pushed it between Albery's legs. "Rene, you don't know what you're doing," she said, contemplating just how long it would take her to wrestle the gun away from Rene, empty the clip in her head, and then make a clean getaway before the cops showed up. She looked over at the clock. Her plane was due to take off in less than two hours. "You don't understand what this man did to me. What he did to my family," Chyna pleaded, trying to fuck with Rene's head. "I'm not the bad guy here. Do you really think I could hurt someone just—"

"I know that you're a fucking monster, and I want my life back!" Rene hollered insanely.

Chyna rose from the bed and took a walk down the green mile. As she got closer, Rene's finger embraced the sensitive trigger tighter.

"You think you scaring me with that gun?"

Rene remained silent.

Chyna moved in closer. "You wouldn't dare shoot me," she threatened.

Rene could hear the ambulance from a distance.

Albery struggled to get the words out. "Kill her. There's a million dollars . . ." he wheezed, "in that safe. It's yours," he uttered painfully.

Chyna smiled, strongly believing that that wasn't an option.

Rene, however, was unmoved. She was in control. She could do whatever she wanted to do right now and get away with it. She considered all she had to gain and all she had to lose. It didn't require much thought at all when Chyna lunged toward her. Without seeing it coming, Rene fired a single shot.

Albery managed to lift himself from the bed. He limped over to where Rene stood. He eased the gun from her trembling hands. "I'll take care of this," he slurred.

Rene looked at Albery, and then down to Chyna who was still clinging on to life. The hole in her chest poured blood as gurgling sounds escaped from her throat. Rene gasped. She couldn't believe what she had done. Part of her couldn't handle allowing a human being to die, but Chyna was no human being, she reasoned. She was pure psycho.

"I'll clean this up," Albery reassured her. "Go on. Get outta here." His voice almost sounded hoarse. "Wait. Aren't you forgetting something?"

Rene looked over at the open safe, then to the bed and at the bundle lying there. "I didn't do it for the money," she said. She started to leave, but before she took another step, she turned back around to witness Albery load three more bullets into Chyna's limp body before collapsing on top of her.

Trent spotted Illusion after rounding the block four times in a row. He wouldn't be surprised if folks thought he was an undercover cop.

Illusion was having one hell of a night. She had just made $400, and now she had another john honking at her. She walked over to the car, but as the window powered down, the smile on her face instantly faded. "Get the fuck outta here, Trent!" she yelled, running back for the sidewalk. "Fuck!" she huffed.

"Illeshia, this ain't you! You know that. C'mon now. Talk to me," Trent said, riding his brakes.

"I don't want you seeing me like this. Please, just go!" she yelled, walking at a much-faster pace.

Trent slammed the car into *Park*, hit the hazard lights, and got out. He caught up to her. "Hold up! Gimme a minute to talk to you."

Illusion wasn't stopping. "What do you want from me?" she yelled.

"Your time," Trent answered simply.

Illusion kept walking.

"Wait. I get it." He began fiddling around in his pockets until he pulled out a wad of money. He shoved the money into her hands. "Here's five hundred. I know that's a little less than what you're used to, but I just want you to hear me out for a second," he pleaded with her. "I ain't asking for nothing else."

Illusion stopped, exhaled, and then rolled her eyes at him. She looked around her as she debated on what to do. "You have ten minutes," she said finally.

Trent let out a sigh of relief. "It'll only take me five," he said.

Epilogue

Eight Months Later

Sand and Rene stood side by side in matching attire as they walked out of the church and down the flight of steps with flowers and ribbon twining down them. Rene wore a beautiful raspberry strapless dress that stopped just below her knees, with an attached chiffon sash. Her hair was styled in a sophisticated bun with pieces of baby's breath sprouting out of it. She looked so beautiful, and this was one of the happiest days of her life. On the other side of her, Sand looked equally stunning in an ivory and raspberry tux. Her hair was faded out, and her diamond princess cuts shined from ear to ear. She was too clean.

Reaching that final step, Rene took her place to the left and Sand to the right. They smiled at each other, knowing what the other had in mind. Minutes later, their attention went back to the double doors in which they'd just come through.

Standing hand in hand were Shun and Carl, the newlyweds. Rene fanned at the tears tempting to fall from her eyes. She lived for this moment since the day Shun told her that Carl proposed. Finally, she was seeing the fruits of her labor. All the hard work that she had invested in planning the wedding, hiring the caterer, and seeing to it that everything went perfect was more than worth the headache.

"Congratulations!" everybody yelled out to them, throwing bird seed as the pair hurried past them and slipped into their waiting white limo, heading off for the airport where they'd be honeymooning in Jamaica.

"Come on, boys," Rene said to her godchildren who joined in on the excitement. They all waved good-bye to their mother and new stepdad.

Illusion slowly got out of the car and walked over to the gray-haired woman sitting on the nearby park bench. She sat watching all the kids that played, but she focused on one in particular.

"Mama," Illusion spoke first.

"Illeshia."

"May I sit?"

"It's a free country," her mother spat coldly. "So I don't see why not."

Illusion tried calming her nerves. She wanted to believe that her showing up here today was not a mistake or a huge slap in the face. "Thank you for agreeing to let me see her." Illusion's mother didn't bother looking up. She kept her attention on her granddaughter who was now swinging. "Be careful, sweetie!" she called out.

Illusion sucked in her trembling lips. Her showing up was difficult enough, and she felt it was a bad idea from the moment Trent suggested she reach out to the woman. She couldn't take it anymore, and the pressure was starting to gnaw at her insides. Maybe she wasn't ready to face her daughter after all this time. What would she say to her? Illusion didn't have any of those answers. All she knew was that she wanted her baby in her life, but she didn't even know where to start. She didn't know how to be a mom. How to care. How to love. She nearly talked herself out of being there. She stood up to leave.

"So, it's that easy, isn't it?" Her mother finally turned to face her in what felt like ages. She looked exactly like her.

"Why?" her mother asked simply.

"I don't know. I don't have all of the answers for why I did what I did," Illusion offered, trying to push past the pain. "Maybe I was afraid of failing you and Zakira . . . maybe I didn't know how to—"

"I'm not talking about *that*," her mother frowned, cutting her off mid-sentence. "I mean, why now? Why today?"

Illusion took a deeper breath. "Because I'm tired of waking up every morning of my life wondering if I died tomorrow, would my only daughter miss me?" Tears made their way back down her face.

Her mother's eyes softened.

"I've lived that life. I've done everything in the book that there is to do. But I've changed. I've grown. I'm ready to turn the pages and move on to the next chapter," Illusion confessed. "I'm ready to be a part of my baby's life and do the right thing by her."

Her mother was quiet. She looked Illusion dead in the eyes when she told her, "I will do everything in my power to protect that child," she said, pointing to Zakira. She retrieved a handkerchief from her purse. "Don't cross this bridge if you aren't ready to see what's on the other side."

Illusion inhaled the smell of autumn. She was ready. More ready than she would ever be. "I'm ready to see the other side."

Her mother placed her hand over her chest. "Zakira," she called out. Her granddaughter came running.

"Yes, Nana?"

She took the eight-year-old by her small hands. "Say hello to your mother."

Zakira looked up at the strange woman. "Hi, Mama."

Illusion bent down, wrapped the girl tightly in her arms, and released a lifetime of regrets. She could barely breathe, let alone speak. "Hi, baby girl," she managed weakly, never wanting to let go.

Sand had been taking it easy since the shooting, and she was thankful that she pulled through perfectly fine. Lying on that operating table, holding on to dear life, had changed her perspective on how she wanted to live out the rest of her days on earth. She realized how for so long she had taken so much for granted and how she had taken risks for the people in her life that meant nothing to her but never gave those who meant everything to her equal gratification. Those last few days she spent caged in that hospital room gave her the answers she'd been looking for all of her life. And now, as she watched the woman who meant so much to her sleep so peacefully sound, she knew that she was making a decision that would alter the rest of her life, but it felt so right. With all the strength vested in her, she refused to wake up tomorrow wishing she would've taken that chance on love.

"Rene, baby, wake up. I have somebody I want you to meet."

Rene wiped her eyes. Staring up at Sand brought a smile to her face. "What time is it?" She thought about the last joke Sand pulled on her, and then checked the clock for herself. "Baby, are you serious? It's seven in the morning."

"Come on. Get dressed."

Rene shook her head and dragged herself out of bed. She went in the bathroom, freshened up, threw on a T-shirt and jeans, then made her way across the hardwood floors of their new apartment, yawning. She saw

Sand hunched over on the living-room floor and immediately thought something was wrong. "Sand!" she yelled. "Are you o—"

Sand took Rene by the hands as she positioned herself on one bended knee. Rene's watery eyes meant that she was all too familiar with what was getting ready to take place. She took a deep breath and tried to relax as best she could. Her hands weren't sturdy, but Sand managed to calm them with her opening line.

"Rene, I love you with all my heart. I've loved you since the first day we met, the first day we kissed, and the first time you allowed me to make you mines. I've loved you over and over again. It took me almost dying to realize that I have the most precious thing that one could ever ask for. I have a woman that loves me. Me, and only me. Rene, I don't want you to ever stop loving me. I want this love we have for each other to last forever, even when our days on earth are done." Sand pulled her mother's wedding ring from her pocket. "This ring belonged to my mother." She sniffed.

"It's okay," Rene said, her aching eyes sympathizing with her girlfriend.

Sand held onto Rene's left ring finger. "She left this to me in her will." As more tears fell, she fought through them and slipped the diamond onto Rene's finger. "Rene?"

"Yes?"

"Will you be my forever?"

"Yes! Yes, I will." Rene wrapped her hands around Sand's face and kissed her. Their tongues danced around each other's passionately. Just as hands began to roam, Finesse came out of nowhere, pretending to clear her throat.

Rene jumped. She hadn't heard or seen anyone behind them. She watched as Finesse wheeled over a white man in a wheelchair. Rene looked confused. She quickly looked up at Sand with questions in her eyes.

"Baby," Sand said, "I'd like you to meet my dad."

Rene's eyes widened with surprise. She was shocked and nearly speechless. "Mr. Ross," she began. She was in such disbelief the words wouldn't leave her mouth quick enough. "It's such a pleasure to meet you, sir." She reached for his hand.

Mr. Ross pulled himself up with Finesse's help. He stood to his feet. "Do you love my daughter, Rene?"

Rene batted her eyes and sucked in her trembling lip. "Yes, sir. Very, very much."

Mr. Ross opened his arms and extended a hug. "Well, now I have two daughters instead of one."

Sand joined in on their hug, and Finesse fell in as well. It was at that moment that Rene knew what it felt like to have a family. She leaned in and kissed Sand again. "Thank you for never giving up on us."

Sand blinked back a tear. "I always knew you were the one. I thank you for giving me time to grow up and letting me come home," she said, placing Rene's hand over her own heart.

"I love you," Rene said again.

"I love you too. Always . . ."

Rene finished the sentence. "And forever."